GATHERING OF SHADOWS

BOOK FOUR
OF
THE HUNDRED HALLS

THOMAS K. CARPENTER

Gathering of Shadows

Book Four of The Hundred Halls

by Thomas K. Carpenter

Published by Black Moon Books

Cover design by Ravven
www.ravven.com

Discover other titles by this author on:
www.thomaskcarpenter.com

ISBN-13: 978-1976544644
ISBN-10: 1976544645

Also by Thomas K. Carpenter

ALEXANDRIAN SAGA
Fires of Alexandria
Heirs of Alexandria
Legacy of Alexandria
Warmachines of Alexandria
Empire of Alexandria
Voyage of Alexandria
Goddess of Alexandria

THE DASHKOVA MEMOIRS
Revolutionary Magic
A Cauldron of Secrets
Birds of Prophecy
The Franklin Deception
Nightfell Games
The Queen of Dreams
Dragons of Siberia
Shadows of an Empire

THE DIGITAL SEA TRILOGY
The Digital Sea
The Godhead Machine
Neochrome Aurora

GAMERS TRILOGY
GAMERS
FRAGS
CODERS

THE HUNDRED HALLS
Trials of Magic
Web of Lies
Alchemy of Souls
Gathering of Shadows
City of Sorcery

This book is dedicated to
those who protest injustice in this world at
great cost to themselves.

GATHERING
OF
SHADOWS

1

The city of Invictus melted beneath the punishing August sun. It'd been fourteen days in a row above 105 degrees, with nary a cloud for comfort or rain. Only the gondolas reserved for the fourth and fifth years dared the pale blue, endless sky, windows winking across the heavens.

For mages of the Hundred Halls, the fourth year was a time of exponential growth. The basics of spell work were mastered, so more freedom was given by the professors as students poured their time and efforts into a specialty. Fourth years were effervescent. During that year, the checkout girl at the Save'n Spend, or the waiter at Applebee's, might call them by the honorific Mage due to their confidence, even though they had not yet earned it.

The group of fourth years that Pi traveled with—her sister included—could have been mistaken for a group of prisoners on their way to hard labor. They'd been holed up in Arcanium all summer, clawing at the walls like vampires in a locked coffin.

No one wore clothing related to the Hundred Halls or Arcanium, nothing to give away that they were mages. Deshawn and Isabella were holding hands, heads huddled close as they whispered to each other. Xi, Tristen, and Daniel brought up the rear, necks craning for an attack, flinching whenever a car passed them.

"Come on, guys," said Pi, hands jammed into the pockets of her leather jacket. "A trip to Freeport Games is supposed to be fun. I swear everything will be okay. Lighten up, you look like kindergarteners about to tour John Wayne Gacy's house."

Aurie gave her that look, the one that was two parts sisterly love with just enough exasperation not to be condescending.

"It's brutal out here," said Deshawn, taking a handkerchief to his forehead. "Does Freeport have a shower in the back? Cause I'm gonna need it after we get there."

"The city smells like hot garbage," said Xi, pinching his nose with his forefinger and thumb.

There were nods from the others. They were wilted.

"Sorry."

She kept forgetting that they feared to use magic while the patron of Arcanium, Semyon Gray, was in his soul-torn coma. Spells that provided comfort in extreme elements were some of the first ones new hall mages learned, but Arcanium students couldn't even cast Arianna's Comfort Skin. And the spells provided by others wouldn't stick. It was like they were allergic to magic.

Semyon's soul had been torn in the battle with the soul thief at the end of their third year. The only known cure was time, but no one knew how long it was going to take, and until he was healed, if the mages connected to him used too much magic, he could die, and those that couldn't handle it would go mad.

"Where's Hannah? I thought she was supposed to meet us outside of Arcanium?" asked Aurie, forehead knotted with concern.

"She was running late, said she'd meet us at the train

station," said Pi, rereading the last text from Hannah to make sure she'd read it right.

The background voices in her head rose in crescendo for a moment, before settling down, like a crowd before a concert. She'd gotten used to having the fragments of twelve other people inside her head, especially since she heard them directly less and less. At first it'd been hard to compete with the sheer number of voices, but over the summer they'd assimilated to the point that when she experienced their memories, it was hard to remember that they weren't hers.

"We should go back," said Deshawn, squeezing Isabella to his side. "It was a mistake to come out. It's not safe for us."

"I'm here to protect you," said Pi, winking.

She caught a few of them looking away. Though they didn't know about the additional souls, everyone knew she wasn't technically part of Arcanium, though not the reason why. So there was an uneasiness as if they knew in their guts she wasn't like them.

Aurie stared at Pi. A little frown hung on the corners of her lips. She'd been warning Pi to stop reminding people that she wasn't in Arcanium any longer.

Her phone buzzed against her leg.

"Shit," said Pi. "Hannah says a group of Protectors got off the train and are headed our way."

They were only half a block from the station. The train rumbled away, squelching as it banked out of a turn, headed deeper into the city. A group of grade school aged boys filtered out of the nearby Spell 'O Mart, laughing and spitting water at each other.

"Maybe it's a coincidence and they're not here for us," said Tristen, who clearly didn't believe his words even as they came out of his mouth.

Pi checked the message again. The time stamp on the text

was a minute old. A knot formed in her sternum.

"Aurie, take them back to Arcanium. I'll run interference."

Her sister had barely nodded her head when the group of Protectors came around a brick building at a jog, implied violence in their predator-like focus. There were four guys and two girls. Fourth or fifth year mages.

Her friends turned to run, but a Voice of Command nailed their feet to the sidewalk. They tugged on their legs, trying to pry them loose as if the concrete had turned to glue.

"Aurelia Maximus Silverthorne!"

The truth magic from Aurie's lips blasted towards the Protectors, knocking them off their feet and bringing a grin of pride to Pi's lips. Her sister was formidable, even without access to the majority of her magic.

"It's her!" said the leader of the Protectors, a rail-thin girl with a braid of black hair hanging over her shoulder. She looked like the kind of girl that would snitch on her parents for slow-rolling a stop sign.

The six Protectors raised twin fists in unison, bringing them down as if they were banging on a table, trying to flip it over. The blast wave that rolled their way, sending up a cloud of dust and debris, was meant for controlling riots.

Pi leapt into its path, calling forth a spell from the Daring Maids—a hall dedicated to protecting women around the world. She intended to deflect the spell, but seeing that it would hit the boys loitering in front of the Spell 'O Mart, she had to let the full force hit her square in the chest, throwing her into a brick wall.

The silver amulet on her wrist disintegrated. The impact was rerouted into it, saving Pi from being turned into mush. She'd hoped they wouldn't run into trouble, but had prepared herself accordingly. She'd have purple-blue bruises across her body, but it was better than a concussion and multiple broken bones.

The Protectors rushed forward. The lead girl had spell dampening manacles in her hands.

Pi was climbing to her feet when Hannah came rollerblading around the corner. Hannah was sporting a blue Mohawk and a fresh sleeve of colorful tattoos. She lobbed a handful of metal balls at the Protectors. As they hit the concrete, they exploded into a web of sticky white goo, freezing the Protectors into place.

Using the opportunity, Pi raced to her friends and countered the charm so they could continue their escape. Aurie started to linger, but Pi pushed her after the others.

"Stay with them, there could be others," said Pi.

Braid Girl snapped the sticky webbing into dust, her dark eyebrows forming an angry *V*. "Brad. Sunil. After them."

Two Protectors broke off, curling away. Before Pi said anything, Hannah charged after them. "On it!"

"Armor up," said Braid Girl.

Fully enchanted body armor snapped into place across the Protectors' limbs, glowing with eldritch runes. A high-pitched whine emanated from them. Another time, Pi might have enjoyed their display of magic because they reminded her of a childhood watching Japanese anime and tokusatsu, but having it arrayed against her brought a healthy dose of doubt.

Pi's mouth went dry at the realization that she'd misjudged the trip. The Halls that formed the Cabal had been testing Arcanium during the summer, trying to get the students to use magic and injure Semyon, but they hadn't resorted to direct attacks.

As if to highlight the unusualness of a wizard showdown in the middle of Invictus, a maroon SUV slammed on its breaks at the other end of the street, its wheels burning out as it reversed in a wobbly fishtail.

"All this for little ol' me?" asked Pi, taking a tentative step backwards.

Braid Girl gave signs to spread out. They expanded into an arc. "No quarter."

"No quarter. What the hell does that—"

The words were barely out of Pi's mouth when the Protectors moved as one. Four force bolts shimmered through the air like invisible fists.

Pi threw herself out of the way. Two of the bolts connected, spinning her down the street. She landed in a tangled heap, sight blurry.

"I think I chipped a tooth," she muttered, rubbing her jaw as she slowly climbed to her feet as the Protectors advanced.

A spell called itself to her mind from the Aura Healer soul. It was a mild anesthetic that would dampen the pain, though it carried risks if she pushed herself too far.

Pi quickly cast it. The searing ache dulled until it was a low throb.

She eyed her surroundings. A head-to-head fight was suicidal with four armored Protectors, and she needed time.

Pi avoided a second volley of force bolts with a spell-aided jump, and kept running, veering down the street the SUV had traveled.

A vial of chalky blue liquid from her leather jacket went down her throat with a little choking and gagging, but as soon as it hit her stomach, a surge of energy filled her limbs. Her senses brightened as if the world had been turned up to eleven.

The Protectors followed, enhanced by their armor. Pi had to dodge more force bolts, zigging and zagging across the street. An attempt at a force shield was blown apart by the impact of four bolts.

She threw herself down an alleyway and pushed herself into a burst of speed. She'd pay for the strain on her limbs later. Already the anesthetic spell was fraying at the edges, bringing needlelike aches to her neck and knees, but she had no room to rest, and she doubled her efforts until she came out the other side.

The street was filled with cross-traffic. The sidewalk teemed with pedestrians craning their necks at the gondolas traveling overhead.

The Protectors charged down the alleyway. Pi was looking for a place to hide when the mathmagics soul gave her an idea.

Pi stepped back into the alleyway and cupped her hands around her mouth.

"How many times were you dropped on your head as a baby to qualify to be in Protectors?"

As expected, they slowed long enough to launch another volley of force bolts, oblivious to the people on the street. Pi threw up a force wall, but this time shaped it into a parabola-like structure. When the bolts hit, they zipped around and headed right back at the Protectors, knocking them from their feet.

"Math *is* useful," said Pi as she ran away, feeling a warm satisfaction inside her mind.

Pi circled back towards Arcanium, noting that she'd heard no sirens or helicopters. There was no way that a full-out mage battle hadn't been reported, which meant it was being suppressed at Police HQ. This was worrisome for many reasons, none she cared to contemplate while they were chasing her.

Three blocks from the alley, Pi cut through a parking garage under construction. Orange cones and tarps blocked the entrance, and far above, the harmonies of stone singers bent stone to their will. Stone singer magic had a primal, gut feel to it, and the reverberations in the concrete tickled her hearing.

Running across the yellow lines that demarcated parking

spots, Pi didn't think much of the strand of wire lying on the concrete. It looped around her ankle as she leapt over, dragging her back to the ground in a hip-twisting yank.

Pi made a slashing gesture to sever the cord, but Protector Sunil stepped from behind a concrete pillar and hit her with Voice of Command from point-blank range, freezing her limbs and giving the cord a chance to coil around her like a constrictor.

He flicked a wad of bubblegum-like substance from his fingertips, and it landed on her hands, gluing them together. Pi thrashed around like a wolverine in a cage.

"Stop moving," said Sunil, eyes dark with purpose as he pulled a cell phone from his pocket. "You'll only get hurt."

"Go fuck yourself."

"Bannon will be so pleased with me," he said, smirking. "I caught both Silverthorne sisters singlehandedly. Maybe he'll even let me keep one of you."

On the other side of the wall, Pi saw her sister lying unconscious, a dreadful cut across her forehead leaking blood into her right eye.

"I'm going to shove that cell phone up your ass if you don't let me go so I can tend to my sister."

Sunil flicked his wrist, which made the substance around her hands squeeze tighter until her fingers were bright red. The circulation was being cut off.

Pi raged against her bindings, straining and pushing. She hated seeing her sister in pain. She started thinking of the many things she would do to Sunil if she got loose before deciding to conserve her energy and focus on the actual act of freeing herself.

Once she relaxed, Sunil snorted softly and typed a message into his cell phone. "Angela is going to be sooo pissed, but this just proves they should have put me in charge."

A cold wind blew through Pi's mind as she considered what was going to happen when they were given to Bannon. She guessed that was why the police weren't involved. A battle between rival halls could be explained as horseplay, or students blowing off steam. No one outside of the Halls knew about Arcanium's predicament. Sure there were conspiracy sites that talked about it, but those weren't picked up by the national media. Pi knew she'd made a major mistake in convincing her sister and her friends to take a field trip to Freeport. Even though Professor Mali had agreed, Pi still felt responsible.

Pi concentrated on the soul fragments, hoping one of them might have a useful spell. When the answer came, she was surprised because she'd thought the Sirène Hall involved meditation.

She focused on her voice, relying on the soul fragment's memory to guide her through the spell. Most spells required a manual component, but Sirène Hall had been experimenting with using their vocal cords to provide structure, much as Stone Singers used music, except they used vibrations rather than notes.

"Sunil," she said, testing her command of the spell.

He looked at her with a slightly confused expression, as if he'd heard her, but hadn't registered his name.

"Sunil. Come here and release my bonds."

Her vocal cords strained under the spell as if she were the lead singer in a metalcore band.

The effect was fleeting. He went back to his typing, shaking his head dismissively.

Pi coughed. Her throat felt like she'd been kicked in the neck. She knew she was doing it wrong, but it was the difference between being told how to juggle and actually juggling. Her vocal cords weren't practiced enough. She was supposed to create the proper vibrations in her throat that would carry the spell energy into the listener's ear. Already it felt like she'd been gargling hot sand.

"Sunil. You must release me, or Angela will take credit for what you've done."

When he took a step towards her, Pi silently cheered, but then he paused as he muddled through his thoughts.

"That doesn't make any sense."

He went back to leaning against the pillar. Pi sensed she was running out of time.

Pi closed her eyes, and rather than focusing on the spell, she conjured the soul fragment to her mind. Gal Shuttlebeam. She was a large woman with curly black hair and a penchant for bright flowery dresses.

When Pi opened her mouth again, she let Gal's memories guide her, knowing it wasn't enough to bludgeon the listener with the Voice, but to construct the narrative so they would find it impossible to disagree.

"Sunil. Please release me so I can tend to my sister. She's hurt badly. If she dies, then Bannon will be very unhappy with you, and I think we both know how bad that can be."

"Yeah," he said blankly. "He's an asshole."

"I promise to behave. I'm worried about my sister."

He nodded absently. "Of course you are. I wish I had a sister. I'm sure it must be nice."

Sunil pulled out a length of chalk, crumbled it to pieces, and sprinkled it over the gummy material that was turning her fingers purple. The springy stuff grew rigid. She tensed her hands and it turned to powder, releasing her hands.

With her enhanced hearing, she knew that Angela and the other Protectors were entering the parking garage.

Sunil was staring at her strangely, as if he couldn't understand why he'd released her hands. Before he could immobilize them again, Pi scooped up a pinch of chalk and flicked it at him. The puff of dust flew into his mouth and down his throat. She twisted her hand and Sunil seized up, arching forward as if he wanted to puke but couldn't muster enough fluid. His fingers clawed at his throat.

Pi broke the wire and ran to her sister. The blood pooled around her head was larger than she first thought. The head wound was bleeding profusely. Pi used a quick spell to stop it, before lifting Aurie up and throwing her on her shoulder.

Angela and the other Protectors were making their way through the tarps. There wasn't much time left.

Sunil was bright purple. His eyes pleaded with her to release the spell. Spittle formed at his lips as he beat against his neck, trying to dislodge the chalk that she'd cemented inside his throat.

"You fucked with my sister."

Before she left, Pi pocketed Sunil's cell phone.

A force bolt whizzed by her shoulder the moment the tarp was pulled down. Pi ran through the lower level with Aurie bouncing on her shoulder. The potion was wearing off, straining Pi's thighs.

She leapt over an orange plastic fence, landing on the sidewalk outside the parking garage. The crenellations of the Tower of Letters on the south side of Arcanium peaked above the windowed office building, giving her a rough idea of her location. She only had a block and a half to make it.

Pi ran full out, dodging across the street between speeding cars to avoid the force bolts. A Chevy got drilled in the rear, spinning it into the opposite lane, causing a pile up.

This didn't slow down the Protectors, who had earlier abandoned their runed armor, and were chasing unaided. But Pi's potion was nearly spent and Aurie's unconscious body was like hauling a sack of wet concrete up a ladder.

The last half block, her legs turned to mush. Aurie's weight grew on her shoulder. The Protectors had almost caught up. They weren't even trying to blast her with a force bolt. The magic-dampening manacles dangled from Angela's fist, bouncing along her side as she ran.

The drawbridge into Arcanium was another half a block up the street. The Protectors had her cut off.

So Pi did the only thing she could do. She leapt into the moat. The fall was brief. Water shot up her nose. Aurie slipped off her shoulder.

Pi grabbed her sister by the hair, dragged her to the side, clung to the mossy rocks, and was able to pull Aurie far enough out of the water that her mouth was clear. The Protectors stood above her on the sidewalk, but none dared to descend into the water. The tentacled creature that lived in Semyon's pool beneath the waterfall had access to the moat, and though no one had ever seen it, she was comfortable that it wouldn't hurt her. That was the hope, anyway.

After catching her breath, Pi edged along the wall towards the drawbridge where there was a set of stairs on the Arcanium side. She was bone-tired by the time she made it. Deshawn and Isabella were waiting for her, and they helped drag her sister onto the landing.

"We were so worry about you," said Isabella in her thick Latin accent.

With water dripping into her eyes, Pi healed her sister, who woke to coughing. Her eyes were red.

"I've got you, sis," said Pi, gasping.

She collapsed onto her side, muscles quivering, cramps forming with the potion having run its course.

"What happened?" asked Aurie, putting a hand to her head as she grimaced.

"An ambush," said Pi, kneading her legs. "Nearly got me

too."

They helped Aurie to her feet. She had to be held up, and Pi let Deshawn and Isabella do the honors, since her limbs were old spaghetti.

"Leaving Arcanium was a bad idea," said Deshawn, shaking his head.

"Sorry, guys. I wasn't expecting that," said Pi, then remembered that she'd jumped into the moat with her phone in her pocket. "Shit."

"What?" asked Deshawn.

"Nothing. Just thought I might have gotten some answers," said Pi.

Isabella said, "You should go rest, Pythia. We'll take your sister to Professor Mali."

Aurie groaned. "If I don't throw up first."

"Hey Pi," said Deshawn, looking over his shoulder as he helped Aurie down the hallway.

"Yeah?"

"You against four fully runed Protectors? That was legend," he said, grin stretched to his ears.

A well of pride filled her. "I guess it was, but it would have been better if nobody'd gotten hurt."

Pi lay on the wet concrete until her legs could be convinced to stand. She was a wobbly foal, and she had to lean on the wall to make it up the stairs, which for all intents and purposes were torture devices.

Back in her room, she took the soaked cell phone out and set it on the dresser for later. Then she grabbed her shower kit so she could wash off the moat water, but had to stop every two steps and let her legs shake uncontrollably. She'd pushed them past their limits, and as inviting as the bed was, she wanted a shower.

"Merlin's tits."

She dug through her cabinet for the remainder of the chalky liquid and gulped it down. The shakes continued their tremors until the potion took hold and her aches disappeared like smoke.

In the shower, the extent of what had happened hit her fully. She'd nearly gotten her friends, and her sister, killed. They had no business being out without magic to protect them. Before, Aurie would have whipped Sunil like butter cream, but now she was worse off than before she joined the Halls. At least before, if she used her magic too freely, the only danger was her own madness. Now, Aurie could kill herself and everyone else in Arcanium if she used it.

It'd been difficult to see Aurie like that. Unconscious. Helpless. She'd always been the older sister, watching out for her. Aurie had always been the more powerful mage with an access to faez that rivaled a patron's.

As the steaming water bounced off Pi's shoulders, she vowed that she wouldn't put her sister or her friends in any more danger. In fact, she'd find a way to get back at the Protectors, make them pay for what they'd done.

Hair dripping against her face with a thick towel wrapped around her midsection, Pi crawled onto her bed, thoughts turning to the battle with the Protectors. That earlier pride came surging upward, making her giddy.

Deshawn had called her battle legendary. She had to agree. And not only that, she felt like she'd barely tapped the potential of what those soul fragments could do for her. The next time she met the Cabal on the streets, she'd be more prepared. They wouldn't know what hit them.

2

The waterfall beneath Arcanium thundered against the pool, mist forming on the surface of the water. Aurie strode across the invisible path, boots kicking up spray, barely paying attention to where her feet landed as she worked through the arguments she'd practiced in her head.

The door to Semyon's quarters was open. Aurie bypassed his office, glancing at his bookshelves. There was a little guilt, too, since she'd pilfered information from his books a few years ago, but that evaporated the moment she entered the room he was convalescing in.

She'd never imagined her fourth year would begin like this, with her patron unconscious and soul-torn. This was supposed to be a year of celebration as an upperclassman. She hadn't even ridden a gondola yet, and classes had started a week ago. Not that that meant much in Arcanium. Their classes were a farce. It felt like they were doing charades rather than magic, and the hall library was constantly filled because the professors were assigning loads of research rather than practical practice.

Semyon's private sitting room smelled like rich coffee dosed with vanilla. It was a circular room with thick carpet that made her feel like she was treading on a sea of marshmallows. A hospital bed had been set up in the center of the room, and Semyon was stretched upon it, stiff with a hollowed-out expression. Wires disappeared into black boxes that beeped faintly as if they were far away. Semyon was alive, but not alive. His skin looked wooden, and Aurie could only imagine that if she held a mirror before his lips a fog would not stir. He was in a sort of suspended animation like a computer waiting for the program to download.

Professor Mali fidgeted from her wheelchair, thumb rubbing the palm of her hand as she worried over their patron. When she wasn't in class, she was down here. He was never left alone, and while there were plenty of people willing to watch him, Professor Mali took the largest share.

"Professor."

Dark eyes flitted up to Aurie, as if she hadn't noticed that she'd entered the room. The professor's steel gray hair was lined with white streaks, and her gaze was haunted by the demands of her position.

"Aurelia. You didn't have to come. I'm perfectly fine watching him tonight."

"I didn't come to take a turn."

The professor studied Aurie's face. She couldn't hide the seriousness of her intentions, and Mali frowned as if she knew she wouldn't like the impending discussion.

"How are you feeling?" asked the professor, clearly trying to delay the inevitable.

"The attack was weeks ago," said Aurie. "I'm fine."

Her lips drew a thin line, motherly, dismissive. "I know you're physically well, I watched as the healer mended you. I mean your state of self. That Protector took you down hard, and that can be damaging, especially under our current situation."

"It's not the first time I've been that vulnerable," said Aurie.

The professor flinched. She'd told the professor most of what had happened last year, especially the parts with Bannon and what they'd endured in Protector HQ.

Aurie stood across the bed from the professor, putting her hand near Semyon's leg, but not daring to touch him.

"Is he getting better?"

Professor Mali tightened, as if her spring had been turned again. "If he is, he's competing with the passage of the seasons or the rising of the seas for slowness. He needs time to heal— we just don't know how much."

"We need to do something," said Aurie. "We can't hide in Arcanium forever. Some of the younger students have been sneaking out. Eventually someone's going to get caught, and they'll trick them into using magic."

"If you're worried about yourself, I think you're strong enough, should that happen," said the professor.

"I'm not worried about me. If they break Semyon, many of my friends will die or go mad."

The professor banged her fist against her leg. "Don't you think I know that?" She looked away, embarrassed by her loss of control. "We'll have to double our guards, keep the younger ones from leaving. I thought after you got attacked they'd stop asking."

"We're young, we believe we're invincible. I'm sure you did once."

It was a low blow. The professor glared back at Aurie. She took a deep breath.

"Have you thought about—"

"No," said the professor. "I will not, cannot. Semyon is our patron. I cannot replace him."

"Then many will die," said Aurie.

"Breaking the links and transferring them to me would kill him. I cannot abide that."

"You don't know that it'd kill him," said Aurie. "You're saying that so you don't have to consider it, and I wouldn't ask if I thought that would happen. There are plenty of examples of patrons transferring their charges."

The professor responded as if each word was a blunt jab. "Not this large of a hall, nor one of the original five patrons. If I were one of the first five, sure, I could do it. But I've only been a mage for thirty years. In the big scheme of things, I'm a pup. We don't know, Aurelia. It's all conjecture at this point."

"Of course, there's a chance it could go wrong," said Aurie. "But it's better than what might happen. Arcanium is scared. I don't think anyone sleeps anymore. I don't want to lose my friends. They're my family now. I don't have anyone else."

Mali tried to soften her expression. Under different circumstances it would have been comical as her facial muscles seemed to resist the desire to be relaxed.

Eventually, she gave up with an exasperated sigh. "I'm not even sure the Hall charter would allow it."

"It doesn't specifically deny the possibility, and legal documents must be explicit in the rights they grant," said Aurie.

"You should have been an arcane legal scholar."

"I had to be one last year," said Aurie.

Mali winced. "I'm sorry. I forget your experiences in the Hundred Halls have been rather abnormal. Have you no desire to live a normal life?"

"Do you?"

"No."

Aurie shrugged. "Me neither."

"I'm sorry, Aurelia. No matter what your argument is, I'm not taking over Arcanium."

"What about one of the other professors?" she asked.

"None of them are strong enough either. Maybe Professor Chopra, he's been here longer than anyone, but he would never do it. He's a firm believer in the rules, almost to the point of fault. He wouldn't be able to handle it anyway."

Aurie paused, gathering herself. She hadn't expected the professor to agree. She'd only pressured her so she might allow what Aurie really wanted to do.

"What about other options?" asked Aurie cautiously.

The corners of Mali's eyes crinkled with suspicion. "What other options?"

"You said it before," said Aurie. "He needs time to heal. What if we could give him more time? Or more appropriately, speed up the passage of his time?"

Understanding grew on the professor's face, until she realized what Aurie was asking, then her expression closed like a door. "Absolutely not. I'm not even sure how you—never mind, it doesn't matter how you learned about it, but no, and no way."

"The Engine of Temporal Manipulation could be the solution to our problem."

Professor Mali barked back. "It might be a solution to *this* problem, but the new problems it would create would dwarf the current predicament. And even so, I would not ask for it, and the guardian would not hand it over, even if Invictus himself returned this morning and asked. There's no use bothering, even if it would work."

"It's worth the risk, both of failure and of being refused. We need to fix Semyon." She glanced down at him, feeling guilty for talking about him while he was suspended in his quasi-death. She wondered if he dreamt, or was even producing memories anymore. "If he dies, it's bigger than Arcanium."

"It's not worth it."

"Without him the Cabal can reform the Hundred Halls with Bannon or Malden at the head. Do you really want that? You might as well give them the title of Emperor of the World if that happens," said Aurie, heart thrashing away in her chest.

The professor looked away. "I am aware."

Frustration filled Aurie until she couldn't take it. "You are? Because it doesn't look like it. It looks to me like you're giving up."

The professor rose up in her wheelchair, thrusting her finger out accusingly. Aurie almost expected a spell to come zinging out.

"I am not giving up. You get the hell out of here. You don't have the right to say those things. Not now, and not ever. Forget about the artifact. Forget about me taking over as patron, and figure out how to keep your fellow students safe. Am I understood?"

Aurie bit back her anger. "Yes, ma'am."

The professor went back to staring at Semyon. Aurie thought about continuing the argument, then realized it was no use. She left through the waterfall, wondering how long it would be until the Cabal raided Arcanium, forcing them to use magic. There'd be no one left in the aftermath.

3

A rainstorm had left the city that morning, leaving wet pavement and a musty, industrial smell as the water pushed the oil in the concrete to the surface. Pi's boots clicked along the sidewalk as she made her way to the Church of the Sprawl in the eighth ward.

She'd left her magical leather jacket in her room, along with every other trinket. She wore a black frilly skirt and a Hundred Halls T-shirt, the ones they sold at the university stores. Isabella had one as a lark, and she'd borrowed it as her disguise, along with a bad Elsa wig that she'd dyed black.

Pi had taken three different trains, crisscrossing the city, to lose anyone following her. She'd been sure there were at least two mages when she left Arcanium, a blonde girl she thought was from Coterie and an Asian-American kid who wasn't subtle about his spells when she passed him in the Green Line train station.

The tracking spells had been easy to scrub. And she'd been wearing different clothes when she left Arcanium, ones with minor enchantments on them, to fool her followers into tracking those. She'd left her spell-laden clothes in the bathroom on the Blue Line that circled the city, replacing them with the touristy fashionable ones.

The Church of the Sprawl looked nothing like a church. It was an internet cafe squeezed between a bakery and a coffee shop, which was about the best place possible for all-night gaming binges. She paused before she went in, regretting her choice of disguise. The wig could easily be slipped off, but her hair had gotten sweaty underneath, and once she pulled it away, she'd have to spend the next ten minutes scratching her scalp.

Pi found the guy she was looking for in the back playing an immersive VR shooter. Dustin Davies. He wore a big heavy helmet with wires that went into a black box with lights inside that rotated between red, blue, and green. What he was seeing inside the viewscreen was being displayed on a desk-sized monitor on the wall. He was standing inside a ring to keep him from falling over, and he kept bumping into the sides as he spun around shooting.

As he fired, he screamed things like: "Eat my cock, you chode-monster!" and "Die, casuals!" and "You lame!"

Between firing, he wriggled his fingers, and his avatar would glitch to a new location. Sometimes he would appear directly behind another player and unload his virtual weapon into their backs, then follow it up with a steady stream of insults, the most common being "You lame!"

Pi watched for about ten minutes before unplugging his helmet from the computer.

He yanked his helmet off, half catching it on his ears, until sweaty and out of breath, he was facing her. His expression went through contortions as he tried to figure out who she was and why she was standing there.

"Who the fuck are you?" he finally asked.

"A girl with a problem," said Pi. "And you're going to help me."

"Go away, tourist," he said, leaning over the ring and plugging the helmet back into the computer. "I've got a kill streak to maintain."

"I can pay, get you a couple of weekends' worth of game time," she said.

He gave her a dismissive shrug. "Who pays?"

He went back to playing, and Pi chewed on her fingernails. Clearly the direct approach wasn't the right one with him. Nor was the offer for payment, which meant he was probably hacking them for credits. She considered using the Voice on him, but it hurt like hell, and using it in public would be too easy to trace.

She eyed the second VR station in the room. She'd played enough shooters to be decent, but Dustin was playing on a competitive map. Everyone in that game could kill her with both their eyes closed. But like Dustin, she didn't plan on playing fair.

Pi spent the next few minutes studying the spell he was using. Without the soul fragment from cybermagics, she'd have no chance to make sense of what he was doing, but the gestures woke enough memories that she could repeat the spell.

She went to the register and purchased three hours of playtime. The attendant walked her through the equipment, shaking his head at Dustin as he explained how the VR equipment worked.

"Shall I put you in a beginner's map?"

"No," she said, holding the helmet. "I want to be in the same game as him."

"Really? You'll get slaughtered. Top pros play on that map," he said.

"I'm a fast learner."

"Whatever. Your money."

The fake reality inside the game was uber detailed. The game map was the burned-out ruins of Stalingrad during World War II. Pi might have been impressed had she not spent the majority of her second year getting killed by giant bugs on an alien planet.

Pi entered her name as CasualN00b. About ten seconds after loading into the map, Pi was killed. Then killed again. She barely had time to figure out the gun controls before getting shot six more times in rapid succession. The other players moved realistically, dodging and weaving and leaping across shattered buildings, while Pi could barely move ten feet without tripping over rubble.

At least one of those times, she got killed by UL4M3, which she realized was Dustin Davies by his catchphrase "You lame!"

Eventually she was able to get into a hiding position so she could figure out how to hack the game like Dustin was doing. When she teleported behind another player and stabbed him in the back with her bayonet, she whooped for joy, only to have her victim call back, "Noob!"

The next two hours, she spent killing the other players with growing expertise. Pi wasn't deluding herself that she was suddenly a top-ranked player—the spell was doing most of the work—but it felt good to get her kills in, making her long—only partially—for a normal life when goofing off playing videogames was a thing she could do.

When the attendant tapped on her shoulder, she authorized another three hours. She hadn't gotten anywhere near killing Dustin, since he was impossible to track. She'd planned on stalking him in-game and challenging him to a contest, but she couldn't even find him, which made her plan ridiculous. She was about to give up when she remembered the monitor in the room, showing exactly where he was located. The only problem was that she couldn't see the screen and play the game at the same time, and he moved too quickly for her to switch back and forth.

Pi took the VR helmet off and pulled a quarter out of her pocket. She enchanted it to act as a mirror of the monitor, and fixed it inside the helmet like a miniature HUD device, using a piece of chewed gum to hold the quarter in place. Seeing both viewpoints was a little disorienting at first, but Pi figured out how to use it to track him.

When she killed him the first time, a revolver shot to the head while he was setting up a sniping location, she didn't say a word. Then she killed him again while he was sneaking up a set of stairs. The next three kills were right as he teleported to a new location.

"Get off my back, glitcher! I'm gonna report you," he screamed in her ear through the mic. She heard the echo of his real speech in the room through her helmet.

"I'm going to keep killing you until you help me."

"Fuck you."

"Nice insult, you infantile Muppet humper," she responded.

He rage-screamed in her ear until she muted him. Then she killed him again. And again. He spent the next ten minutes teleporting around the map trying to avoid her, but she kept fragging him over and over until she saw the message "UL4M3 has left the game" appear in the corner of her vision.

When she dragged the helmet off her head, the wig went along with it. He was staring at her with suspicion.

"Who the hell are you? How are you casting our proprietary Hall spells?"

"Who I am doesn't matter. What matters is that if you don't help me, I'll stalk you in whatever game you play, making sure I spend my every waking moment murdering your avatar in rapid and continuous fashion from now until the heat death of the universe."

"Wow. If that wasn't so fucking psycho, I'd say that was awesome. Until the heat death of the universe—I'm going to have to remember that one," he said.

Pi was a little thrown by his sudden change in tone. He didn't seem as mad as she thought he might, given what she'd done.

"Will you help me? Like I said before, I can pay, or we can trade." When his lips started to curl upward, she pointed her finger towards him. "Say it and I'll put my Sketchers up your ass."

He smiled congenially, spreading his hands. "I'll help you, assuming it's something I can help you with, *if* you tell me how you knew exactly where I was going to be in the game."

"Sure. *After* you help."

He stuck his sweaty hand out. Pi stared at it for a few seconds before shaking. "Deal."

When he set his helmet down, she scrubbed the sliminess off her palm against her black skirt.

"So where'd you learn how to do that?" he asked as they took a table in the back of the room. Dustin ordered a pair of energy drinks from a touchscreen that appeared.

"I knew Bala," she said, which was true, but probably not in the way that Dustin expected, but she wasn't going to tell him she had a piece of his soul in her head.

He did a double take, then kneaded his hands together. "You knew him? Man, I miss Bala. Fucking bad luck that it was him last year."

A memory from Bala's life that involved Dustin wavered into her mind. It was them lying on their beds in their hall, talking about growing up. Dustin had lived in a trailer outside of Kansas City, raised by a single mom who worked long hours.

"I miss him, too," said Pi.

A familiar warmth moved through her mind. Bala and

Dustin had been best friends, and losing him had been pretty tough on Dustin. She thought about telling him about the soul in her head, but decided against it, in case he grew attached to her.

"We met on some old forums, before the Halls, and we used to trade spells back then," she said.

"What hall?" he asked.

"Coterie."

"Whoa," said Dustin. "So what do you need?"

She pulled out the cell phone she'd gotten from Sunil, and accessed the information she'd been able to restore from it after getting dunked in the Arcanium moat. Besides some nasty pictures Sunil had taken of drunk girls passed out at parties, there was a lot of other information that proved the things they'd suspected about the Cabal. She'd read through group text chains talking about the rewards offered by the professors of their halls if they could get Arcanium students to use magic. There was talk of a raid on the hall, though most seemed apprehensive about the protections enchanted into the physical structure. Even without Semyon aware, the school itself was formidable.

"I acquired this phone. But the owner unconnected it from their apps, emails, and other stuff. I want to reconnect it into their text chains so I can monitor what goes on."

Dustin chugged from his energy drink, then set the aluminum can down hard on the table as his eyes whirled with thoughts.

"That's a tough one," he said. "Bala would be able to do it, for sure. He was our best hacker. Almost as good as our patron."

"Could you walk me through the idea of what I might do?" asked Pi. "Like, maybe, assume I had Bala's skills."

Which was kinda true. She had some of his memories,

but she didn't have enough of them to accomplish the task. His fragment was thin, and filled with major gaps. Like an amnesiac trying to rediscover their life, she was hoping to trigger the right memory.

"You'll need to jack the data stream and spoof the encryption to accept this phone as the real deal."

She waved him to a stop. "You're gonna need to slow it down. Less techy speech."

He shook his head, disbelieving. "I don't know how you're planning on accomplishing this then. Sounds like you're not even a script-kiddie, but okay, I made a deal." He paused, shook his head again. "Hacking using magic isn't so different from hacking using a computer, except magic is a tool that has certain advantages, but you still have to understand the code. Like there were some French hackers that used a drone with a camera to fly it up to a window in a corporation, and had it read the blinking red light on the server to figure out what it was transmitting. Using magic is like that. It's a way to bypass the normal rules, if you're creative enough."

"So you're not 'seeing the Matrix' or anything like that," she said.

"No. But it does allow you to hack in ways not accessible to regular coders. Like in the game, I was using a coded spell that allowed me to move to any location in the game as if I were sysadmin."

"What if I wanted to jump into a group text?" she asked.

Dustin tapped on his chin. "That's simple. You only need the password and login."

Pi opened her mouth to ask a clarifying question when a trickle of knowledge floated to the surface. Suddenly, she understood what she needed to do, or more importantly, Bala had regained the knowledge.

"Got it," she said, smiling. "I'm good now."

"But I haven't really said anything," he replied, face scrunched.

"Like I said, I'm a fast learner."

"Whatever." He tapped his energy drink on the table. "Your turn."

Pi retrieved the enchanted quarter from the inside of the visor. As soon as he saw it, he understood.

"Wow, yeah. I'm an idiot," he said. "Maybe you're better than you make out. That's hacker thinking. Why brute force it when you can work around."

She left when he returned to his game, content that she could access the text chain so she could monitor the Cabal students. She thought about sharing her discovery with Aurie, but decided against it in case that encouraged her to leave Arcanium again. The attack a few weeks ago had taught her that Aurie and the other students were too defenseless to leave the school. Whatever Pi decided to do against the Cabal, she'd have to do it on her own.

4

Aurie found Pi in the map room, staring at the representation of the city of Invictus, fiddling with a cell phone that she shoved into her pocket the moment she realized she wasn't alone. Aurie didn't recognize the cell phone, but decided that if her sister wanted her to know about it, she'd tell her.

"Hey, sis," said Aurie, giving a hug, catching the sharp perfume she was wearing. "New scent? I like-y, but that fruity one's kind of your thing."

Pi ran her fingers through her blue-streaked dark hair and looked away. Aurie noted that her sister looked older than her nearly twenty years, possibly due to a change in makeup, or the new perfume, but she couldn't pinpoint the exact reason.

"Not anymore. Whatcha need?" asked Pi.

"I need your help this afternoon. Outside Arcanium."

"You can't go out there," said Pi. "Too dangerous. If you give me a few days to prepare, maybe we can go, but you have to warn me about this stuff."

"That's sweet, sis," said Aurie, trying to control her annoyance at being lectured at, "but I've already taken care of it. We'll be fine, but that's why I'd like you along, in case I missed something."

Pi touched the pocket in which she'd placed the cell phone reflexively. "It's worse than you think. Trust me. I've been doing some research, let's call it some counterintelligence. The Cabal can't wait to get their hands on an Arcanium student. They've given them free rein to try and take someone. I guess this kind of thing isn't forbidden by the charter, harkening back to the early days of the school when they warred with each other."

"I'm going. You can either come along or not," said Aurie, crossing her arms.

She hated playing the big sister card, but she hadn't involved Pi with her preparations on purpose. Since the attack on the way to Freeport Games, Pi had been downright annoying with her mothering.

"You're not playing fair," said Pi, shaking her head. "At least give me a chance to go change. You should too. They're set up for tracking enchantments leaving the building, so we need to strip ourselves."

"I'm leaving right now," said Aurie, enjoying her sister's discomfort. "You can keep your leather jacket on."

Pi ran to keep up with Aurie's long strides, her black boots clicking against the hardwood flooring. Along the way, Aurie stuck her hand in her pocket and rubbed the smooth stone in it, feeling the memory in her head brighten. When they ascended the drawbridge and a black limousine bracketed by two black SUVs came into view, Aurie couldn't help but smirk.

"You could at least try not to act so smug," said Pi. "Are you sure we can trust her?"

Rather than answer, Aurie raised an eyebrow. When they hopped in the back, Violet greeted them with a little hand wave as she finished up a conversation on her earpiece. She wore a black pants and jacket combo, and her hair had been brushed to golden silk.

"Hey, Silverthornes," said Violet, smiling warmly. "Looking good."

Aurie chuckled. "We look like a dumpster fire compared to you." Pi interjected with protests that her jacket was uber-sweet. "Things seem to be going well for you." Aurie flinched. "I'm sorry, that came out badly."

Violet reached across the space and patted Aurie on the knee without a trace of contempt, which seemed like a miracle considering their shared past. "Don't *ever* apologize. My mother was a grade-A bitch with outsized ambitions. She got her comeuppance. While I mourn her, I'm not blind to the fact that she was willing to hand the city over to Bannon Creed, the creepiest of creeps."

Aurie nodded. "Thank you for helping out."

"Helping out? I'm in this boat with the rest of you. If Semyon goes down, I'm screwed too. And while I've got a media empire to run, the board members are well aware of what's happening in Arcanium. Every one of those old farts hated my mother, and now that I'm in charge, they've stopped hiding their contempt. I don't go anywhere without multiple layers of bodyguards, and I'm not even sure of their loyalties considering the stakes. If it's not the Cabal, it'll be one of my own."

Aurie already knew this from her texts with Violet, but assumed she was explaining it for Pi's sake. Her sister wasn't saying anything, which was probably a good sign. After last year, and especially after experiencing Violet's memories about her childhood, Aurie understood why Violet acted the way she had.

"How is everyone doing?" asked Violet.

Aurie knew exactly what she meant. "A little shaky. Xi has terrible nightmares. Deshawn found him wandering half naked through the library last week. Drake has reoccurring hiccups that he says are from not using magic. You?"

Violet looked out the window at the passing city. "I have moments when I forget what happened to Semyon and start to cast a spell. Even when I remember, I still *want* to do it, like a compulsion." She chuckled at herself. "A few nights ago, I tried to walk through a wall, thinking that I had some magical ability that allowed it."

"It's only going to get worse as the year goes on," said Aurie.

"So where are we going?" asked Violet.

Aurie told her the address, which she relayed to the driver. While they drove, the three of them caught up, and at times, Aurie found it hard to believe they'd been enemies for the first three years of school, based on the way they reminisced. Violet didn't ask about the purpose of the trip, which could have been a side-effect of her destination, or she was trying to be careful, assuming that whatever Aurie was doing was important enough she shouldn't know about it. Aurie guessed it was a bit of both.

When they arrived at the destination in the twelfth ward, Violet asked before they got out of the limo, "Do you need me to pick you up?"

"Won't be necessary. Getting home after this will be much easier," said Aurie.

Violet surprised Aurie with a hug, Pi included, before they left. As they waved goodbye to the limo and two SUVs, all heavily enchanted, Aurie felt her shoulder blades itch with the feeling they were being watched.

"Why did you have her drop us off in the middle of a dump?" asked Pi, doing a slow circle.

It wasn't a dump, but an old industrial area in which most of the buildings were half collapsed, trees growing right out of the middle of them, bushes chewing through the concrete sidewalks, turning them to chalky dust. Rusted chain-link fences were bent, where squatters had probably jumped over in years past, though she couldn't imagine anyone living in these now. The buildings looked out of the '50s, or earlier, and probably hadn't been used since. The air didn't smell like oil or waste, but sweet, as if the rot had consumed it, and the section of the city was returning to nature.

"I think the term is post-apocalyptic chic," said Aurie, heading towards the end of the street, where a boarded-up wall was covered in signs. She pulled the stone in her pocket out and kept it in her fist. She could feel the magic of the area warring with the enchantment on the stone.

"Superfund site?" asked Pi. "What are we doing here?"

Something clanged nearby, metal on metal. A couple of black birds took flight.

"Looks like we have guests. I'll explain when we get there. Can you?" she asked, gesturing towards the chain and padlock.

Pi's spell made quick work of the barrier. The boarded fence swung open. Aurie slipped in, and upon finding that Pi had not followed, had to go back out. Her sister was wandering away with a dazed look on her face.

"Pythia," said Aurie sharply. "Come here."

"What? Why aren't we leaving?" asked Pi, perplexed.

Aurie grabbed her sister's arm and dragged her towards the open gate. Through the skeletal buildings on the far side of the block, she saw people headed their way. "Come on."

Pi resisted her effort, but not enough that Aurie couldn't maneuver her through the gate. Inside the fence, the buildings were worse than outside. Old rusted barrels leaked bright green fluid onto the street. Radioactive signs with yellow hazard symbols were placed everywhere. Aurie's skin felt warm despite the cloudy, cool day.

Her sister clutched at her jacket, frantic, looking back the way they'd come as if it were her lifeline. "We shouldn't be here. It's not safe."

Aurie felt it too. There was a pressure on her, forcing her out, but she was determined to go forward. She squeezed her sister's arm, dragging her ahead, keeping a firm grip on the smooth stone. Aurie imagined that if she had a Geiger counter, it would be pegged into the red. Walking past the florescent green liquid gave Aurie the creeps even though she didn't think it was real. If she was wrong, then she'd probably doomed them to death from radiation poisoning.

About a hundred yards from the entrance, the pressure relented, almost as if it'd popped, and Aurie stumbled forward.

"Wait," Pi said, suddenly looking behind them. "What just happened? How did I get here?"

Aurie experimented with the stone, putting it back in her pocket to see if the enchantment on the area erased her memories, but she didn't lose her thoughts.

"We're past its defenses," said Aurie. "I can explain now."

"Explain what?" asked Pi. "I'm so confused."

"We're here for the Engine of Temporal Manipulation. I think we can fix Semyon with it."

"Here? In this radioactive junkyard?"

"I'm pretty sure it's an illusion, a really powerful one. Plus there's another enchantment that makes you forget this area, and also another that compels you to leave. It's taken me months to find it and figure out how to get here, especially without magic." When she saw her sister's look, Aurie pulled out the stone. "It's a memory stone, allows you to remember something you don't want to forget. It's really simple, but it worked."

"What about the illusions and the enchantment to make us want to leave? If it'd been me alone, I would have never come here."

"The thing that's going on with Semyon, making us a little allergic to magic? Well, that helped me resist. Since you can use your magic, it affected you strongly. Basically it keeps anyone with magic out, who would be the only people who could see through the illusion in the first place. A neat trick if you ask me."

"And I clearly did not," said Pi, grinning.

About twenty yards after the place the compulsion left them, the illusion faded away, leaving Aurie breathless.

"Merlin's tits," said Pi.

Aurie shivered with excitement. An autumnal forest, brilliant with vibrant oranges, fiery reds, and glowing yellows greeted them. The spaces between the trees let shafts of sunlight trickle through, illuminating motes floating through the fresh air. It was a cathedral to nature, making Aurie wonder if they'd stepped into Fae.

"How is this not visible on satellite maps?" asked Pi as they strolled through the wide spaces.

"That should give you an indication of how powerful the enchantments are."

Pi nodded, pulling her leather jacket around herself protectively. "Gotcha."

After a twenty-minute walk, they spotted a cottage nestled in a hollow, basking in a beam of sunlight as if it were trying to get warm. The rustic building had an uneven roof like a hat knocked partially off and gray walls made of misshapen stones. A wisp of smoke curled from the chimney.

"I smell bread," said Pi. "Like that good bread that releases steam when you break it in half."

Aurie's face felt tingly and light. "I'm suddenly regretting coming here."

"Another enchantment?"

"No," said Aurie. "It was cloudy before, but I can see blue

sky through the trees. I'm feeling like a couple of kids in a fairy tale, you know, the ones where they're eaten by the wicked witch."

In an exaggerated motion, Pi cracked her knuckles. "That's why you brought me, sis. The girl who took on four Protectors in runed armor."

"Don't get cocky," said Aurie, glancing around. "I don't think whoever or whatever is creating this is in the same league."

"Dooset daram," said Pi, nodding.

"Dooset daram."

As they approached, Aurie noticed a second building, similar to the first, back a ways. No smoke leaked from its chimney, no light burned in its windows. The stone was gray. Shadows collected around the edges in drifts.

The second cottage gave Aurie the shivers, but she had no further time to consider it when the door of the first cottage opened.

"Be silly to come all this way and leave, right?" asked Aurie.

Pi glanced back the way they'd come. "Wouldn't hurt my feelings."

They went inside. A man sat cross-legged on a wooden rocking chair, skin as black as night, knitting an afghan blanket with deep blue yarn. He was focused on the tips of the needles, hooking the yarn with efficiency. His colorful shirt matched a rainbow chopped out of the sky and woven into fabric.

Two stools sat opposite him. A second rocking chair was shoved into the corner. He uncrossed his legs and pointed his toe at the stools. Aurie took hers with Pi close behind.

A low table between the chairs held a ceramic pot, steam leaking out the spout, with three cups waiting. A bitter tang caught the back of Aurie's sinuses.

"It's been a long time since I've had visitors. Drink. The palith root might make you sneeze, but trust me, that's the most enjoyable part," said the man in a voice that could have come from a cabbie in Philadelphia.

"Thank you..." said Aurie, pausing, wondering what to call him when a name appeared in her mind, "Oba."

Aurie placed the cup against her lips and took a tentative sip in case the liquid was too hot. As advertised, the drink was bitter but pleasant, tickling her sinuses until she had to set the cup down before releasing a quick sneeze in her cupped hands. After the sneeze resided, a pleasurable wave passed through her.

Beside her, Pi sneezed as well.

"Merlin's tits, that's amazing," said her sister.

"It's a stressful experience coming here," said Oba. "A cup of palith takes the edge off."

Rather than take a second sip, Aurie set the cup down and really studied her host. His features were unremarkable, average even, but she felt her gaze roll towards him as if he were a valley and she were a river flowing to the center.

"Get out of my head!" said Pi, standing up, backing away.

Oba frowned, setting his needlework against his crossed knee. His lips were flat, disapproving. "What's one more? I was only curious. Is this a thing now, to adorn oneself with slivers of souls like jewelry? What a terrible price for vanity."

Pi bent at the waist like a trap sprung, hands to her ears. "Stop!"

Aurie stood up. "You're hurting my sister. She didn't ask for those souls. She was saving them."

Oba tilted his head. A presence brushed through her mind, suggesting vastness so large it made the Grand Canyon feel small.

Pi collapsed on her rear, but removed her hands from her ears. She was breathing heavily and looked like she'd been through ten rounds with a box of snakes.

"You shouldn't peek in other people's minds, not without asking," said Aurie.

"Like you did with Violet Cardwell's dreams?" responded Oba without delay.

Suddenly, Aurie regretted coming. Whoever or whatever Oba was, he was a power unto his own. She'd assumed that anything within the city was there with Invictus' permission, but she doubted that assumption now. She shared a glance with Pi, who was white with concern.

"My apologies, Oba," said Aurie. "We're guests in your house. I shouldn't have lectured you."

Oba cackled, setting his needlework against his knee as mirth left his lips.

"I suppose that's what passes as groveling these days. You're lucky I don't care about such things anymore. Speak now, Aurelia Maximus Silverthorne, student of Semyon Gray. Why do you risk much coming here? Do you seek wisdom? Or perhaps the sad story of my life?"

Aurie paused. Either his ability to read her mind was not absolute, or he was testing her. She decided to go with the idea that he already knew, and was only following the protocols of conversation for her sake.

"We came for the Engine of Temporal Manipulation."

"And you shall leave without it," he replied.

"We need it to save the Hundred Halls. I assume you were a friend of Invictus'; otherwise, you wouldn't be hiding in his city."

"Were?"

Aurie paused. How long had Oba been hiding in the cottage? "He's dead. It's been almost sixteen years, and now

Semyon is...well, he's not well, and the Engine would help us fix him, I hope."

Oba slowly set his needlework on the table, moved to the window, and stared into the forest. Pi motioned at Aurie, asking what they should do. Aurie shrugged, putting her hand on her heart.

"Were you and Invictus friends?" asked Pi.

Without turning around, Oba said, "I was ancient before he was even born. He was a minor nuisance for a long while, and then by chance, I had reason to let him live. It was a fortuitous decision, as he showed me there were other ways."

"So he *was* a good man," said Pi, almost a question, but filled with self-doubt and deep reflection.

"Good? No. Better than most at the time, but that's like calling a lion gentle because he sleeps most of the day. It's hard for me to imagine that he's dead, but it happens. It used to happen more until he had this crazy idea to start a school and bind mages together"—he turned his head a little as if he anticipated their questions—"not me of course, but the Halls was his gift to humanity, a path to real civilization."

"Then you understand how important it is that we preserve his legacy, keep the Halls alive," said Aurie.

Oba turned back, putting his hands on the back of the wooden rocking chair. "The Halls were his project, not mine. I helped him because I owed him, but now that he's gone, my debts are paid."

"Then you don't need the Engine of Temporal Manipulation," said Aurie, clasping her hands together. "Give it to us. Let us deal with the Halls."

"You don't understand the danger they represent, or even how it works. I'd be giving a nuclear weapon to a baby," he said, a frown on his lips.

"I know how it works, and it's not a nuclear weapon, at

least how I want to use it," said Aurie, shaking her hands at him. "The only thing that can heal Semyon is time, and we need more of it, fast. I want to speed up his time, and nothing else. There's no danger."

"Ha!" he said, swishing his hand through the air as if he were slapping her. "This proves you are ignorant of that which you seek to possess. If you speed him up, something else must balance out. It's a scale, and time is immutable. There must be equilibrium. Unless you've had a few millennia to understand your craft, you should not think about using it. Even Invictus did not dare. That is why he gave it to me, in exchange for services rendered."

"Bullshit," said Aurie, waving her sister off when she reached out to calm her. "You wouldn't have hunkered down here in the middle of a heavily enchanted forest disguised as a junkyard if you were the owner of it. You're holding onto it for a reason, and Invictus is letting you use it, but it's still his, and with his death, his belongings pass to the Halls. So you've got our property, and I want to use it."

"You've overstepped your bounds," said Oba coolly.

Power simmered beneath the surface of his skin, warping the air around him like shimmers on a hot road. He could squash them like a bug, could have done it before they even stepped onto the grounds, but he hadn't, and Aurie clung to that idea, hoping that it gave her a chance.

"No, you have. You're hiding here," she spat back, then jabbed her finger at the forest outside the window. "That's why it looks like late fall outside, even though it's only the end of summer in Invictus. You've frozen time here, which means that something else is going faster. Like you said, it's an equilibrium, a balance."

"I shouldn't have let you come," said Oba gravely. "I was bored, needed a distraction, but this is insolence. I should turn your skin inside out and run you through the brambles."

She believed him, but did not relent. If she failed at this, the school was doomed. She had to try, even if it was fruitless.

Aurie thought about the second cottage. Looked around the room at the second rocking chair, the blanket that he was knitting. Realization came to her like a lightning strike. Before Oba could stop her, she ran out of the cottage, heading straight for the second building. Before she'd gotten halfway across the space, Oba appeared by her side and knocked her to the ground.

"I forbid!"

His power pinned her to the ground—she felt like a gnat in a hurricane. She felt him waver between letting her go and crumpling her like a tin can.

"Get off my fucking sister!"

Eldritch bonds whipped through the air, attaching to Oba's limbs like an angry glowing octopus. Pi's magic crackled around Oba. The pressure released Aurie, giving her a chance to run. She hoped she hadn't made a foolish decision.

Oba quickly sliced through the bonds and knocked Pi away like a paper doll. But by the time he turned to stop Aurie, she'd made it to the cottage door, throwing herself inside.

The second cottage was identical to the first, except a featherbed filled the space occupied by the rocking chair in the other one. Deep within the covers lay a woman with skin like cream, fiery red hair, and freckles across the bridge of her nose.

At the top of the bed, resting on a little shelf, sat a runed brass tube. A deep-seated hum that made the back of Aurie's teeth hurt emanated from the device. It wasn't much to look at, but she knew what it was the moment she gazed up on it: the Engine of Temporal Manipulation.

Oba burst in with his arms poised for action, but when he

saw Aurie standing over the woman in the bed, they fell, while his expression tightened.

Aurie spoke before he could rebuke her. "It's not the land that's being held in time, but this woman."

The way Oba looked at the woman in the bed outlined their relationship. He would do anything for her, and clearly had.

Pi stumbled into the room behind Oba. Her hair was covered in leaves, and her nose was bloody, but otherwise, she looked unharmed by his magical strike.

"Her name is Boann. She is my beloved, and she exists in the last hours of her death."

"What about the equilibrium?" asked Aurie.

Oba strolled to the side of the bed and traced his fingers across Boann's cheek. The weight of his love for her was borne in his tight shoulders.

"What's a few centuries to an old man that's seen so many? I bear this burden with pride," said Oba.

"Is there a way to heal her?" asked Aurie.

He shook his head tightly.

"The blanket you're making is for her, isn't it?" He nodded. "Why? She's going to die."

Behind her, Pi hissed for caution. Oba looked at her, eyes murderous.

"You're being selfish," said Aurie. "A whole city, a whole world, is at risk while you sit here in your private garden making a blanket for someone who can't even enjoy it. Give us the Engine. We can do something good with it."

"What do I care about good and right?" he asked, sneering. "I destroyed cities for spite, murdered whole peoples for bowing wrong. She was my beloved. Mine. Why should I care about you and yours? I'll sit here until the end of time if I want, and there's nothing you can do about it."

"Then you'll die a lonely man," said Aurie venomously.

Oba swiped his hand at them, and the cottage disappeared, replaced by the junkyard outside the autumnal forest. He'd teleported them over a mile with only a gesture.

But Aurie was not deterred. She readied herself to march back in until he was ready to give up the Engine of Temporal Manipulation. She opened her fist to check for the memory stone, but it was only dust. Oba had destroyed it.

Immediately the memory of why she'd come disintegrated, until she was staring at the radioactive sign with deepening confusion.

Beside her, Pi was scratching her head. "Why did you want to come here again?"

Aurie glanced around, trying to catch something that might trigger her memory. Her palm was dusty, so she wiped it on her pant leg. Then she noticed Pi's bloody nose.

"Did you get hit by something?" asked Aurie.

Pi touched her nose, and came away with crusty blood. "I...I'm not sure."

Aurie shook her head. The day was getting warmer, and the sun was breaking through the clouds. She had the impression she'd forgotten something, but it flitted at the edge of her memory like a butterfly tickling a flower before darting away.

"I guess whatever it was that I wanted isn't here. We should get back to Arcanium before the Cabal finds us."

They headed out on foot to the nearest train station, two miles away. Aurie looked back at least a dozen times before she convinced herself that it hadn't been that important to come to the twelfth ward.

5

The phone buzzed awake, the electronics showering her room with light. Pi struggled over the mass of blankets collected on her bed, scooped the device from the table, and quickly typed in the code. The little icon displaying the number of texts received had a red number thirty-five inside.

"Shit," said Pi, stumbling out of bed, quickly scanning the messages that she'd missed. She'd been monitoring the text chains between various members of the Cabal. The students were mostly talk, going on with great exaggeration about how they'd "show the Arcanium dorks what real magic was" or how Semyon Gray was the weakest patron of the original five because he'd gotten taken down by Camille Cardwell before she died. This was wrong, of course, because he'd been attacked by the man she'd thought was her uncle—Liam, the soul thief—but it told Pi how much the patrons involved their students in their plans, which was, not at all.

Except for the attack when they'd tried to go to Freeport Games, the Cabal students' bluster had barely reached the level of the darkest internet message boards.

But this conversation was different.

Rather than attack Arcanium, which was a suicide mission

for this group of fourth years, they'd figured out that Isabella's parents lived in the city, on the east side of the ninth ward, and planned to take them captive, forcing her to come out to them. Isabella's parents had no ability with magic. She was the only child of their six kids that had exhibited the talent, which was not uncommon. The science behind why certain people had access to faez and others didn't was largely unsettled.

Pi had to stop them. She'd prepared for this possibility—not the kidnapping specifically, but that she might have to leap into action at a moment's notice—leaving out a pair of jeans, a plain white T-shirt, and her magical leather jacket, along with a few potions, protective charm bracelets, and a couple of packets of exploding powder.

She left without informing Aurie, who would only slow her down. She considered going directly to Isabella, to warn her not to fall for their trap, but knew that wouldn't work either. Isabella would want to save her parents, and Pi wasn't prepared for what she would have to do to stop her.

The only problem was she had no reliable way to leave Arcanium without being spotted. If the attack had happened during the day, she could have used the pizza guy trick, or called Violet for a ride, but it was 2:54 a.m., and none of those things would work.

Pi went to the roof and outside the garden dome, then scanned the surrounding buildings for one close enough that she could reach it through magic, or a magic-assisted jump, but Semyon had chosen this spot wisely, and the moat around the building created separation, and even if she could get across to the other buildings, it was doubtful she could make it across the city in time.

The phone kept buzzing with conversation. Sunil was the leader of the little group, which involved an Alchemist, two Assassins, and two Coterie mages, whose names she didn't recognize, indicating they were younger. She sensed he thought this trick might get him back in everyone's good graces after letting her and Aurie get away last month. He was already telling the others how much he would be able to help them once they'd accomplished the task, as if it were a school project and not kidnapping and torture. It was driving Pi crazy not to respond to his idiotic, and clearly disingenuous, influence peddling.

His latest text read: [I'm going to introduce you to some important mages after we do this!]

They were meeting at an all-night diner near Isabella's parents' house in twenty minutes, which didn't give Pi much time to get there. She thought about just leaving Arcanium, daring them to come after her, but that would only drag more Cabal students into the fight. One against six was already going to be terrible odds.

When the floating candle-like gondola approached overhead, Pi had an idea—a stupid idea, she decided, but an idea nonetheless. The gondola was headed towards Arcanium, albeit at a distance of a hundred meters above the Hall, and even in the slight direction of the ninth ward.

She looked around the roof for something she could use to propel herself up to it, but the opportunities were pretty thin. There was only another twenty seconds before the gondola would pass overhead and be out of reach.

When she pulled the packet of explosive powder from her inside pocket and weighed it in her hand while simultaneously weighing the idea she had in her mind, she knew what she was going to do was irrevocably stupid.

Pi touched her charmed bracelet for luck, set the explosive packet on the ground, and placed the soles of her boots on top. If she missed, the landing was going to be messy.

At the precise moment the gondola passed over Arcanium,

Pi jumped into the air, formed a concave force shield beneath her feet, and steeled herself for impact.

The packet detonated when she snapped her fingers, throwing her straight up. The acceleration shoved her chin into her chest, rotating her forward. She was headed right for the gondola, but her body was tilted, facing downward, so she'd have no way to grab the loading rail that went around the bottom. Pi leaned into the spin, doing a full flip, coming around right as she went past the gondola, overshooting it by ten feet.

Inside the gondola were a couple of identical pale-haired fourth years in robes, who pressed themselves against the window as she shot past. Seeing that she was going to plummet back to the earth, Pi used a pulling spell on the gondola, which failed to move the vehicle, but since she was untethered, shot her towards it. She hit the glass and barely got her fingers around the metal rod before her weight wrenched the sockets in her shoulders painfully.

Hanging from the bottom of the gondola, Pi had no way to open the door or use her hands to create a spell that might help her. She'd come all the way up, but hadn't thought about how to get inside.

The window opened, and twin pale heads were stuck out.

"'allo down there. Have we got a hitchhiker tonight?"

The guy sounded like the Swedish chef, making her laugh, which wasn't good considering her situation.

"Can you help me up? I can hold on for a while longer, but I'd rather ride in the gondola."

The twins looked at each other. The second one said, "But you're not allowed in the gondola, and we don't want to break the rules."

Pi gritted her teeth. "I'm a fourth year, you knuckleheads, otherwise how would I have managed that stupid trick. Let me up. I needed to get somewhere fast, and this was the best way."

When no answer came, Pi started figuring how she might lever her legs onto the rail and pull herself up. Then a pale rope came slithering down the side of the gondola. Pi grabbed hold, testing it for strength, then put both hands around it.

The rope pulled upward, and upon cresting over the lip of the window, she saw the rope was the hair of the twins, grown magically longer.

Finally on her feet inside, Pi wiped her sweaty hands on her jeans before offering her hand to the twins.

"Thanks, guys," she said.

The nearly albino twins were familiar to Pi. She remembered them from her Merlins at the beginning of her first year. They'd been playing mock Five Elements against each other while waiting for the tests, and then later, had joined Violet's team during the anti-gravity battle in the bug room. They were cute, in an androgynous way, and she wondered if they had supernatural heritage.

"Very sorry. We don't like to touch. I'm Arvid, and this is my brother Björn."

"You're from Oestomancium?" she asked, pointing at the pins on their robes showing a circus tent made of bones.

"It is okay," said Björn, "you may call it the Weird Circus."

"I'm Pi."

They both nodded.

"We know," said Astrid. "You and your sister are famous in the Halls. Very sorry we did not recognize you hanging from the gondola."

The Spire at the center of the city was passing them on her right, which meant she had a couple of minutes before the gondola reached the outer wards. Pi examined the control panel.

"How do you work this thing? Is it like a glass elevator kind of thing and I can change directions?"

The twins took position on either side of her, which was unnerving, only because it was like being surrounded by human mirrors.

"The elevator once sent on its heavenly journey cannot deviate," said Astrid, or Björn, she couldn't tell.

"Where is it headed?"

"A gondola station near our Hall."

Pi pressed her face against the glass, trying to ascertain their direction. "Ninth ward, right?"

"Eighth," they said at the same time. Stereo weirdness.

"Shit," she said, checking the group text for status. She did some quick math and realized she'd be late if she rode the gondola to the station. "I need to get off, like soon. It's an emergency."

"There's no way to change our destination," said the twin on her right.

Pi moved back to the window. "Then I'm going to have to jump, or something." But when she looked out into the darkness, seeing how far below her the streets lay, a pit of vertigo opened inside her. A car passing below didn't even look like a toy, just a tiny bug crawling across the ground with lighted eyes. It was a lot farther than she'd thought.

The twins huddled on the far side of the gondola, speaking quietly to each other.

"Great," she muttered to herself. "They're having a Weird Convention."

Pi looked back out the window and started going through ideas, hoping one of the soul fragments had a spell that might work. When she heard creaking, like old wood warping, and a low moaning, Pi paused, thinking about all the horror movies she'd ever watched, with the sinking feeling in her gut that she wasn't going to like whatever the twins were doing.

When her curiosity finally got the best of her, she learned she was right. Arvid, she thought, was stretching his arms, growing them outward like silly putty. It might not have been so bad, had his eyes not been rolled into the back of his head in either ecstasy or agony. Björn was crouched on the ground like a mushroom, his hair growing into a coil at the center of the gondola. It looked like he was churning butter with his head.

"I hope this isn't a weird murder fetish thing," she said.

Arvid opened his eyes briefly and said, "We help you get down."

When they had completed their bodily modifications, Arvid was a human scaffold attached to either end of the gondola, while his legs had wrapped and entwined around Björn.

"Throw the hair out the window and climb down."

"Rapunzel, Rapunzel. The fairy tales had it all wrong," she said as she slipped out the window, after a spell to strengthen her grip.

Swinging beneath a gondola that was riding on invisible wires, while hanging from human hair wasn't the strangest thing she'd ever done, but it was pretty close. When she got about twenty feet above an apartment building, Pi dropped, hit the roof hard, and rolled into the forward motion.

A quick check on her cell phone told her she had a few minutes to spare if she hurried. Pi waved to the twins before vaulting down a set of metal fire stairs that rattled like an earthquake.

A potion from her jacket provided an energy boost, allowing her to run the six blocks to the all-night diner without breaking a sweat.

When she arrived, Sunil and his cohorts were filing from the diner, headed towards Isabella's parents' house, which was only half a block away.

Pi watched from the shadows. She had no intention of letting them get close to the house, but one against six would be tricky. She had to find a way to tip the odds in her favor. There was also the question of how lethal she wished to be. Pi had no doubt she could kill the six of them before they could react, but then what kind of person was she? But trying to take them out without killing them would open her up to major risk. It sucked fighting fairly, especially when your enemy wasn't going to. Pi could hear Aurie's lectures already about how sinking to their level makes sure they win, even if you defeat them, by destroying the thing that you're trying to protect. But what if there's no other way?

Pi zipped up the front of her leather jacket. She wasn't prepared to go that far, yet.

Using Ashley's memories, Pi layered an enchantment on herself, being careful to hide the anchors in case one of them had faez-seeing glasses on. The spell was a nasty bit of business that would only work once, so she had to make it count. It also assuaged her concern about attacking first.

Pi jogged to catch up to them when they were crossing the street.

"Hey, you shit-for-brains cockswaggles, where do you think you're going?"

Sunil turned first, gesticulating as he conjured his response. The others followed his lead, using the most basic spells of the Five Elements. The sharp smell of faez hit the air like an impending rainstorm as energy crackled from the six Cabal students.

Pi prepared a flashy spell of her own, full of menacing flame and screaming shadows, something that might have come from a demon's mouth. The spell was all show and no impact, but she didn't want them to think about their response to her sudden arrival.

The spells didn't hit her simultaneously, but they were pretty close. She wasn't even entirely sure what they were, but a color storm of magic ripped through the air, buckling the pavement between her and them. The girl Assassin, wearing thick black glasses, was the only one that pulled her spell, which told Pi she hadn't hidden her reflection spell enough.

Five spells hit her like a freight train, then rebounded, heading directly back to their casters. The mages were blown off their feet, screams and curses filling the city street.

The remaining mage pulled two knives from a hidden pouch and threw them at Pi before she could react. Her reflection shield was spent, and even if some had remained, it wouldn't have stopped the physical blades from seeking her throat.

One blade bounced off her leather jacket, while the second sunk into her thigh. Pi had little time, as the Assassin girl came running with a katana as tall as she was in her hands.

With the knife sunk into the meat of her thigh, Pi transformed a disc of metal into a shield to block the sword blow. The girl came at her relentlessly, grunting and swinging.

Half limping, Pi kept the shield between her and the girl, the blows ringing off the metal time after time. Each step drove the knife further into her thigh, until she managed to grab the handle and yank it out.

Pi nearly blacked out from the pain. She blocked a low sweep, which forced her to bend her leg.

The other mages were stirring. If they joined the fight, she was done.

When the Assassin mage brought the sword down for an overhead strike, Pi folded the shield around it and the girl's arms. Pi pushed her away, and she fell to the street with a clatter, trapped.

Pi put a numbing bind on her wound, and limp-sprinted the other way. Her jeans were soaked with blood, but she had no time to spell the wound closed.

As she cut across the street, a car went past, the passenger's wide-eyed stare almost comical in its exaggeration. She hoped to Merlin that the guy been drinking so he wouldn't go to the cops.

The mages were about half a block behind her, and catching up. Pi found an idyllic park nestled between the buildings, and she slipped into an exquisitely shaped stone pagoda with sweeping gold and crimson painted roofs and wooden railings. It looked like something an artistic Stone Singer had created for wedding pictures.

Pi crouched behind the wall and placed no-look enchantments overtop herself. She wanted to fix the wound in her leg as the blood loss was making her dizzy, but she couldn't risk detection.

"I think she went in here," said Assassin Girl, standing at the entrance to the park.

Pi wished she'd broken the girl's glasses. She probably saw the traces of faez in the park.

Her pursuers entered the park carrying magelights that spread their illumination across the grass, turning the area to daytime.

"Spread out," called Sunil. "We have to find that little bitch."

Crawling around the inside of the pagoda, Pi fixed explosive packets to the support structures. If she blew them at the same time, they could provide a last-second distraction while she sprinted out.

When she was finished, she tried to figure out where the mages had gotten to. Pi was peeking over the rail when a blade was pressed against her throat.

"Move and I bleed you like a pig," said Assassin Girl.

She had a bit of a country accent, and Pi gathered that the threat was real, and filled with experience.

Pi nodded slowly to show she was cooperating.

"She's over here!" yelled Assassin Girl.

While the others approached, Pi tried to think of a spell that would solve her current predicament, but nothing came. The soul fragments were completely silent.

"Not a good time to disappear, gang," Pi said under her breath.

"What?" asked Assassin Girl.

"Nothing."

When the others arrived, Sunil placed bindings on her arms and legs, suspending Pi between two concrete pillars like an "X." Then he put a spell on her throat that kept her from speaking.

"Can I borrow that knife?"

Assassin Girl shrugged, handing it over to Sunil.

"Keep an eye out, make sure no one sees what's happening here," said Sunil.

The corners of her eyes creased while her lips pursed with thought. She finally shrugged and jogged into the darkness of the park.

When Sunil moved up close, she saw his right eye was bloodied from the spell rebound. A lingering rage lurked behind them.

She had fifty pithy things to say, but no way to say them, since he'd silenced her. Which was probably a good thing, because she'd probably get herself killed with a comment.

"Video this," said Sunil. "We're going to send a message to the sister."

A mage in back, shorter, with a dark complexion, said, "We've got her. Why get the sister?"

"Cause clearly this one's not in Arcanium, or she wouldn't be able to use magic. Come on, Darrell, use your brains for once," said Sunil.

Sunil leaned down, examining her thigh wound while the others watched. He stuck the tip of the blade into the cut and wiggled it back and forth.

She nearly blacked out. Her mouth opened, sweat forming on her brow, but no sound was produced. When he pulled the knife out, she panted.

Sunil examined her face, leaning in so close she could smell his hot breath. He smelled like fast food and diet soda.

"I don't think that's good enough," he said, looking back into the cell phone being held up as a camera. He held the knife up for the video, then jammed it into her shoulder.

Blacking out would have been a relief, but that never came. The tip of the blade impacted her bone, the flesh splitting as he pressed against the hilt. If he'd used magic, her charm bracelets might have absorbed some of the impact, but she had no protections against physical damage.

"Did you get a good shot?" asked Sunil, looking back as if they were taking prom pictures or something much less mundane than torture.

"Got it," said Darrell.

"Send it to her bitch sister, and let's see how fast she comes running. Make sure you explain that if anyone else shows up, little Miss Pi is dead."

Pi thought that was going to happen either way, based on the amount of blood she'd lost. She was feeling rather cold suddenly, not a good sign.

While Darrell was typing away at his phone, Pi eyed the explosive packets she'd hidden on the stone columns. She hadn't planned on triggering them while she, or anyone else, was in the pagoda, but she couldn't let them send that video.

Sunil stuck his face in hers again, leering at her with his side-cocked grin. "What do you think about that?"

Pi couldn't speak, so she spit in his face. Before he could register his outrage, she triggered the packets with the snap of her fingers.

She was thrown to the earth, stone and concrete flying around her. The heavy roof crashed down, chunks splitting and falling into the park. A piece the size of a desk narrowly missed her head.

After the collapse was finished, Pi was lying in a bush, a hunk of stone over her like a lean-to. Her hearing was shot, and the wounds in her shoulder and thigh were throbbing.

"Fuck," she whispered to herself, which was a good and bad sign. She could talk, which was a plus, but she'd heard herself through a tin can. She'd probably blown out her eardrums. But it also meant that Sunil was incapacitated, since his spells were no longer affecting her.

"Guys?" came a voice from outside the collapsed pagoda. "Sunil? Cynthia? Darrel?"

It was Assassin Girl. She'd been in the park, and had avoided being smashed by the falling roof.

"Oh, god," she exclaimed, which meant she'd probably seen one of the bodies.

When Pi didn't hear anything further, she assumed that girl had left. Pi extricated herself from the bush and closed her wounds with a spell so she didn't bleed out. The rest would have to be dealt with later.

She stumbled out of the stone lean-to and surveyed the damage. Sunil's lifeless eyes were peeking from beneath a chunk of golden concrete. Limbs poked out from the destruction.

The cold realization hit her: she'd killed five people.

It didn't matter that they'd been torturing her and planning to capture her sister. It didn't matter that they would have killed her. They'd been alive, and now they were not, and Pi had caused it.

Her hands shook with the realization. She wanted to vomit. She could feel it in her gut, but she didn't have time for self-recrimination. She had to get away, fast, or their deaths would become her immediate problem.

Pi chugged another potion. The aftereffects would be hell on her body, but she needed the energy to get away before the authorities arrived. Before she left, Pi looked through the rubble for Darrell. She found him under a chunk of concrete, ignoring the pool of blood leaking out. His cell phone was lying nearby, screen cracked, but still showing the video and message unsent. Pi quickly deleted the message and shoved the phone in her pocket.

After she got a few blocks away, Pi called a cab. She made it back to Arcanium around sunrise, fixed the worst of the damage with a few Aura Healer spells, and collapsed in bed. It'd been a long fucking night and she wanted to sleep for a week.

6

A gust of rain battered against the window of Aurie's bedroom. It'd been raining for the past three days, a wet beginning to the month of October. Normally, it'd have been a great time to get schoolwork done, but without the practical side of magic taking up her every waking moment, she'd had to resort to finding things to do.

Aurie was working on a spreadsheet of spells on her laptop while drinking chamomile tea and listening to the Breaknecks on her phone. Piles of papers and files sat by her desk while she cross-referenced the spells she was familiar with by usefulness, complexity, and location of tome. During her time at the Hundred Halls, she'd found a lot of interesting spells that she thought might come in handy later, but had never gotten around to cataloging them. And while she couldn't cast any of the spells at the current time, she hoped that her work would be put to good use later when Semyon was restored.

It was hard not knowing when that would be, especially with her sister running around the city battling the Cabal single-handedly. Last night, the fourth time in weeks, Pi had come stumbling into her room, bloody and bruised. She never talked about what happened on her excursions, but it wasn't hard to figure it out by the articles in the *Herald of the Halls*. Violet did her best to suppress mention of Pi, but there were other news sources that had nailed the description of her sister enough that she had no doubt. The Cabal had to know too.

Three nights before, Pi had needed help putting a broken arm back into place so she could spell it together. The time before that, one of her kidneys had been turned to gelatin. It'd taken a visit from Hannah's friend in Aura Healers to reverse the curse.

The situation made it all the more important that Semyon be healed, but it didn't seem like that would happen any time soon. In fact, Aurie kept thinking she was forgetting something that she'd been working on, but she couldn't put her finger on it.

A bang on the door startled Aurie.

"You in there?" asked Deshawn.

"Yeah."

"The professor wants to see you. The usual place."

Aurie paused. "I'll be there. Thanks, Deshawn."

After putting on respectable clothes, as she didn't think her Hello Kitty pajamas would be acceptable to the professor, especially in the context of an unknown request, Aurie left her room only to find a strange runed cylinder sitting on the table in the common area between rooms.

Aurie eyed it with concern. Something tickled her memory, like an itch between the shoulder blades that she couldn't reach. Did Deshawn bring it? But that wouldn't make any sense.

She banged on Pi's door. "Hey, did you leave something on the table out here?"

When there was no answer, Aurie rattled the handle. Locked.

Hands on hips, Aurie surveyed the item. She was already

heading to Professor Mali, maybe she would know what it was.

As she touched the cool metal, a surge of thoughts ran through her mind, like a life on fast-forward. Images she didn't recognize flooded her memory, then disappeared.

Aurie rubbed her hand as if it'd been painful. It hadn't, but the item clearly contained magical powers. It wouldn't be safe to accidentally activate an unknown trinket.

Using a towel dampened with water and olive oil, which was a wonderful inhibitor, Aurie wrapped the cylinder up and hurried to Semyon's apartment, concerned that whatever the item was, it was important.

Professor Mali was slumped in her wheelchair, and for a moment, Aurie thought the worst until the professor stirred, yawning and stretching her arms above her head. The professor had a sleepy expression until she saw who was standing in her room, and her face hardened.

"Miss Aurelia. Thank you for seeing me on such short notice."

"Of course, Professor."

She wanted to add, *it's not like I have anything else to do,* but decided that snark wasn't the appropriate response at this time.

The moment the professor straightened in her wheelchair, Aurie knew it was going to be bad. She might as well have spit in her hands and hauled an axe out for chopping, for what she was about to say next.

"Miss Aurelia." She paused. "Aurie. I'm afraid I'm going to ask that your sister leave Arcanium."

"What? Are you kidding me?"

The professor's eyes went wide with surprise. She tilted her head in a dangerous manner. "Excuse me? Would you like to rephrase that?"

Aurie choked back her anger, but it was hard. It was like

she'd shaken up a bottle of champagne and was trying to open it without making a mess.

"I'm sorry, Professor." The title was said with a hard emphasis. "But my sister has been the only thing keeping Cabal students from messing with Arcanium. Like a month ago when they tried to kidnap Isabella's parents, or the time they put a spell on Felix through his open window. If she wouldn't have been around, Semyon would likely be dead, along with the rest of us."

A muscle in Professor Mali's jaw pulsed. "I am well aware of your sister's contribution to the defense. However, she crossed a line when she killed those mages."

There'd been no proof that it was Pi who'd caused it, and Aurie wasn't about to admit it to the professor, but her resoluteness suggested that she had learned the truth.

"If she killed them, a big if, I might add, it was entirely in self-defense," said Aurie.

"The issue is not whether or not it was in self-defense, but that she killed them, and because of that, she has to go," said the professor, crossing her arms.

A blind rage welled up in Aurie's chest. It was like her sister was being taken from her, and she didn't want that to happen. Aurie swallowed down her fear and responded as sanely as she could muster.

"Please, Professor. She's my sister. She has no place to go. I'll make sure she doesn't go out anymore. No more excursions, no more battles with the Cabal."

The professor's eyes rounded with sadness. "I'm sorry, Aurelia. It's not about her anymore. It's about the safety of the Hall. The other major halls have requested that we turn her over to them. They seek retribution."

"For what crimes? I thought we were immune from such things? My trial last year was only because of the public's outcry and Camille's maneuvering."

"You're absolutely right. Hall mages are immune from prosecution for self-defense, or other magic related events, within reason. But this is not about crime. Five mages died, representing the other major halls, which puts her in a precarious position politically, and second, your sister is not a member of any hall. Pythia is free game to them, and by harboring her, we put Arcanium at risk."

"But she's still tied to them through..."

The words trickled to silence when she realized the problem. Pi had renounced her spot in Arcanium, and the Halls didn't recognize the soul fragments. She was technically a member of the Hundred Halls through her many souls, but legally had no standing.

"Merde," said Aurie, squeezing the towel-wrapped tube against her chest.

"You understand now."

"What will we do without her? Can't we hide her or something?"

"How can she defend the Hall if they know she's here? And the moment they come barging into Arcanium with the full authority of the Halls, don't you think they might cause mischief? Leaving enchantments or other charms to lure away our students in the thick of night?"

"Fine," said Aurie, shaking her head. "But why do I have to tell her?"

"Because you're her sister. She'll listen to you. And because you asked that she could stay, so she's your charge. And lastly, having to deliver this kind of news is good training."

"Good training for what?"

"Leadership. Being able to deliver bad news is an important skill."

Aurie wanted to tell the professor where she could shove

that skill, but kept her mouth shut. Or maybe she didn't have to say anything. She could leave with her sister. Why did she have to stay in this place anyway?

"Aurelia. I can see what you're thinking. You'd be a fool to leave. They'd hunt you down and force you to use magic. You know the right thing to do is stay in Arcanium. Just like you did when you stayed away from the Engine of Temporal Manipulation. You're a good student. There's a reason Semyon spoke so highly of you."

Engine of Temporal Manipulation. Memories from her visit to Oba came rushing back, revealing the meaning of the object in her arms. Why did she have it? Did that mean he'd given up on Boann? But why?

"Yeah," said Aurie, swallowing, mind whirling. "I...I have a question about that."

The professor's lips went white.

"Uhm," began Aurie. "The guardian you mentioned. Is he—or she—a dangerous person, or thing?"

"Why are you asking?"

Aurie tried not to look at the towel in her arms. "Curiosity. I did the research to find that it existed, and I was wondering about the guardian. Not that I'm going to do anything about it. Honestly, your warning last time spooked me off it, but I am my mother's daughter, and artifacts were kind of a thing for my family."

The professor gave her a suspicious side-eye. "You're not trying to pump me for information so you can try and get it, are you?"

"No, Professor. Curiosity only."

It could have been because the professor felt bad about making Aurie tell her sister to leave Arcanium, or due to her exhaustion at watching over Semyon day or night, but the request worked.

"Without getting into specifics, I can tell you that the guardian is extremely dangerous. Let's say that Invictus was a clever man, and eliminated two problems—the guardian and the artifact—without resorting to direct measures."

"Invictus tricked the guardian into watching over the artifact?"

"It keeps him from causing trouble. We have enough complications without him running around in the world," said the professor.

Though she couldn't prove it, Aurie suspected that Invictus had caused whatever had happened to Boann so Oba would watch over her. He was a selfish, self-absorbed man-god, and Aurie had unleashed him on the world.

But he had given her the artifact, which in her eyes had been worth it. At least until she knew the full extent of the price, which was hopefully never.

"Professor Mali. Could I watch him for a while?" she asked, nodding towards Semyon's lifeless body.

"I'm perfectly capable of overseeing him," said the professor, a little peeved.

The wrinkles around her eyes had deepened, and shadows haunted the grim set of her lips. Aurie could see the guilt in her stiff shoulders. The professor felt responsible for what had happened to him.

"It's not that," said Aurie softly. "I need some time to think before I give my sister the bad news. This is as good a place as any, and maybe it'd be like he was listening to me, and I might figure out what I need to do."

The professor's lips lost their hard edges, and her eyes rounded. After one succinct nod, she rolled out of the room.

Aurie waited until the front doors to his apartment clicked shut, then she unwrapped the runed brass cylinder. It looked so simple, so innocent, but it was a frighteningly powerful artifact because it could manipulate the relative speed of time. Aurie worried that she wouldn't know how to use it, but as soon as the questioning started, the answers appeared in her head, another gift from Oba.

Keeping the damp towel between her hands and the artifact, Aurie set it on his chest. She wouldn't be able to keep it there, or the professor would find out, but that was the best place while she activated it.

"Time belongs to no one, it is a master unto itself, we can only use what we have until it's gone."

The activation phrase seemed contradictory with the device's purpose, which indicated the sense of humor of its maker.

Aurie traced the runes with her forefinger, keeping a set of matching patterns in her head. No false memories blew back through her.

When she finished, the runes glowed like embers, and time stutter-stepped like an irregular heartbeat, or a case of rapid déjà vu. The moment between the stutters, when time for her stood still, was horrific. It was as if she didn't exist and was aware of that feeling at the same time.

The runes cooled until they were back to their original brassy shine. As far as Aurie could tell, she'd performed the activation ritual correctly. Next, she hovered her hand over it and whispered the command word "white rabbit" while moving her hand across the length of the tube as if it were a slider bar, adjusting the flow of time for Semyon Gray.

Concerned that she might not be able to control it, Aurie kept the setting low. She could always make the cylinder run faster as she understood how well it was working. Plus, she was turning up Semyon's time, but the balance had to go somewhere, which meant something else was slowing down, but she didn't know what. That part of the instructions had been left out.

Aurie looked for a place to hide it. It only had to be near Semyon. She placed it under the medical bed, sticking it in the place between the frame and the mattress. The hum it created was hardly noticeable, and she knew what to listen for.

"That's the best I can do for now," she told the lifeless body of her patron. "I know the professor thought this way was too dangerous, but I had to do it. I hope when you wake up that you understand why. Now, if you'll excuse me, I need to find my sister. And to let you know, because I'm certainly not going to tell this to anyone else, I'm not telling my sister she has to leave Arcanium because Professor Mali told me to do it. I'm telling her so she'll be safe, not us. If she stays, something will happen because she thinks it's her duty to protect us."

Aurie paused, the weight of her words heavy on her shoulders.

"I hope to god she understands."

7

Pi woke to a knife of pain in her side. It felt like her ribs were rubbing together, which wasn't a good sign if it were true. She'd rolled over in her sleep. A spot beneath her right shoulder, on the side of her ribs, felt like it had been attacked with a jackhammer. She moved her breast out of the way and examined herself while buried in her covers. A massive purple nebula covered her whole right side, the flesh mangled and leaking blood. After digging out of the covers with ample groaning and air-sucked-between-teeth grimaces, she realized her blankets were soaked.

"Great. I need new bedsheets again," she said, rolling over, which only took her breath away as she pinched her side.

She'd placed a pain blocker on it before she passed out last night, but had forgotten to fix the wound.

Last night hadn't gone as well as she'd hoped. The Cabal students had figured out that she was spying on them, and they'd laid an ambush. The only thing that had saved her was that she'd been late, a result of her constant exhaustion. A few minutes earlier, and they'd have captured her with a Rathbone's Miniature Cage Spell.

There was a knock on her door as she downed a couple of

aspirin. It was Aurie.

"Hey, we need to talk," she said.

"I'm getting ready," yelled Pi. "Give me a few."

"I'll be out here."

Pi checked herself in the mirror over her dresser. She was a wreck. She thought she looked worse than she felt, which seemed impossible, considering that warmed-over garbage would have felt better.

She tongued a back molar that had come loose in the fight last night. The back of her hair had been singed off by a fireball. She threw a Yankees hat on and tucked her hair beneath. Channeling so much faez through her body had taken its toll.

After stopping the bleeding with a bandage—she was too tired for magic—and throwing on a pair of jeans and a Meatloaf T-shirt that she didn't care about if it got dirty, Pi joined her sister in their common area.

Aurie was waiting with a plate of falafel flatbread wraps with a spicy tahini sauce drizzled over the top.

"I thought you might want something to eat. Sounded like you were out pretty late."

"Oh, god, thank you," said Pi, hastily shoving one into her mouth, even before she'd taken the plate. "I didn't realize I was so hungry," she said between chews.

Pi recognized the wrapper. "Isn't this from the street vendor down on Merlin and Fifth?"

"I paid a kid to run for them."

While Pi devoured the falafel wraps, Aurie sat on the couch and watched with heavy eyes. Pi knew her sister had something important to say—it was why she'd brought the food first—but Pi was too hungry to care.

After wiping her mouth and chugging a mug of cool water, Pi collapsed back on the couch, rubbing her belly.

"I'd like to sleep for another week."

"Why don't you? You can't keep this up forever," said Aurie.

Too tired to argue voraciously, Pi instead doled her words out between stretching her stomach. "I'll keep it up as long as I must. You're kinda my only sister."

"That's why I'm worried about you," said Aurie. "Between the late-night battles and the faez exhaustion, one or the other, or maybe both, are going to kill you. You can't keep doing this."

Pi wasn't going to tell her sister how lucky she'd been to survive the previous night after that comment.

"Yet, I do."

"Pythia."

Pi scowled. "Don't try that mom shit with me. I know what I'm doing."

"I'm not saying that you don't, but there comes a point when you have to pull back, get some rest."

Pi knew there was something more going on. Like the time she'd taken her to a run-down industrial park for no reason, risking her life for a meaningless field trip. If there was anyone who needed rest, it was Aurie, who spent her days and nights buried in books, trying to delude herself that there was a way to fix Semyon.

"What gives?" said Pi. "I see you've got something to say. I'm too tired to guess what you want, so please just say it."

Aurie looked into her hands as if the answers were there. "I think you should take a break from the defense of Arcanium. It'd be best if you found another home for a while. Somewhere you can be safe."

"I'm safe here! Hell, I'm keeping *you* safe. That's what I want to do."

"Arcanium's not safe for you any longer, not after what

you did to those mages."

There was no question in Pi's mind what Aurie was referring to. "I didn't mean to kill them. It was in self-defense. Remember, I had to see their bodies afterwards. I'll never forget that. Never."

Pi got up and faced the door, crossing her arms, flinching when the movement wakened the wound in her side. Every night when she went to sleep, no matter how tired, she saw their faces. It didn't matter what they were planning on doing to her, she'd still killed them.

Her sister spoke softly. "I know. I know. I'm sorry. I...I don't know what you're going through. I can't. But the way you're going isn't healthy. I love you, sis. I'm worried that you're pushing yourself not because of us, but because of them, that you're punishing yourself."

This line of thinking wasn't something Pi had thought of, but it was hard to deny it once Aurie had said it. Yet, to truly admit it would be to acknowledge what had happened.

"You're still asking me to leave."

"For your protection."

Pi spun around. "My protection? What about yours?"

"We'll figure it out."

"Figure it out? Professor Mali spends her time moping in the basement, the other teachers are just going through the motions. Do you wonder why we haven't had any alumni come to our rescue?"

Aurie blinked, looking a little stunned. "I'm sure they're too busy. They can't come running to our rescue every time there's a crisis."

"It's not that," said Pi. "The Cabal isn't pressing Arcanium in the Hundred Halls only. They're making sure no one dares to come here—legally, financially, whatever they can do. Coterie mages own a third of the damn Fortune 500 companies, it's not like they don't have the resources. Plus, everyone assumes that Semyon's time is done. That there's no way to save him."

"There is," said Aurie. "But it's going to take time."

"Time that Arcanium doesn't have. Which is why you need me."

"What I need is a live sister. One that hasn't gone so far over the line that she can't ever come back."

When Pi spun around to rebuke her sister, the wound in her side set off a fit of coughing, which was like getting stabbed again. After she was finished, her sister was by her side.

"You're hurt," said Aurie, trying to lift up the side of Pi's shirt.

"What does it matter? If I'm hurt I can't kill anyone else."

"That's not what I mean and you know it...Merlin's tits— you're a mess. Let me fix this," said Aurie.

Pi pulled away, catching a wounded glance from her sister. "It needs magical healing. I'll fix it when I'm rested."

Aurie clasped her hands in front of her. She was pensive with thoughts. "You don't need anyone, do you?"

"I need *you* alive, sis. Believe me." Pi searched around for a rag to wipe up the leaking blood, found a pile of napkins from Wizard Burgers, and dabbed the fluid away, repressing her grimaces. "I wish Semyon would have been a little more ruthless, then maybe we wouldn't be in this situation. At this point, the Halls are practically irrelevant. Once Semyon dies they'll reform it into something different. I wish I knew how it'd gotten so bad. I thought at one time the patrons of the first five were friends."

Aurie had sunk back onto the couch, hands in her lap. "If it was possible, do you think I could take over for him? I know I'm strong enough to survive without the Halls. He told me that I was strong enough to be a patron."

"Would you want to?" asked Pi, genuinely curious.

"No...maybe. Probably. I don't know. It would mean that Semyon would never come back. Since he's not awake, taking the link would kill him. I've argued that Mali take it, but she wants nothing of that path. I'm not sure I do either."

"It might be the time has ended for the Hundred Halls. Not everything lasts forever, and without Invictus, I'm not sure anyone can hold it together," said Pi with a shrug. "Once you're out of danger, I'm probably not staying around here. It's too much of a mess."

Rather than answer, Aurie noisily slurped from her soda.

"I wonder what happened," said Aurie. "Like you said, they'd been friends once, but no one has ever explained why they had a falling out."

"I can't imagine Bannon and Semyon hanging out, or Celesse and Priyanka. Maybe that's just a fiction that Invictus told people because it sounded nice. Anyway, power corrupts, and the rest of them are as wicked as they come."

"I'm not sure," said Aurie softly.

"I am. I loved the Halls when I was growing up, or I should say, I loved the idea of the Halls. Now that I'm here, my eyes are opened. It's a feudal system designed to keep people in line."

"A little organization is not a bad thing. Like you said, power corrupts, or have you forgotten about Liam already?"

Pi tapped on her head with her forefinger. "How can I ever forget that?"

When her sister went back to staring at her with those big sad eyes, Pi said, "You really want me to leave, don't you?"

"Not forever," said Aurie. "Just until this blows over. It's not like I'm going to be in the Halls for the rest of my life. This is our fourth year, remember?"

"If you haven't forgotten, I'm kinda not a part of this school anymore."

"Is it getting any easier? You know, the fragments?" asked Aurie.

"It's still strange. The other day I was going to shave my legs, but I almost put the blade to my cheek. Or when I tried to go into the men's bathroom. Little things like that."

A moment of quiet passed between them. It was uneasy. They'd always been able to exist in each other's space without having to work at it, but it felt different, like they'd grown apart in the last year. Pi didn't know if it was the soul fragments or the march of time, but either way, it was real.

"You really want me to leave Arcanium?" asked Pi.

"No. I'll be worried sick while you're gone, but I think it's for the best," said Aurie.

Pi nodded, trying not to let her sister see how much it hurt. "Okay, I'll go, but only because you asked."

"Where will you go?" asked Aurie, biting her lower lip.

A hundred possibilities passed through Pi's mind. "Not sure yet. I won't leave the city, if that's what you're worried about. Not yet, anyway. I'll message you when I get there, wherever that is."

"Don't leave until you're healed."

"Yes, *Mom*."

Aurie cringed. "Sorry, I'm the worst."

"No, you're the best big sister anyone could have, even when you're a pain in the ass. In fact, it's probably because you're a pain in the ass that makes you so good."

"I'm not as great as you think," said Aurie. "I'm probably an idiot for telling you to leave Arcanium."

"I'm surprised actually. You won't be able to watch over me when I'm out there, keep me in line."

"That's what I'm afraid of," said Aurie without a trace of sarcasm.

Truthfully, that worried Pi, too. Her nightly battles had

been getting pretty harrowing, and the fact that she'd killed five mages hadn't changed either. It was another reason she had to leave the city of sorcery—it was changing her and, she was worried, not for the better.

"I'll be fine," said Pi. "Maybe I'll lay low and stay out of trouble, you know, sort some things out in my head, figure out what I'm going to do with myself once this end of the Hundred Halls thing blows over."

Aurie gave her a reassuring smile, but neither of them believed it.

8

The request for a meeting had been a surprise. The message had come through Violet, who'd brokered the meeting, setting up the terms and ensuring Aurie's safety while she was out of Arcanium. The possibility of betrayal was more than zero, which left Aurie fidgeting in the back of the limousine on the way to the meeting location.

It wasn't just the meeting she had on her mind. Pi had left Arcanium a few days ago, which put a stone in Aurie's gut, leaving her to wonder if she'd made the right choice. She checked her cell phone to see if her sister had sent a message indicating where she'd ended up, but there was only an emoji heart from late last night indicating she was safe and alive, no location given.

Aurie hated the idea of not being able to watch over Pi. Even when Pi had been in Coterie, Aurie had at least understood that the structure of the Hall would keep her relatively safe. Though it wasn't her sister's physical safety that worried Aurie, but her emotional one. Pi'd always pushed the boundaries of what was right and possible, leading to unintended consequences.

Aurie adjusted her shirt, thinking about the wisdom of

her own choice of attending a meeting at a Cabal Patron's request. The only reason she'd agreed, besides the condition of safe harbor, was that she thought there was still a chance to turn one of them to their side. The original patrons had been friends once, long ago when the school was still new. If there was any way to leverage that into an agreement that preserved Arcanium, she had to try.

The limousine dropped her off in the heart of the third ward, the high-end shopping district that made the Avenue des Champes Elysées in Paris jealous because you couldn't purchase the kind of enchanted garments that you could on the Avenue le Fay.

A few passersby wrinkled their foreheads in confusion when she appeared from the long black vehicle, as if they were expecting someone famous, not a twenty-something girl in jeans and a dark V-neck blouse. The only stylish adornment she'd allowed herself was a jade necklace that doubled as a fail-safe should the meeting not go as planned.

The Elysium had tinted white privacy windows that made it difficult to gaze upon them. The front of the business was unassuming, except for a model-looking woman in a tight flowery dress who opened the door for Aurie, avoiding eye contact as if she had not been given permission.

Inside, the scented air was a delight, not at all the cloud of perfume in the makeup areas that haunted the malls of the Midwest, the only experiences Aurie had with pampered boutiques, which was like comparing a shelter mutt with a prize-winning show dog. Aurie wasn't even quite sure what the Elysium was selling as there were no products displayed.

The blonde girl who had let Aurie into the Elysium indicated to follow her down the hallway. Through the first window, Aurie spied an older woman in a garish maroon dress, seated on a giant cushioned chair, drinking a bubbly orange liquid with blue streaks and having her feet rubbed by a chiseled shirtless man-hunk. She was giggling like a ten-year-old even though she had to be on the far side of sixty.

In the next room, a 1920s' flapper theme, a team of stylists fitted a rail-thin woman in a dress made of aluminum soda cans, cut and fashioned into links. The stylists buzzed around her like a cloud of gnats with tape measures and metal snips.

The next window had been tinted nearly black, so Aurie couldn't see through it, but a deep pulsing music that went into her gut throbbed against the glass. Between the beats, Aurie thought she heard screams or moaning, it was hard to tell which.

After the hallway of twenty rooms or so, Aurie got into an elevator with her blonde escort. There were more floors listed on the control panel than Aurie remembered from the outside of the building, and when the elevator went up, there was little shaking, and almost no press-on-the-shoulders feel of gravity while the numbers ticked across the brass plate. The door opened when the number seventeen lit up. Aurie's escort did not exit the elevator.

Aurie went out alone, steadying herself with a cleansing breath. Her heart was hammering, something she was going to have to get used to while she was in enemy territory.

The little octagonal room she'd stepped into had no door. For a brief moment, she had visions of being dropped into a pit, or gassed into unconsciousness without ever seeing the patron.

One of the eight panels surrounding her disappeared, and a man wearing a bulletproof vest stepped into the room with her. Mirrored sunglasses hid his eyes, but the Protector pin on his vest told her everything she had to know about him. He had a gun clip at his hip, and he kept his hand hovering over it as he circled her, examining every inch of her body through the sunglasses, presumably checking for enchantments.

He stopped at the bracelet on her wrist. "You'll have to take that off."

"It's only for protection."

"Take it off."

The command was given without a trace of wiggle room. Aurie sighed and unclasped it, handing it over. "I better get this back when I leave."

He made no indication this would be the case. He looked ready to let her through when he did a double take, focusing on the jade necklace. He ran his fingers across the chunks of jade, and her heart rate doubled in time.

"There's faez residue on this," he said. "What is it?"

"I don't know," she stammered. "It was a gift from a friend, maybe it's from when she made it."

The mirrored sunglasses hid his expression, except for a slight tightening of the forehead. He was listening to instructions in an earpiece, Aurie realized. She feared he'd take the necklace, leaving her defenseless.

He took his thumbnail and scraped it across the chunks of jade, looking for hidden compartments, his frown deepening as he worked. Aurie tried to look impatient and put-upon, hoping the visual language of the elite might convince him to hurry his investigation.

When he slid his arms around her neck towards the clasp in back, Aurie said, "At the very least you could have eaten a mint before you stuck your face in mine."

He pulled his arms back after a few seconds and said to the air, "She's clean."

When she followed him into the next room, she didn't know if the jade necklace was still around her neck until she caught her reflection in a mirror in the short hallway, showing it was still there. He opened a door and beckoned her through.

Aurie had met Celesse D'Agastine on two separate occasions during her trial by magic. Pi had met her once, when she was making a delivery for Radoslav. Neither her experience nor the one relayed to her prepared her for meeting the patron of the Order of Honorable Alchemists on her home turf.

The facade Celesse had presented in the Court of Threes, like Malden, was not her true self—or at least the true self she'd become with magic. It was not uncommon for the wealthy to modify themselves, mold their features until they appeared youthful and beautiful. Celesse had taken this ideal to the extreme, with wide doe-eyes, golden hair, and features smoothed to silk, yet almost alien in their perfection, making it difficult to gaze upon her, as if she were a goddess.

Aurie was aware that the sweet perfume in the air had traces of alchemical agents, making her more susceptible to Celesse's looks. Pangs of lust echoed through her midsection, a strange, artificial feeling that Aurie was able to resist because of her allergic reaction to faez, a reaction she doubted Celesse would be aware of.

"Aurelia Silverthorne," said Celesse, leaning seductively against a high-backed divan in her sculpted white dress.

Aurie sensed the patron wasn't trying to seduce her directly, but lay the groundwork for a favorable negotiation.

"You can call me Aurie," she said, hoping it conveyed the proper amount of awe and subservience.

Celesse smiled softly, and Aurie was aware the lizard part of her brain wanted her to fall down on her knees before the patron.

"Aurie. Welcome to my home."

When Celesse motioned to the room, giving permission to look away, Aurie was able to take in her surroundings. The decor was Egyptian oasis, complete with palm trees, white furniture, golden accents, and a small pond at the center. The vaulted ceiling towered overhead.

"I'm honored."

"I'm almost surprised you came," said Celesse. "I made the offer to check all my boxes. Yet here you are. This is a bold, but probably foolish choice from a fourth year student in these difficult times. Even if nothing had happened to Semyon, you'd be no match for me."

The dryness of Aurie's mouth matched the sandy rim around the little pond. She'd thought there might be some back and forth before the challenge.

"You offered sanctuary."

"And you believed me?" asked Celesse, placing her long fingernails against her chest in faux indignation.

"I didn't come without protections."

Celesse scoffed. "My bodyguard removed that trivial item outside."

Aurie hated to have to play her hand early, but Celesse wasn't giving her a choice. "That wasn't the only one."

"A bluff," said Celesse, stepping forward, producing a crystal decanter with an icy blue liquid inside. "I can make you drink one of my custom cocktails and you'll burn yourself out in a blaze of glory, killing Semyon in the process, and then the charter can be reformed with more favorable terms."

"What about your feelings for Semyon?" she asked.

Her surprise at this revelation was hidden skillfully behind a mask of indifference. "Feelings, yes. But not enough to blind me from opportunity."

"Were you always this cold and calculating? Or did you trade your soul for luxury over time?" asked Aurie.

Celesse's lips squeezed to a thin line. "A girl with little experience should not judge someone who has lived a much longer life. The world is a cruel place. If you aren't prepared to be ruthless, then you'll never be old enough to gain the wisdom necessary to understand."

"But wasn't that the point of the Hundred Halls? So that mages could work together instead of fighting? Look how far humanity has come in the last century. Magic has given the world a reprieve from war and misery. Why risk a return to that?"

"There will be no wars."

"Are you sure? Once the charter is dissolved, won't there be a battle for power? Who's to say another charter will ever be forged? The only reason the Halls exist is because Invictus brought you together."

A snide chortle of derision slipped from Celesse. "Invictus brought us together? A fiction. He may have bested us, formed the Halls through us, but most of us were friends long before him."

It was Aurie's turn to be surprised. The history of the Hundred Halls was well known, or at least she'd thought so. Of course, there were no pictures from that time. The records had been lost, or maybe destroyed to preserve the tale presented as truth.

"Are you sure you can trust the others? They've each tried to take the Halls for their own. Why would they want to share power?" asked Aurie.

Celesse waved the crystal decanter dismissively. "If you came here thinking you might pit us against each other, you're more naive than I thought."

"I came here to save the Halls, to appeal to the patron you used to be, not the one you've become," said Aurie.

"Who's to say that I've changed? That any of us have changed? The old saying, that power corrupts? Not true at all. Power only brings out the person who was really underneath. What you see here is what was there all along."

Celesse wandered past Aurie, running a fingernail across her shoulder, bringing a shiver of pleasure. "Of course, how would you know? You might actually be a good person inside."

"I could have said your name to Malden last year during the trial, and pit you two against each other."

"If you really thought it might work, then you were a fool not to. Those not willing to play the game ruthlessly don't play long."

"But then it's a race to the bottom," said Aurie, "as we destroy the foundations of what keeps us together. That's why I didn't say anything. It does us no good to fight each other."

"Fight each other? Isn't it Semyon who's defied the rest of us? It was he that should have bowed to the consensus of the group, not us," said Celesse.

"You killed Invictus," said Aurie.

"You should try learning the truth before making accusations."

Celesse was trying to play her, but Aurie would have none of it. She steeled herself.

"I can still say your name to Malden. He'd believe me."

"As if I would let you do that after you placed yourself in my care." She swished the decanter at Aurie. "Maybe it's time to be done with pretense."

As Celesse's long fingers curled into the beginnings of a spell, Auric stepped forward. "You cast that spell and you kill us both."

With a hint faez in the air, Celesse paused. She raised an eyebrow. "Liar."

"I would not have come here if I hadn't prepared for betrayal," said Aurie, growing serious.

Celesse cackled, putting a hand to her chin. "And what will you do? Truth magic won't save you. The wards alone in this room would kill you before you threatened me."

Aurie moved a few feet away from Celesse. "I assume you are familiar with batrachotoxin?"

Batrachotoxin was a poison harvested from western Columbian tree frogs. The material was used in alchemical mixtures involving transmogrifications. Aurie had broken into Arcanium's store and created the necklace with a little help from her fellow fourth years.

Celesse's eyes searched Aurie. She stuck her chin out, daring the patron.

"If you try to scratch me, or move against me, I will burn your lungs out with fire," said Celesse.

"And you will die." Aurie patted her jade necklace. "This isn't jade, but a hardened matrix of batrachotoxin that will turn to a particulate with any significant use of magic. So if you try to attack me, you'll trigger it to explode. Or if you try to run away, I'll trigger it with truth magic."

"You'd die too."

"A risk I'm willing to take, though I don't think it'll be necessary. You enjoy living as much as I do."

Celesse stiffened, clearly unnerved by the predicament. She had not expected this, and did not hide her concern. The thin line of her lips revealed her utter lack of options.

"A stalemate," said Aurie. "What is it that you really wanted to ask me?"

"An offer."

"I'm listening," said Aurie.

"Eventually you and the rest of your friends in Arcanium need to face the truth that Semyon isn't coming back. Remember, we have a connection to him through the charter. We know he's all but gone. The longer you wait, the more dangerous it'll become for you and your fellow students. This is the flip side to faez madness. You have that connection, but you can't use it. It'll be like a dam building up until it explodes, killing everyone in Arcanium."

"You can't scare me," said Aurie.

"I don't need to scare you," said Celesse with a respectful nod. "You're not the scaring type. But you are logical, as you have demonstrated by the conundrum your necklace represents, so I'm appealing to your intellect. Eventually Arcanium will die. There's no two ways about it. Not only would it be a terrible waste, but it could cause considerable damage to innocents in the area."

"Let me guess, you're the only one that can save us."

"I'm the best of your options. If you give me access to Semyon, I can transfer the students of Arcanium to me, safely, I might add. Then Semyon can heal on his own time, and if he recovers someday, then he can return to the Halls," said Celesse. "This is something that only one of the original patrons can do, I might add."

"How generous of you."

Celesse gave an exquisite sigh, as if she were a soap starlet preening for the camera. "Semyon is not going to recover, which leaves the other original members of the Halls as your only hope. Would you rather pledge yourselves to one of them? I may be a bitch, but I know I'm a better option than the others. Or were you hoping for Bannon?"

Aurie was beginning to wish that she hadn't come, only because Celesse was right. Semyon wasn't getting better, and she was the least horrible option of the patrons if it came to that.

"Why did you make this offer to me?"

Celesse snorted derisively. "Do you really think Old Ironsides would listen? Or even come here? And the rest of the professors are your typical smug elitist types who hate to dirty themselves with reality. None of the students would listen to them, even if they suggested it. You're the one they'll listen to.

You're the one they'll follow, even if it's into my waiting arms."

"No," said Aurie, right away. "Not you. Not ever."

"You'd doom them to death then?"

Would she? Was it fair to answer for them?

"I can't trust you," said Aurie. "Look what you were going to do when I came here."

"True. But I would be willing to sign a magical contract between us to ensure no cheating."

Aurie thought about her friends in Arcanium. They were despondent, listless with grief. Yeah, everyone was trying to put on a brave face, work their faez-less spells as if nothing had happened, but it was like watching a mime work after a two-week bender.

"What's in it for you?"

Celesse looked away, presenting a noble figure. Aurie didn't know if it was on purpose, or not, but it was impressive. It reminded her of those old Hollywood actresses.

"As cutthroat as I can be, I have no interest in seeing students die. It would be a terrible waste, both for them and for the Halls, or whatever the Halls will become."

"And you gain new followers, professors too."

"Well, I *am* a calculating bitch. Proudly. You don't survive this long otherwise."

Every bit of Aurie wanted to agree, to say yes to Celesse so that the slow nightmare of their existence in Arcanium would end. But in the end, she couldn't. She couldn't betray Semyon, she couldn't effectively doom the Hundred Halls by her decision, handing them over to the Cabal. There was no hope of Semyon recovering, but she couldn't give up.

"I'm sorry, but no. I can't support this."

Celesse's gaze narrowed. "You don't have to support it. Take this back to your fellow students. Let them decide. Or are you afraid of the answer?"

"I'm not telling them," said Aurie. "I put my life in danger coming here to hear what you had to say. I heard you. Now, I'm going back. I won't be your pawn."

"Very well," said Celesse, turning to walk away.

Aurie almost went back towards the elevator, then she remembered her necklace.

"I wouldn't go much further."

Celesse froze mid-stride, shrugged, and turned back. "I'd hoped you'd forgotten."

"I'd love an escort back to Arcanium," said Aurie, keeping her voice annoyingly light. "There's a nice limousine waiting outside."

Celesse looked ready to say something else, but changed her mind and nodded.

"Shall we," said Aurie, motioning towards the exit.

They entered the elevator together. As Celesse stepped inside, her modified self disappeared beneath her older version. Aurie rather preferred this one, though it wasn't real either.

As they walked out the bottom floor, Aurie asked, "What is it you sell here?"

"Experiences you cannot find anywhere else," said Celesse. "I mix the potions myself, tailoring them to the desires of the customer."

"Don't you have a team to do that for you?"

Celesse gave the barest hint of a shrug. "It keeps me on top of my craft."

Aurie did not doubt that. This whole visit had been tailored for her benefit. Aurie wondered if Celesse had known about the jade necklace all along, and had gone along to deliver her message. This made Aurie worry that there was another level of gamesmanship that she hadn't considered. It was too late now.

The limousine was waiting outside. Before Aurie got in,

Celesse said, "If you change your mind."

"I won't," said Aurie.

"I'll be here when things get worse and you realize there's no other way. You know how to get ahold of me."

The patron of the Order of Honorable Alchemists disappeared inside Elysium, and with that, Aurie had no doubt that her visit to Celesse's business had been scripted to sow doubt. The worst part was that it'd worked. If Aurie couldn't figure out a way to save Semyon, then maybe pledging to Celesse was the best way forward.

9

The Goblin's Romp was darker and dirtier than Pi remembered from last year. Her starry-eyed view of her "Uncle" Liam had blinded her to the fact that the establishment was barely above a combination ale trough and urinal.

Eyes followed her as she went into the back. Pi stepped over a dead mouse among the drifts of peanut shells. The place smelled like a horse barn.

Pi ignored the muted whispering as she adjusted her backpack covered in Hello Kitty! buttons and went around the bar to the dark archway. Radoslav's rune got her past the chew-lipped bouncer with a neck bigger than her thigh. As she headed into the stairwell, she caught a shadow of movement, a thick head of hair and a dirty face. She didn't bother speeding up, but kept her pace until there was a foot scuff.

She paused on a landing and called out, "Unless you'd like to learn what your asshole tastes like, I suggest returning to your nest and enjoying a piss-warm beer. Or maybe just piss, it certainly smelled like it up there."

Her follower didn't comment, so she pulled a piece of cloth from an inside pocket, placed a temporary enchantment on it, and placed it on the nearest step. The fabric-snake slithered up the staircase and after about twenty seconds, she heard someone cursing and running back the other way.

"What a waste of a good towel," she said and continued down.

Big Dave's Town was an improvement from the bar above, but she knew that was a bit of projection. This little spot of civilization in the Undercity was her destination, at least until she could figure out a better place to live, giving her a case of renter's Stockholm Syndrome. The only problem was she didn't know anything about Big Dave's Town.

She'd spent the previous couple of weeks moving around the city, staying in hotels, but the Cabal kept finding her after a few days. She'd thought about contacting Hemistad, but he still hadn't forgiven her and Aurie for what had happened the year before, and Radoslav was out of the country on business, which left no safe places in the city. When she realized that she couldn't keep up her hyperawareness forever, she decided to move to the Undercity, where the denizens of the Halls held less sway.

There wasn't much to the cobblestone streets, as she learned by walking around. Big Dave's Town was laid out like a hashtag, with two sets of streets crisscrossing each other. At least three roads went in different directions, heading through caverns that connected to the large one the town existed in. There was an open-air market that sold fruits, vegetables, fungi, and other edible goods, run by a couple of fungusfolk in tie-dyed Grateful Dead T-shirts. A buzzing neon sign splattered its bright pink lights over another street, announcing the Devil's Lipstick was open and served cold beverages. Other establishments had their signs, but Pi didn't see anything that looked like an apartment building or real estate office. The whole place had the feel of a town in the Old West.

Pi waffled between talking to the fungusfolk and checking

out the Devil's Lipstick, but went with the latter because she'd had a bad experience with Voodoo Jake. As she paused at the door, a ruckus from near the open-air market caught her attention. A fungusfolk with a bright red beard of lichen was throwing green apples at a group of fleeing shapes that flickered like shadows from a windmill as they escaped the cavern.

Pi was too far away to hear what he was saying, but she had the impression the creatures had stolen something from his market. Probably something valuable if he was so irate. She had no idea what the creatures were. They seemed to move in stutter steps, jumping across patches of light, before disappearing down a side passage.

When they were gone, Pi checked the street. The whole way here, she'd had the feeling someone was following her, but her spell work uncovered nothing, so she marked it down as nervousness about her new adventure.

Shrugging away the momentary distraction, Pi went inside. The bar was nicer than she'd expected, though the clientele was seedier than a motel that charged by the hour. There were a lot of physical modifications, either deliberately or due to curses. A woman near the entrance had a head of porcupine quills that ruffled as she slurped soup. It was early morning above ground, but the Undercity kept its own time. Judging by the busy tables and people eating and drinking at the bar, it seemed like dinner-time.

Pi didn't want to sit at a table. It would have felt weird to be alone like she would be expecting Aurie to come strolling in at any time.

There were a couple of empty seats at the bar. The nearest was next to a tall gentleman in a cowboy hat and duster, but she didn't want to sit near the door. Another was next to someone in a red hoodie and as Pi moved towards the spot, the guy or girl, she couldn't tell, moved their backpack onto the spot. She ended up having to take the seat on the far side of the bar, near the window where the two waitresses picked up meals for their customers.

As Pi sat down, a tray of cinnamon apple crisps went past, making her salivate in anticipation.

The bartender, a woman with big hair and a Garbage Kings T-shirt, slid over to Pi.

"Drink or food?"

Pi tapped on the counter. "Information?"

"Drink or food."

"Right," said Pi.

The food smelled delicious, so Pi ordered a bacon cheeseburger and crispy mushroom fries along with an energy drink. She caught the girl—Pi realized as she heard a feminine throat clear—watching from behind her red hood, but could only see the green tips of her hair and dark eyes.

The bartender screamed the order into the back, startling Pi from her examination. The cook responded, "One of these days, Delilah, you're going to blow out a vocal cord."

Before Delilah could move away, Pi asked, "Information now?"

The woman checked for other customers that needed service and when she saw none, made a hand gesture.

"I'm looking for a place to live. Is there a real estate office or something?"

Without hesitation Delilah answered, "You can't live here."

"I've got money."

The bartender looked her over, dismissing her as so many had before. Though Pi knew when she was older she'd enjoy her youthful looks, at the current moment, it seemed like a curse.

"Money don't matter. You need a sponsor."

"Sponsor?"

Delilah nodded. "A bonded member of Big Dave's Town."

"And how does one go about getting sponsorship?" asked Pi.

"You don't," said Delilah.

"Are you a bonded member?"

Delilah nodded. "It's my place, after all."

"Could I pay you for sponsorship?" she asked.

"I told you. It's not about the money. We keep a tight ship down here, and we only take in people we trust. Since we don't know you, well, you get the picture."

"Tight ship?" asked Pi. "When I was coming in here, I saw the fungusfolk get hit by some thieves or something."

Delilah half growled, glancing back towards the cowboy with animosity. The cowboy didn't seem to notice. Pi caught the tin star on his chest. He was an honest-to-god sheriff, which explained the look she'd given him.

Before Pi could ask any more questions, Delilah left to pour another beer for the guy two seats over. Pi's dinner arrived a little while later, and the burger was as delicious as it smelled. It was bubbling with grease, and the bacon was a perfect crispiness that exploded on her tongue.

She was wolfing down the shroom fries in twos and threes when the bartender called out while pointing behind her, "Pi!"

After dropping the fries onto the plate, Pi spun around, fingers gesticulating, carving a mini force bolt from midair to throw at the girl with the green hair in the hoodie approaching with something wrapped in a sack that could have been a knife or a gun.

Right as the spell knocked the girl off her feet, Pi's mind reinterpreted the bartender's words, especially as she saw the go-box that had been in the girl's hands flying into the air, spilling a wedge of apple pie, which landed unceremoniously between her legs.

Every eye, a katana from behind the bar, and at least three guns were cocked in Pi's direction. She held her hands up and quickly said, "I've made a terrible mistake."

Delilah held the katana like a baseball bat, so Pi didn't think she had to worry about her, but the guns could kill her before she got a spell off.

The sheriff approached with a big gun in his hand. His forehead was wrinkled with disappointment.

"Care to explain yourself?" he asked in a Jersey accent.

"I'm sorry," said Pi, rushing through her explanation. "My name is Pi, short for Pythia, and when she called out 'Pie,' I thought she was saying 'Pi,' warning me about something behind me. I'm so sorry, so very sorry."

While trying to look as contrite as possible, Pi covertly eyed the doorway. It was too far away to reach.

"You alright, Jade?" he asked the fallen girl.

The girl in the red hoodie picked bits of broken apple pie crust from her clothes. "A little shook up, Vincent, but otherwise I'm fine."

"I'll pay for a replacement pie, and your dinner. I'm really sorry," said Pi, trying to get a look at the girl's face to see if she was going to press charges, or whatever they did in Big Dave's Town, but she was still knocking apple gunk from her hoodie.

Vincent slipped his gun into his holster. "What'dya think?"

Jade climbed to her feet, and seeing more exploded pie on the way up, she tugged off her hoodie, throwing it on the table behind her.

Pi thought someone had hit her with a bean bag the moment Jade looked at her. Pi's interests cast a pretty wide net, but she'd never been interested enough to move beyond a couple of dates or a one-night stand.

Jade had a dark complexion, exotic—as if she had a touch of supernatural—with kissable lips, long eyelashes, and a sleeve of flowered tattoos on her left arm. She had that practiced indifference that young movie stars got when they turned from cute TV stars to old enough for R-movies smoking hot.

"Not hurt, or anything, and I'm cool if she pays for dinner, and the *whole* pie," said Jade.

"I'm really such an idiot," said Pi, shaking her head, trying not to imagine kissing Jade, or running her fingers through her dark hair with green tips. "I'm happy to pay for it."

Delilah, who had the katana on her shoulder, yelled into the back, "One apple pie!" Then to the restaurant when she realized everyone was still watching, "Show's over, and it won't cost you a cent—this time."

Conversations and the clank of silverware on plates resumed. Vincent looked like he was revving up to deliver a lecture, when one of the fungusfolk tie-dyed hippies came through the door and went straight to the sheriff.

"I got hit again," he said, scratching at his beard of ochre mushrooms, knocking a few caps onto the floor. "Damn things are robbing me blind."

Vincent adjusted his cowboy hat. "I'll come by and take a look, Bear, after I'm done with dinner."

"I don't need you to check on my produce. I need you to stop them," said Bear, wringing his hands.

"My jurisdiction extends to the edge of the cavern, and no further," said Vincent.

"What the hell are we paying you for then?" asked Bear. "First you won't let me be bonded, even when I've been here as long as the rest of you, and now you won't stand up to the agreements. I pay my fair share of taxes. If you won't help, I'll take my market elsewhere."

Delilah said, "Hey, whoa, don't get so hasty. Vincent, are you sure you can't do something? Bear provides great fresh food. You like your apple pies, amiright?"

"It's not my call," said Vincent, spreading his hands in a what-can-you-do pose. "I'm not supposed to leave the caverns on official business, even if I wanted to."

"Dammit," said Bear, slapping his leg. "Then I'm leaving."

"I'll help," said Pi, hearing the words echoed from a few feet away. She shared a glance with Jade, who shot back an annoyed expression.

"I can take care of it," said Jade. "For the right price."

Pi turned to Delilah. "I'll do it if you sponsor me."

"What the hell?" asked Jade. "First you blast me on my ass, and now you're horning in on my business?"

Vincent put his hands out. "Whoa, ladies. I'm not sure this is the kind of work a couple of young girls could handle."

"Go fuck yourself," said Jade as she hit him in the arm.

"Handle?" said Pi, right after. "Why don't you shut the hell up before I take that handle, shove it up your ass, and break it off."

Jade stifled a snort, then resumed her serious demeanor when Pi glanced over. Vincent blushed and pushed his cowboy hat down on his head as if he were a turtle trying to go into his shell.

"Deal," said Delilah, smacking the counter with an open palm. "You stop whatever these things are and I'll sponsor you."

Jade threw her hands in the air. "What about me? I've lived here longer than her!"

"Sorry, honey. I'm not paying you for what I can get her to do for free, and judging by that spell work of hers, she can handle herself," said Delilah, chuckling and looking at Vincent when she said "handle."

Pi slipped off her backpack. "Would you hold onto this while I take care of this?" Delilah stuck it behind the counter. Pi paid her bill. "I'll be back as soon as I'm done."

Jade followed Pi out of the Devil's Lipstick. "I don't know who the hell you are, but you can't just do this."

"Do what?" asked Pi as she oriented herself. Her plan was to check the area around the market for signs that she could follow.

"I needed that money."

Jade had her arms crossed. Her hair was falling into her face, and Pi wanted to tuck it behind her ear.

"Could you really stop them?" asked Pi.

Jade blew a breath out dismissively. "With my hands tied behind my back."

"Prove it."

"Why?"

"I don't know the area and I could use the help," said Pi, silently questioning her reasons for asking Jade along.

"Are you going to pay me?"

Pi nodded.

Jade rolled her eyes like she wasn't going to do it, then sighed and took a stance as if she were about to play Five Elements. Her finger work was tight, no sloppy curved fingers when the knuckle had to be held at a ninety-degree angle. At the end, Jade blew air into her cupped hands, revealing a ghostly whip-poor-will that trilled a quick song before leaping into flight, disappearing over the Devil's Lipstick in three short wing bursts.

"You're hired."

"Thanks," said Jade. "I guess."

Bear met them at the market. The stalls were wooden with bright canvases overtop. The air was sweet with the smell of fresh produce. A few people were strolling through the rows of produce, including a man with bright blue skin and a forked tongue that tasted the air every few seconds.

"I much appreciate your help," Bear said, though he looked skeptical about their chances of success.

"Where did they hit you?" asked Pi at the same time Jade asked a similar question.

Bear looked between them before finally answering without looking at either.

"They hit the far side. Took a whole bushel of peaches, two trays of strawberries, a container of apples, and some radishes. Don't sound like a lot, but it costs a pretty penny to get stuff hauled down here, especially as fresh as it is."

The stall that had been pilfered from looked like it'd been hit by a bunch of toddlers. There were empty spaces where the food had been, and the rest was knocked around as if the thieves had been blind.

When Pi couldn't find any signs through simple examination, she searched her pockets for the correct reagents, coming up empty.

"Got any salt?" she asked Bear.

He went two stalls over and returned with a shaker of rock salt. As he handed it over, his face wrinkled. "No demon summoning."

"Don't worry," she said.

Realizing she couldn't grind the salt and hold her hand out to collect it, Pi handed it to Jade.

"Can you grind this into my hand?"

"Sure," Jade said, performing the deed with a practiced annoyance.

Standing so near Jade while the salt poured into her palm made the little hairs on the back of Pi's neck crackle with pleasurable static.

When she had enough salt, Pi pulled a ceramic cup from

her leather jacket, dumped the salt in, and set it on the smooth cavern floor.   She heated the salt using magic; the semi-difficult part was keeping the heat inside the cup.   The white crystals sparked and crackled until the whole mixture turned into a white brick.

Then using a needle shoved into the center as a fulcrum, Pi balanced the puck in the cup and used a sharpie to make an "X" on the salt side sticking up.

The divining spell was the simplest part.   After it was cast, she hovered the cup over the area, and the salt puck spun with a wobble.   When she moved it away, it slowed.

Pi had been so focused on her task that she'd forgotten anyone else was nearby.   When she looked up at Jade, Pi caught a moment of soft wonder on her face, which was quickly slammed behind a wall of indifference.

"Okay," said Pi.   "We'll take it from here.   Not sure where this will lead us, but we'll let you know what we find."

Bear nodded and returned to his market with a wave and a parting comment for good luck.

Following the trail of faez required a back and forth pattern, watching for the spinning "X."   The further she got away from the trail, the slower the disc spun, the closer, the faster.   Pi got the hang of tracking pretty quickly.

About halfway out of the cavern, Jade said, "They don't like Hall mages in Big Dave's Town.   Especially rich ones who didn't earn their money."

Pi stopped so abruptly, the salt puck almost went flying out of the cup.   She grabbed it with her other hand and glared back at Jade.

"I quit the Halls last year, and I earned this money," said Pi.

"I doubt it," said Jade, eyes smoldering with anger.   "I'm gonna take a big guess that you grew up in suburbia to some rich parents who probably also went to the Halls."

"I—I...that's not—I did," said Pi, and in trying to find her words, growled. "Yes, fine. I grew up wealthy, but then my parents got killed by some homicidal maniac, and my sister and I got shipped off to the orphanage, then shuttled around foster homes for like forever, until we got into the Halls ourselves."

Jade had appeared ready to fire back a new insult, but as Pi spoke, her anger deflated.

"I'm sorry," said Jade, the phrase almost a question.

They resumed the search in silence. The trail led them out of the cavern to a passage that was only as tall as they were, requiring them to duck occasionally, and lit with magelights. A sign at the beginning explained the passage went in the direction of the Bright Anvil. They moved quickly since Pi didn't have to weave back and forth to find the path.

"Can you tell how far we have to go?" asked Jade, glancing behind them.

"Not really," said Pi. "With more tools I could build a faez detector that would tell us the strength, but right now, the spinning disk will have to be enough."

"I'm sorry about your parents," said Jade. "I saw the jacket, and the arrogance of privilege, and I figured you for a rich girl."

"I suppose that was almost me," said Pi.

"Why did you quit the Halls?"

"It's complicated. But let's just say I learned how corrupt they were," said Pi.

Jade's eyes widened. "You said you had a sister? Is she still in the Halls?"

Pi nodded. "Arcanium. That's where I was for two years, Coterie for another."

"Two halls? Wow. I've never heard of that."

"Were you in the Halls?" asked Pi.

Her expression darkened as if a cloud had formed over her. "I never had the money to test. I know I could have passed too. My ability should have been enough, but it wasn't. System is rigged for the rich."

From what Pi had learned, she knew this to be true. Jade walked beside her with fists clenched and jaw pulsing with anger. This would have been her if she'd never gotten into the Halls.

"The magic earlier," said Pi. "Do you have a patron?"

Jade shook her head. "No way. I'm not going to be beholden to anyone, especially the nut jobs in places like the Undercity who offer protection. And the risk of faez madness isn't as much as you think. They just say that so people will depend on the Halls."

They came upon a crossroads. The spinning salt puck led them to the left, down a set of connecting caverns filled with jagged stalactites and stalagmites that required more care to move through without cutting themselves on the sharp stone.

"What about you?" asked Jade.

"No nut jobs for me either."

They shared a smile. Pi found it hard not to imagine kissing Jade, and judging by her look, she might be doing the same.

Pi had an idea there would be water ahead when she smelled the cool air. The underground lake went into the distance, at least a couple hundred meters, based on the dim phosphorescent lichen that clung to everything in the cavern. The surface of the water was like a black shimmering mirror, with no currents or wind to disturb it.

The spinning disc led to a sandy beach at the water's edge. Signs of people pushing a small boat into the lake were evident by the markings in the sand.

"Not going to get much further without a boat," said Jade,

staring at the footprints.

Pi reviewed the possible ways she could get across the lake. All of them required getting wet, an option she was willing to take if it earned her a spot in Big Dave's Town.

"There are ways..."

"Great," said Jade, speaking loudly, suddenly cheery as she looked around. "Let's get started."

Pi was digging through her pockets looking for a rubber ball when Jade said, "This really sucks."

There was a wrongness in Jade's voice that stopped Pi cold.

"What sucks?" asked Pi, catching a glimpse of Jade pulling something from her pocket.

"I think I like you," said Jade. "But I can't trust that you are who you say you are."

The first part brought heat to Pi's face. She wanted to respond that she liked Jade too, when Pi realized that the object in Jade's hand was a gun and it was pointed right at her.

"Jade?"

"I'm real sorry about this. You kinda messed the plan up." Jade tilted her head back. "You can come out now."

Shapes moved from the shadows. There were five girls, weapons in hand. Some of them had deformities, which suggested curses or other incurable magical injuries.

Pi wondered how they would have known that their plan had changed until she remembered the ghostly whip-poor-will. She should have known it was a message bird.

"Double dipping on your thievery?" asked Pi, hoping to delay the inevitable.

"A little food, a little money." She raised her eyebrow at Pi. "And a really nice magical jacket, which I dare say will look better on me than you."

Despite the circumstances, Pi found it hard not to disagree.

"It won't look that great if you blow a hole in it."

Jade lifted the gun and cocked the hammer.

"Not if I shoot you in the face."

10

Aurie was sitting on the desk in the library next to the Biblioscribe, staring at her phone hoping for a message from Pi, when Deshawn came running in.

"There you are. I've looked all over. Mali is going to kill me," he said, heaving.

Aurie almost asked why he didn't use a spell to find her. "What's up?"

"I don't know," said Deshawn, chewing on his lower lip. "She seemed pretty peeved, and I mean, like nuclear-grade peeved."

Aurie had a pretty good suspicion about what had set her off, and her stomach twisted thinking about what the professor was going to do. She'd known this day was coming, but thought it might be much later, like hopefully after he'd improved, so she would see the benefit of her decision.

"Is she in Semyon's room?"

"Yeah, how'd you know?"

"She's always there these days," she said, though that wasn't it. She had to assume that the professor had found the Engine of Temporal Manipulation.

Aurie gave the phone one last look and shoved it into her

pocket. The last message from her sister had been that she was going into the Undercity, and that was a day or so ago. She hoped everything was okay.

"So you going?" asked Deshawn.

Aurie hopped off the desk. "I'm going. Don't worry. I'll tell her why you couldn't find me."

He started to walk away, then stopped. "Are you going to the Spring Formal?"

"Wait? Spring Formal? Isn't that like months away, or am I missing something?"

"Yeah, it's still October, but Isabella is planning it now, to give everyone something to look forward to."

Aurie nodded, knowing how desperate they were to find reasons to be hopeful.

"I'll be there."

Aurie left the library and headed to the hidden pool beneath the hall. The waterfall thundered against the water, spray forming a mist that kissed her skin as she passed through.

Even before she reached Semyon's room, she felt the vibration in the back of her teeth. The Engine of Temporal Manipulation was working harder than a few weeks ago when she'd come back to check on Semyon. Then it'd only been a slight vibration beneath the bed that could have easily been dismissed. No wonder Professor Mali had found it.

"Aurelia Silverthorne."

Professor Mali was sitting upright in her wheelchair, gray hair pulled back in a ponytail so tight it yanked her eyebrows upward. Her knuckles were white as she gripped the rests.

The Engine of Temporal Manipulation had been set on Semyon's chest. He appeared no different than before, still the same grayish manikin masquerading as her patron.

"I'm sorry, Professor," said Aurie, cringing as she entered

the room and the full force of the vibration hit her. "I'm trying to help."

"Help?" asked Professor Mali in mock surprise. "You think this is help? No, you've made things worse. Can you not hear that or are you as thick as this decision?"

"It wasn't doing that before."

"Brilliant observation. I told you not to mess with Oba and the Engine." She shook her head. "This problem isn't even the worst of it. If we have the Engine then it means that Boann is no longer, and the world has one more problem. A big one."

"Who is Oba?"

"Who is Oba, she asks, after letting him free. A question you might have tendered before such foolishness. As you may recall from your history lessons, the world was a terrible place before the Halls. Unchecked power can lead people to very dark things, and in the annals of history, Oba was one of the worst."

"Which is why we need to save the Halls, so there is a system that keeps us together," said Aurie.

"System? Systems are made of people, and people are flawed," said the professor, shaking her head. The constant vigilance had clearly taken its toll on her.

"Maybe so, but look what it did for the Halls. The Cabal want to destroy it, but they haven't, not yet. Not while he's still alive."

The professor was staring into her lap. Words seethed from her lips in gut-wrenching command.

"Turn it off."

Aurie searched her memory. Oba had given her the knowledge of how to turn it on, but not how to turn it off. Had he done this on purpose? Without Invictus to oppose him, was he sabotaging the Halls as well?

"I can't."

The professor bored her eyes into Aurie. "Turn it off!"

"No. I can't. I don't know how."

The Engine whined to a higher pitch like a motor on its way to failure. It was like getting a root canal from a jackhammer. Aurie doubled over, wondering if this was the moment it failed. After a few seconds, which felt like a lifetime, she was able to think again.

"You've doomed us," said the professor. "Professor Chopra was right. We should have locked Semyon's apartment down and not let anyone in, not even students."

"No," said Aurie. "Maybe it's working harder because it's fixing him."

"Where is the time exhaust going? The Engine can't generate time or take it away," she said. "It's got to go somewhere."

A tightness formed in Aurie's chest. "I don't know where it's going."

"You've got to fix it, or something," said the professor. "We can argue about the stupidity of your decision later, but for now, it needs to relieve pressure or it's going to explode, and I can't even fathom the repercussions of that."

Aurie nodded, understanding.

"I'll see what I can do. He left me instructions. Maybe if I adjust the settings, it'll fix it."

She reached her hand out towards the Engine of Temporal Manipulation. The air around it vibrated with an energy that made the hairs on her arm stand up.

Aurie imagined the symbols that she'd traced before, seeing them as an instruction manual. Her fingers dangled towards the runed brass cylinder.

"I think maybe—"

The words died in her throat. Her whole body compressed,

then like a rubber band pulled back and launched, she felt instant dislocation, a thousand times worse than when she'd traveled through portals.

Aurie landed in a pile of crunchy leaves. She was in a forest past the death of its foliage. It was a world of brown. She shivered against the cold, warding away the sun in her eyes to survey the surroundings.

"Where the hell am I?"

The Engine of Temporal Manipulation had transported her somewhere, probably north, judging by the weather and the colors of the trees. In Invictus, the leaves were in mid-change, which meant further north, the transition had already happened.

Aurie knocked the leaves from her clothes, thankful that getting thrown halfway across the continent was the only thing that had happened. She was probably in Canada, which was going to be difficult to explain when she crossed the border, but it was better than the alternatives. With the kind of power surging through the Engine of Temporal Manipulation, it could have torn her apart or done all sorts of strange things.

She smelled the faint burning of wood, and spied a curl of smoke winding into the clear blue sky. She headed towards what she hoped was civilization.

On the way, she pulled out her cell phone, but there were no bars. "I must be at the arse end of the world."

The smoke was coming from a small camping fire. She saw a solitary man warming his hands on the flame. Aurie stayed back, trying to get a read on him before approaching, but he turned and looked directly at her. Before she could think about hiding, he gave her a hearty grin and a friendly wave.

Aurie joined him at his fire. He was sitting on a log in homemade breeches and a dirty white shirt of a style she'd seen in historical reenactments. Even sitting, she could tell he was tall. He had crisp blue eyes, dark hair, and a pair of dimples that put a warm center in her gut. He was studying her with curious eyes.

"Um, hello?"

"Madam, I am pleased to meet you."

Her mouth went dry at his formal words. The idea that he was a reenactor was fading quickly, leaving an alternative she didn't want to consider.

"And you as well," she said.

"May I inquire about the nature of your attire? It is unlike that which I have ever laid my eyes upon."

She was wearing a flannel shirt and jeans. "It's common where I come from."

"Which is?"

"Philadelphia."

"Franklin's home," he said with a wistful smile. "Have you ever had the good fortune to meet him?"

A knot of tension formed in her neck. Now she was sure she wasn't in Kansas anymore. But she also knew that time travel wasn't possible based on Einstein's Third Law of Magic, which left the most likely scenario that she'd been thrown into some alternative universe near her own, which if it were true, was very bad, as she'd never get back. There were other lesser possibilities, but she was too shell-shocked to think about them.

"Are thee well?" he asked, looking genuinely concerned.

She tried to console herself that at least she'd encountered a charming and attractive man on her arrival, a thought which suggested a bit of escapist fantasy on her part. This suggested that it might not be an alternative universe.

"I've traveled far, and I'm a little tired," she said.

"Please, have my seat..." he said, standing up, leaving

a space at the end of his sentence for her. He was at least six four, built like a lumberjack with powerful forearms. She didn't realize he was asking her name until he gave her an expectant head nod.

"Oh, I'm Aurelia, Aurie for short."

"I'm Beecee," he said, moving around the fire to a spot against a tree. He placed his forearms on his bent knees.

Aurie warmed her hands on the crackling fire. "Where are you headed?"

"I'm meeting friends," he said.

The smile stayed on his lips, but faded from his eyes. Dark thoughts traveled across them like clouds on a sunny day. He seemed to realize his sudden sullenness and cast it away.

"And you?"

"Traveling home."

"To Philadelphia?"

She nodded.

"Your path takes you by a circuitous route," he said.

"I'm lost, if that's what you mean. I'm looking for a place to stay."

"No pack? No gear. It is strange for a lady to travel alone and without her belongings," he said.

"I ran into some trouble."

"Ran into?"

"A figure of speech. I had belongings earlier, but now they're gone."

"Ruffians?"

"Sure," she said.

He smiled like he understood, but his eyes said otherwise. He seemed to be weighing a decision.

"What"—Aurie started to ask what year it was, but realized that would be rather odd—"news is, well, new? I've been out of touch for a while."

"I'm afraid I'm in the same situation, I've been deep in the territories, so I've not been privy to the news of the day," said Beecee.

"May I travel with you? At least to the next town."

"Certainly," he replied. "I was about to put out the fire before you arrived. Could you assist me and then we'll be on our way?"

When she nodded, he gave her a water bladder and pointed down the slope to a creek gurgling through the forest. The water was freezing cold on her hands.

Aurie swallowed the spell that came to her lips, a reaction to the discomfort. If she had her magic, she would have made her hands impervious to the temperature. Then she realized she wasn't in her home world, or time, or whatever. Aurie closed her eyes and focused on the well of faez inside, finding it right at the surface, and strong. There was no trace of Semyon at the edges, no anchor inside her mind.

Was he truly gone? Or was this a trick by the Cabal to get her to use magic?

But the clues of her new existence tempted her sorely. The spell erased the needles in her fingers from submerging them in the cold water.

The taste of faez was in the back of her throat, like an addict taking a hit of a cigarette after a long absence. Aurie ached to let loose and feel the flow of magic through her limbs, washing away the ever-present anxiety.

But she didn't want to disturb her new friend, who would not understand. If Ben Franklin were alive, that meant she was in colonial times, which was before the Hundred Halls had been founded, when magic was not generally a known thing, or at least not by the public. A man or woman finding their power, but not enough to defend themselves, might end up being burned as a witch or warlock.

When she returned, the fire was out, not even smoldering or trailing off smoke. Beecee seemed almost embarrassed by the state of the fire. She handed him the water bladder.

"I'm ready if you are," she said.

He led the way with long strides eating up the distance. She kept on his heels, relishing the chance to be outdoors. Aurie'd been so cooped up in Arcanium that she'd forgotten what it was like to walk in a single direction for more than a hundred feet. She knew her muscles would be sore, but it would be worth it.

After an hour, they crested a ridge into a valley. Multiple streamers of smoke trailed into the sky, announcing they'd reached the town. Coming up through the trees, they heard the banging of metal on metal. It rang through the air.

The town was no larger than fifteen-odd buildings, a dirt road heading out of the valley, and farms in the surrounding area. The houses were made of logs, with white pine coverings and smoky glass windows. Men and women moved through the town. The women wore dresses with aprons and dirty hems, and the men were dressed similarly to Beecee, but dirtier. The town reeked of horse manure, a pungent assault on her nose.

Aurie tugged on her shirt, wishing she had something less conspicuous. A woman in a light blue dress carrying a basket gave her a nasty glance as she tromped by.

The woman wasn't the only one. The men in the nearby fields stopped their harvest to stare before returning to the sweaty work.

Beecee checked back with Aurie. He seemed to ask with a raised eyebrow whether or not she was going to stay.

"Could I travel with you a little further?" she asked.

"Certainly," he said, "though I plan on acquiring more supplies before traveling on. It'll only take a short spell to barter. I can afford a little extra if you'll be needing it."

"That would be very kind and generous of you."

Beecee stopped a woman outside her house, inquiring about purchasing supplies. Aurie stayed back, as her presence aroused suspicion in the locals.

While she was waiting, a little red-haired boy with a constellation of freckles across his nose and cheeks came running up until he was about ten feet away, then stopped and glanced back to his mother. He had a carved wooden figure in his right hand.

"Hello there," said Aurie, giving a little wave.

The freckled boy didn't speak. He smiled cautiously, eyes glittering with wonder. He kept glancing back to his mother, the woman bartering with Beecee, as if he knew he wasn't supposed to be near her.

"What's your name?" she asked.

"In-jen," he said, in halting speech. "In-jen."

"In-jen?" she asked.

He pointed at her. "In-jen. In-jen."

It hit her what he was implying. She'd forgotten how dark her skin was compared to these folks. The boy thought she was a Native Indian. It wasn't her clothing that bothered the townsfolk but her skin tone.

She pointed to herself. "Persian."

"Per-jen?" he replied.

"Persian. Per...oh never mind," she said, sighing.

The boy ran away when the woman called his name in a high screech that Aurie couldn't understand. She dragged the boy into their house by his ear. Beecee came back to her.

"A petite moment and she'll bring us what we need. I asked her for a blanket so that you might warm yourself at night. It's a three-day journey to the next town," he said.

"Thank you," said Aurie, feeling embarrassed she had

nothing to offer.

After ten minutes, the woman in the dirty dress with the red-haired son came marching up to them with a basket and a blanket over her arm. The smell of fresh bread beneath the covering in the basket made her stomach gurgle embarrassingly loud, receiving a searing look from the woman.

Beecee took the basket and threw the blanket over his shoulder. "Many thanks, Misses Butterton."

"May the Lord keep his watch upon your road, Mister Beecee."

As they moved away, headed out of town, Aurie found herself mulling over his name. Something about the way Misses Butterton had said it made Aurie realize she'd been hearing it wrong.

When they were about half a kilometer from the town, she asked, "Is Beecee short for something?"

He chuckled lightly. "My initials. B and C."

Something about those letters triggered a moment of fear, though she couldn't pinpoint why. She looked at him again, wondering if she knew him.

"And they stand for?"

"Bannon Creed, but my friends call me B.C."

11

The end of the gun barrel looked like a big black tunnel to Pi. A tunnel that led to the end of her life. There were a lot of things that magic could do to prevent the bullet from smashing through her face and blowing shards of bone through her brain matter, but they required time and preparation. Two things she didn't have.

Out of the corner of her vision, she saw the other girls approach. The one on the right had an arm made of cracked stone, striations of gray threading through her body. The girl on the left, wielding a baseball bat, had skin that pulsed translucently. If Pi wasn't staring at the end of her life, she might have focused her attention on the girl with the see-through skin.

The only thing that gave Pi hope about getting out of the situation was the fact that the gun barrel was shaking. It appeared Jade wanted to shoot her as much as Pi wanted to be shot.

"There are better options," said Pi, keeping her hands wide and her fingers straight. She didn't want to give the impression that she was performing any magic, or Jade would kill her.

Had it only been Jade, using the Voice would have been a possibility, but not a good one. When she'd used it on Sunil, it'd taken multiple attempts to get right. She didn't have that kind of time now.

"There are always other options," said Jade, facial expressions contorting with inner decisions. "For a rich girl."

"I was an orphan. I told you," said Pi.

"But you were born rich, with all the advantages it entailed. You just got unlucky for a while. But had you been poor from the beginning, you would have never been able to work your way back to the Halls," said Jade, clearly trying to convince herself to pull the trigger.

"Was she really an orphan?" asked the girl with the stone arm.

"Shut up, Nancy," said Jade, then she turned back to Pi. "I bet she got special treatment because her parents were in the Halls."

She opened her mouth to refute her, but she knew the truth. Semyon Gray had gone out of his way to help her sister because of their parents.

"My sister did," said Pi, nodding softly. "I can't change who I am."

"And neither can we." Jade nodded towards Nancy. "She got that in the Merlins. They used a cursed trap with no known counter. And Sasha." Jade motioned towards a dark-skinned girl with a loose afro and ghostly blue eyes. "When she didn't get into the Halls, it bankrupted her parents, and afterwards, they never wanted to see her again."

"I get it, you hate the Halls."

"No, you don't," said Jade, shaking her head, much to the agreement of the others. "You got in, probably on your first try. The only thing the news ever talks about is the people who succeed because of the Halls, never the failures. Even if you make it to the third day, the rich kids always gang up on the poor ones. And then if you get in, sometimes they run you out like Bethany."

Jade indicated the girl with semi-translucent skin. Hearing the story reminded Pi of something she'd heard once.

"Were you in Coterie?" Pi asked.

Bethany nodded.

"I heard about you. You were two years before me. I can't tell you how many times they tried to kill me," said Pi. "I bet it was the same for you."

Bethany's face lit up. "Me too. One of the second years did this to me, and then after that, they saw me as an easy target. I had to leave before the first semester was over, or I'd be dead by now."

"Shut up, Bethany. We're not making friends with her," said Jade, who didn't look completely convinced herself.

"Why not?" asked Bethany. "She seems like one of us."

Seeing an opening, Pi stepped to the side to speak to Bethany directly, but Jade shook the gun at her. Pi stayed put but asked a question.

"Tell me this," said Pi. "If you all hate the Halls so much, what have you done to get back at them?"

Jade sneered, giving a throwaway shrug with her right shoulder. "It's what we're going to do right now."

Sasha twirled her afro with her fingertips. "What have you done?"

"I killed five members of the Cabal."

"There's no such thing as the Cabal," said Jade, who'd brought the gun to chest level, keeping it halfway aimed. "That's just a rumor."

"I was a member of Coterie before changing to Arcanium. I can tell you that the Cabal is real. If you want to blame someone for your pain, it's them. They want to take over the

Halls."

They shared glances, and Pi met their gazes one by one, convincing them with her sheer force of will.

"You really killed five mages?" asked Jade apprehensively.

"I was defending myself," said Pi. "But yeah."

"Is that why you're hiding in the Undercity?" asked Sasha.

"The Cabal kept tracking me above ground. But they're afraid to come down here. I'm staying as long as my sister needs me, and then once things are better, I'm leaving the city."

Heavy thoughts were brewing behind Jade's eyes. "If we let you live, would you help us?"

"Help you with what?"

"Tear down the Halls."

She understood their pain.

"It's the only way to stop them," said Pi.

Jade looked to the others. "What do you think? Keep her or kill her?"

"Kill her," said Sasha right away. "If she was in Coterie, we can't trust her."

Bethany gave Sasha an annoyed look, right as she flashed see-through, and Pi saw a pulse of rich red blood surging from her heart. "I say keep. She survived Coterie and got the hell out."

Jade raised an eyebrow at the girl behind Pi. She was a wisp of a thing with pale hair. She looked like a vanilla lollypop. "Sisi?"

"Kill."

The way she said it gave Pi the shivers.

"Yoko?"

The Japanese girl looked pained to have to make a decision, but she eventually said, "Keep."

Before Jade could ask, Nancy said, "Keep."

Jade looked back to Pi. "Two kills, three keeps, and now it's down to me. I suppose since I've got the gun, and I have to pull the trigger, this means whatever I decide will go." She paused, sighed, and shook her head. "And I really wanted that jacket. Keep."

Pi tried her best not to appear relieved, but her knees nearly gave way and she had to stagger back to standing. They crowded around her and patted her back or gave her side-hugs, as if she'd just joined a sorority.

Jade returned her gun to safety and shoved it into a back pocket. The black handle and bulge disappeared, except when she moved. If Pi concentrated she could see flickers of the gun.

"See something you like?" asked Jade sarcastically.

"How are you hiding the gun? Is that camouflage?" Pi snapped her fingers. "That's how you steal from the market. Magical camouflage."

Bethany ran behind a stalactite and pulled out a piece of canvas that had painted white and black lines across one side.

"I came up with it when I was in Coterie, but I've never gotten it to work completely. There are copper wires going around the outside, and the runes keep getting worn off, and I have to put them back on."

The underside had tightly drawn runes in purple paint marker running around the inside of the bottom. The craftsmanship was crude but effective.

"I guess you don't have a lot of materials to work with. Aren't you worried about faez madness?"

Pi's question was met with a concert of eye rolling.

"You believe that?" asked Sasha.

"Absolutely."

Sasha scoffed. "That's just what they want you to think so you'll stay in that patron system. It's another form of slavery if you ask me."

Bethany asked, "Do you have a patron?"

"No. I'm solo."

"Then aren't you worried about madness?" asked Bethany.

"It's complicated."

None of the women seemed to believe her, but they weren't ready to challenge her either.

Hoping to change the subject, Pi asked, "Where do you all live?"

Sasha put her fingers to her lips, blowing a sharp whistle. A rowboat appeared from around the corner on the lake.

"We have a camp on the other side, built from stuff we've stolen or salvaged. Yoko did most of the building, all by hand since none of us know a thing about Stone Singing. It's not much, but it's ours," said Sasha.

Except for Jade, the others had smudges of dirt on their arms or faces. Their body odor was pungent in the still air of the cave.

Bethany tugged on Pi's arm. "We can show you."

Pi was prepared to follow until Jade said, "Actually, we need to go hunting. We need to find something or someone to blame for the attacks on the market."

"Why not just tell Bear that we found some drifters and ran 'em off? The attacks will stop. End of story," said Pi.

"But how will we get food and supplies?" asked Sasha, crossing her arms. "That was our best trick."

"I'll front the money for now," said Pi.

"Spoken like a rich girl," said Jade. "I'd rather earn it."

"I'd rather eat," said Yoko, to agreements from Bethany and Nancy. Sisi and Sasha appeared skeptical.

"You earned it because I promised that money for stopping the attacks. They are hereby stopped. Therefore, I owe you the cash. But don't worry, I'm sure we can figure out a better way once I get settled in town."

Pi turned towards the exit only to find Sisi blocking her way. The pale waif had big luminous eyes like moonbeams. Pi felt hypnotized by them.

"Yes?" asked Pi when Sisi didn't say anything.

"If you don't come back, I'll find you and kill you."

Pi didn't think Sisi had enough magic for the job, but something in the earnest way she'd said it made her nervous.

"Don't worry. I'll come back," said Pi.

"I'm going with her. Don't worry. If she betrays us, I'll put a bullet in her back," said Jade, halfway joking.

The pair left the cavern as the rest of the women loaded into the rowboat. On the way back, Pi kept trying to strike up a conversation with Jade, but she seemed distracted, so Pi gave up. When Pi had come to the Undercity, meeting someone was the last thing on her mind. Now she was trying to decide how sane it was to have a crush on a girl that tried to kill her.

12

The young Bannon Creed caught the fear reflected in her face. "Is something wrong?"

"Nothing," she said. "Your name reminded me of someone."

He took her at her word and continued without remark, leaving her in the wake of her realization. Could this be the same Bannon Creed? She had to assume it was. Just like Celesse D'Agastine, he'd changed his appearance, though Aurie didn't know why, since he'd been a handsome young man, not the enormous version of a Jersey mobster that he was in her time.

He also seemed genuine and not at all the psychopath he'd become. Was this reality true? Or had she slipped into an alternative universe? She wondered if these friends he spoke of were other mages.

Could it be that the Engine of Temporal Manipulation had sent her back to this specific time for a reason? Otherwise, it made no sense that she would appear in the same location as one of the original founders of the Hundred Halls. There had to be a connection to Semyon Gray, and she needed to find out what it was. This gave her hope that there was a way back, a way out.

"B.C.," she said, getting his attention. "You mentioned

that you're going to meet friends. Since we've got a couple of days and I've been away from people for quite some time, I would love to hear about your friends. It would pass the time."

His eyebrows wagged with indecision. "I am uncomfortable speaking about them."

"Is it because you and they can do magic?" she asked.

He recoiled from her, glancing into the forest as if demons were hiding there. "Do not speak of witchcraft. The world has eyes and ears."

She faced off with him.

"I know you used magic to put out the fire, and to convince Misses Butterton to give you supplies without paying for them," she said.

"You cannot prove it," he said warily, like a boy caught passing notes in class. His innocence and naivety confused her, since she knew the man he would become.

Aurie picked a brown leaf from the ground, held it in her left hand, and cast a simple levitation spell on it. She let it dance through the air while he watched with wide fearful eyes.

Eventually, the display became too much for him, and he grabbed the leaf from the air, placing his hands protectively over hers. "You should not be so daring. Even out here, it's dangerous to use it."

He put special emphasis on the word 'it' as if he were afraid to actually say magic. When Aurie pulled away, he tensed up as if he were expecting her to attack.

"Who are you?" he asked.

"Exactly who I said I was. Aurie. A lost girl who's trying to get back to civilization."

"I thought your strange speech and clothing indicated things had changed much since last I came this way, but now I see that you are quite different, and not in a good way. Are you a Rider, here to waylay me on my journey?"

"A Rider? Who I am is complicated, but I'm not a Rider, whatever that is."

"You knew my name," he said. "When I said my full name, you recognized it. There is much you are hiding, Aurelia of Nowhere. Are you a demon? Or some other foul beast that I have no name for? Explain or I will put you to rights."

Aurie backed away, keeping her hands up. "I'm not a demon, or a Rider. I...wasn't expecting to meet you here."

His hands hovered at his side like a gunslinger readying to duel. She knew she was no match for the Bannon Creed of her world, but could she take him when he was young?

But if this was a previous time, what would happen if she killed him? Would the Hundred Halls cease to exist? Would she disappear since her parents met at school?

"I'm not your enemy," she said, though she wasn't so sure.

His response died in his throat when they heard muskets being fired in the distance. They looked towards the town.

"You were sent to distract me," he said.

A woman's tortured scream reached them. They stood at the crest of the ridge near the valley. Though they couldn't see the village through the trees, the trails of smoke were an easy marker.

Bannon turned to run back towards the town. "If you try and stop me, I'll kill you."

"I'm coming with you," she said.

He kept to the far side of the road, constantly watching her for signs that she would attack, but when they reached the village, he stopped. She nearly fell over her boots in horror as she surveilled the scene. It was hard to believe they'd left the village less than a half hour before.

A log cabin on the far side of the village near the fields crackled with fire, half consumed. An ox pulling a broken plow meandered through the street, bleating, lost and confused.

From where they were standing, she could see at least ten bodies, mostly in the street, but a few in the fields, sprawled like discarded dolls.

"Lord have mercy," said Bannon breathlessly.

He set his pack down and marched down the hill towards the village proper, his brow set with determination and his fingers twitching at his side.

Aurie searched for the cause of the destruction, but saw nothing. The air had grown still as if the world were troubled by what had transpired. Above it all, a child's crying could be heard, somewhere in the village.

She caught up to Bannon when he reached the main street. A man lay against a water trough. His gurgling cough suggested he had massive internal injuries. While Bannon looked around the houses, searching for the perpetrator, Aurie knelt by the fallen man's side. He had fear in his eyes, which were bloodshot and white to the grave.

"Help...me..."

Aurie wished it was Pi here, not her. She had no skill to help the man. Pi had the soul fragment of an Aura Healer.

"What did this? Who attacked you?" she asked, smoothing back his hair with her fingers, trying to comfort him as he died. His midsection was a mess of thick black blood and he smelled like acrid fear. Aurie avoided looking at the wound, keeping her gaze locked with his.

"I...she..."

The light in his eyes was fading fast.

"Was it a mage? Did they use magic?"

He recoiled from her, which set off a fit of wet coughing. He looked at her as if she'd been the one to hurt him. The coughing turned to retching, and when he vomited up blood, Aurie left him. She could do nothing for him.

Bannon was standing at the corner of the only two-story

house in the village. The lower half was made of stone, the upper of cedar logs. He was peering around the corner.

"Do you see anything?" she asked when she caught up to him.

He was looking at a horse barn with an open front. The sun was behind the barn, so the entrance was cloaked in darkness.

"Something's in that barn," he said.

Before Aurie could ask, a child's scream erupted from ahead. The red-headed child that had approached her came running out of the darkness of the barn, only to be snatched backwards.

Aurie wasted no time, rushing ahead.

"Careful, you fool," said Bannon from behind, then she heard him break from the corner and follow. "It's a trap," he said between breaths.

Aurie knew as much, but didn't care. She reached the entrance. The barn was only about thirty feet deep and twenty at the sides. Sunlight filtered through the cracks between the wood slates, leaving sheets of light.

There was a wet smell like a sewer emanating from the barn. Aurie stepped to the entrance. Two horse stalls with thick ropes hanging from the sides were on the right. The left had farm implements hung on the wall. Piles of grass lay in the back.

A scream cut through the air, but not from the barn. Back on the street, someone was clearly being attacked.

Without another word, Bannon ran back that way. The sharp tint of faez hit the back of her throat as he created shimmering armor around him. A ghostly sword appeared in his fist. He looked like a Knight of the Round Table rushing into battle.

But Aurie refused to abandon the child to whatever was

in the barn. Her hands shook, and her mouth was as dry as sandpaper. Aurie stepped inside. She could hear whimpering, but couldn't tell where it came from..

She made it to the first stall and peered around the corner, wishing she had something solid in her hands like a sword. Magic was powerful, but until it was unleashed, it left her twitching with agitation.

There was a lump in the back of the stall, sticking up from a pile of dry grass. It was the boy's wooden figure. Aurie reached down and picked it up. The carving looked like a soldier. The bottom half was wet with warm blood.

Aurie caught movement behind her, and she spun around, dropping the wooden figurine. The center of the barn was empty.

She crept around the first stall, craning her head to see into the second. The freckled boy lay motionless in the back. Aurie rushed to his side. She checked his pulse, finding it weak. He was breathing and didn't appear injured. Probably unconscious from fright.

She wanted to carry him out of the barn, but that would tie up her hands. Maybe whatever had attacked him was gone. That could have been the movement she'd seen, the creature escaping.

Aurie knew better than to believe this, so she searched for a better way of getting the boy out without losing her best defense. That could be what the creature wanted all along, to keep her busy so she could not use magic, which suggested that it knew she was dangerous.

A horse blanket hanging on the far wall caught her interest. She crept across the barn, plunging through the bars of light, and snatched the blanket from the wall.

She paused for a moment, peering through the opening to the town to see how Bannon fared, but she saw nothing that would indicate his success or failure.

Back in the stall, Aurie fashioned a sled using the blanket and rope. She maneuvered the unconscious boy onto the sled, then hooked the rope around her midsection, right under her breasts. The coarse rope chafed as she marched forward like a plow horse, but the boy slid forward, the motion made easier by the loose hay on the dirt floor.

Aurie kept her hands in a forward position, fingers itching to carve a spell out of the air and do battle. She kept her head on a swivel, expecting an attack from every mote or shadow.

A whisper of wind on her neck was the only warning she got before something landed on her, pinning her to the ground. A heavy fist pounded into the back of her head, bringing stars to her vision.

Trapped on her stomach, she couldn't even use truth magic. The creature pounded on her shoulders, wailing in a woman's voice. Aurie tried to turn over, but the rope harness worked against her. Her feet were tangled in the blanket and rope.

The crazed woman, Aurie realized, was mumbling the same phrase over and over as she pounded away. "Defiler! Defiler! Defiler!"

Aurie managed a crackle of lightning from her fingertips, an over-the-shoulder Five Elements spell, knocking the woman off. Aurie rolled half onto her side, right as the woman leapt like a cougar, teeth bared, fingers as claws.

It was Misses Butterton, the woman who had sold them goods for their journey.

Aurie's second spell was interrupted by Misses Butterton's punch. She was covered in blood, which made wrestling with her difficult, as her limbs were hard to grab. Aurie took two punches to the jaw as she scrambled to defend herself.

Before Aurie could stop her, Misses Butterton pulled a

dinner knife from a pocket of her dress and drove it into Aurie's shoulder. Aurie screamed herself hoarse as Misses Butterton pulled it out and jammed it in a second time, the tip entering the spot between her shoulder and arm socket, driving them apart.

Through the pain, Aurie could see the woman's crazed face. It was the mask of a demon, every muscle straining with hate.

Misses Butterton brought the knife down a third time, aiming for Aurie's chest. Aurie got her arm in the way, deflecting it to lodge in her ribs beneath her right breast.

"Defiler. I see you, Defiler," said the woman, slaver dripping from her lips.

Aurie tried to form truth magic, but she had no air in her lungs to form the words, no energy to resist.

Misses Butterton wrestled the blade from Aurie's ribs, yanking it high into the air, ready for the down strike. Aurie's world was black with pain, spots forming at the edge of her vision, rapidly connecting as her world dialed down to a pinhole. In the last moments before Misses Butterton drove the knife into Aurie's neck, a glowing sword came soaring out of the darkness, lopping off the woman's head.

13

The stone island at the center of the undercity lake was more comfortable than Pi expected. Jade's gang was more resourceful than she'd initially given them credit for, building a brick oven that doubled as a heat source, since the chilly water made the air in the cavern late-fall cold.

There were six small buildings made of wooden pallets, lashed together and covered in tarps. There was no weather to worry about, but the tarps provided privacy. The insides of the crated homes reminded Pi of a sheik's tent in the desert, with luxurious bedding strewn about. Each one was filled with personal items, which included a generous number of books. There was no internet access to distract them.

Jade was applying a fresh shade of purple to the tips of Pi's hair, while Sasha was grilling steaks and fresh asparagus, and the others were seated on camping chairs. The whole thing felt like she was at a women's camp.

"Those steaks smell amazing. I'm so hungry I could chew my arm off," said Nancy, fake biting her stone arm.

"I can't remember the last time I had steaks," said Bethany. "I could kiss you for them."

Pi was sitting still as Jade applied the coloring paste,

fingers dutifully separating strands, pulling them away from the ear. Though the others couldn't hear it, Pi caught snatches of humming from Jade, along with buffets of minty breath against her neck. It was terribly distracting.

"You're welcome," said Pi. "I'm happy to help."

They'd treated her coldly on previous visits. Pi'd hoped the offering of good food might smooth the way to better relations. They ate the steaks earnestly, washing the meat down with beer from a magically cooled bucket.

Sisi belched like a fog horn, bringing laughter from the group. Bethany and Yoko tried to match Sisi's volume, giggling between tries, until they gave up and crowned the blonde waif the winner.

After the belching contest, they talked about which Halls they'd placed on the Tome of Selection before the Merlins. Pi sat quietly, nursing her third beer, since finishing the second had made her light-headed, and listened to their conversation.

Though she was the youngest of the group, Pi felt significantly older, and not just because of the soul fragments. Everyone was at least twenty years old, but they sounded like they were still teenagers. Maybe she was being hard on them, she decided. Not getting into the Halls had left them always wondering what might have been.

Pi was lost in her thoughts when she realized the whole group was staring at her.

"Yes?"

"Which Halls?" asked Nancy.

"Oh. Coterie and Arcanium."

"Jesus," said Sasha. "Only two, and both major Halls. You're one cocky bitch."

Pi couldn't tell if the "bitch" was an insult or compliment. And there was no way she was going to tell them that she had originally planned to only put Coterie. "I was seventeen. I had more chances if I failed."

"How'd you even get in Coterie?" asked Jade, a level darkness in her gaze. "Bethany told us you have to get sponsored."

Everyone leaned forward to hear her answer. "I...I did something to impress an alumni, and he sponsored me."

It didn't appear Jade believed her.

"Who was it?" asked Bethany.

"Eugene Hickford," said Pi. "He wasn't very popular with the other alumni. Having him as my sponsor was a disadvantage."

"That's what all the rich kids say," said Jade, frowning.

The rebuke stung. Pi didn't know what to make of Jade. One minute she was flirty, the next cold and angry. Pi liked her, but the wildly swinging feedback was giving her whiplash.

"Why did you want to join Coterie?" asked Bethany. "Don't take this the wrong way, but you don't seem like the type."

Pi sighed with relief. This was the kind of question she felt comfortable answering. "I wanted power. My parents were killed by another mage when I was a kid. They were good people, trying to do right by the world. If they were free to get murdered, and no one would do anything about it, then what protections would I ever have? So I wanted to make sure that never happened to me."

The others nodded in agreement, except for Jade, who was staring directly at Pi with a fierceness that bordered on anger.

"So rather than fix the system, you decided to join the very people that killed your parents?"

"You can't fight them from outside the system. They wield too much power," replied Pi.

"Unless you can't get in," said Jade.

"But you wanted to. You tried to join the Halls. Look, I get the frustration. I really do. But I wanted to protect myself."

Jade slammed her beer down. "So it was 'I got mine, screw the rest of you'?"

"Hey," said Pi, "that's not fair. We were orphans. Getting into the Halls, and especially Coterie, was never a done deal. I made sacrifices. It's not like I knew you all then."

"But by joining them, you propagate the very system that oppresses those who cannot," said Jade. "They use the Merlins to justify manipulation of who gets in and who doesn't. The powerful get more powerful, keeping out those they don't like, maintaining a stranglehold on their position."

"The Merlins require skill. Not everyone should be a mage. It's dangerous to give that much power freely." Then Pi saw the looks on their faces. "Wait, I didn't mean it like that. You all should have been in the Halls. For sure. But you have to admit that not everyone deserves it. There has to be some minimum."

Sasha crossed her arms. Her afro danced as she spoke. "Why should someone else get to decide if I'm ready to learn? And it might be acceptable if it was done fairly, but it's not fair. Look at who gets into the top Halls, and who doesn't. You have to have money or connections."

"Arcanium doesn't do that," said Pi.

"And look what happened to Arcanium," said Jade. "The Halls maintain the illusion of being a mcritocracy by allowing the people they don't like to join Halls that don't matter."

"They matter to the people that get in," said Pi.

"Exactly," said Jade. "Those people are just happy to be allowed a taste of power. Subservient to their masters, who give them a little more leash room than the rest."

Pi thought of her friends in the lesser Halls. "Not everything is about power. There are a lot of happy people in those Halls, many of them my friends. And they provide a service necessary to society."

Jade stood up and stalked away, before turning back around. "Wake up, Pi. Why can't you see it? The Hundred Halls controls how much"—she made air quotes—"power gets doled out to the masses. Why do you think there's no Hundred Halls anywhere else in the world? They have a monopoly on teaching magic. Anyone that allowed a school to get set up in their country would get cut off, probably invaded. Back when magic was still in the shadows, Invictus cut deals with the major world leaders, giving them access to his power in exchange for control. Think about it. The patron system could work anywhere, but it's only legally valid here in the States, and specifically in the Hundred Halls. If you take a student outside of the system, then you're illegal and subject to fines, jail time, and removal of your abilities."

"It's not a perfect system," said Pi. "I'm not trying to defend it."

"It certainly sounds like it," said Jade. "I thought you hated the Halls?"

"I do, but you can't just tear it down and expect a better system to pop up in its place," said Pi, realizing she was sounding like her sister. "We need to improve the system, not destroy it. That was one of the reasons I joined."

Which wasn't completely true, but she found it hard to admit she'd fantasized about having a dragon or other supernatural creature as a patron. Illegally, of course.

"Then why are you here?" asked Jade.

Why am I here? she asked herself, but when she looked at Jade, she knew. "We can do both. Our choices don't have to be binary. We can damage the Cabal, keep them from consolidating power."

Jade narrowed her gaze. "You're still trying to save Arcanium."

"Those are my friends there. My sister, too. Look, I want

a new system as much as you all, but there has to be more than anarchy," said Pi, getting up from the circle and stalking to the edge. "And it's not like you're doing anything about the Halls down here. You're barely surviving, stealing apples and living in a glorified cave. I've hit the Cabal where it hurts. I've survived their ambushes and outthought them. So don't talk to me about philosophy. It sounds great down here in the dark, but the real game is up there, and it's mean and nasty, and full of sharp elbows and deceit. At the end of it, no one says 'good game' or 'get 'em next time.' They're usually dead, or out of power. If you really want to do something, then stop worrying about what happened four years ago when you didn't get into the Halls, and start thinking about now. Because I know how to hurt the Cabal, and hurt them good. If that's what you want, then come find me in Big Dave's Town. If not, then good luck to you, because I didn't come down here to hide."

On the way to the rowboat, Pi wiped away a tear and had to fight to take a breath. She really wanted to blast a fireball into the lake, relieve some stress, but didn't want them to know how much she hurt.

She was so intent on leaving, she didn't hear Jade come up from behind and grab her arm.

"Let me be," said Pi, pulling away. "I get it. I'm a part of the system. You don't need me."

The look on Jade's face was somewhere between deadly serious and introspection.

"Hey, I..."

"Don't need me," said Pi. "I get it."

Jade wrinkled her forehead. "That's not what I was going to say. I'm good at being angry, but, what you said back there."

"I'm sorry, that was pretty rough."

"No. Not at all," said Jade. "I was being a jerk. We all

were. I'm just so angry, and, well, you got into the Halls and I didn't."

"I'm sure it could have been the other way around. Anyway, we didn't know each other back then."

"But we know each other now."

Jade stared at her as if this was supposed to have meaning. She stepped closer. A warmth rose up in Pi's chest. The skin on her face tingled.

"What are you, uhm, going to do...?" asked Jade.

Before Jade's features had been angry slashes, but they'd rounded into a delicate softness. Her lips were bunched. Her eyes wide.

"I don't know. I didn't really have a plan when I stormed off."

Pi reached out to Jade, but as her hand crossed the expanse between them, she got nervous and put it back by her side.

"What about you?" asked Pi.

"I'm sure they'll stay up drinking," said Jade. "Not like they got much else to do."

At that moment from the other side of the island, a host of girlish laughter rose up like birds taking flight.

"Not them. You."

Pi moved half a step forward.

The too-tough Jade caught herself licking her lips and looked away, a smile hiding in her eyes.

"I'm free tonight," Jade said in a husky voice.

"What a surprise, so am I."

Pi brushed her finger against the back of Jade's hand, which quickened her breath.

"Do you...?"

Jade nodded emphatically.

"Where?"

"Not here," said Jade right away, then she added with a grin, "I'm loud."

"Oh, shit," said Pi, and not because the idea surprised her—she kinda assumed Jade was the talkative type—but more because it was really happening.

Jade floated near, her minty breath giving her the shivers. Pi curled her hand around Jade's mane of black hair, cupping the back of her head and pulling her so close there was barely enough room for a piece of paper between their lips. When the kiss finally came, it lasted until morning.

14

It'd been three weeks since Aurie had awoken in her bed at Arcanium, bandaged and in great pain. Professor Mali had been there when she woke, grim-faced and solemn, promising to explain what had happened at a later date.

Dr. Fairlight had been brought in for healing, but Aurie's allergy to magic had reduced the effectiveness of the spells. So Aurie had to heal the old-fashion way. During her convalescence, she'd sent her friends for books from the library.

No one asked her about what had happened. Aurie assumed the professor had made them swear not to ask, and she wasn't about to explain, since she didn't know the real answer. Her selection of books did raise some eyebrows. She had them fetch books about time travel, which confirmed what she'd already known—it wasn't possible. The Engine of Temporal Manipulation didn't alter time, rather it transferred the dilation from one object to another.

Frustrated with her reading, Aurie had been relieved when Isabella appeared in her room. Her hair was pulled into her face, so she was looking at her through a curtain.

"Professor Mali wants to see you," mumbled Isabella.

"What happened to your eye?" asked Aurie, sitting up on the couch.

Isabella's chin dipped towards her chest. She reflexively fixed the strand of black hair, hiding the black eye.

"Jacqueline had a major freak-out Monday. She said spiders were crawling out of the walls. Wanted to burn the place down. We kept her from casting any spells, but I got this in the tussle."

"Is she okay now?"

"Mostly embarrassed about it," said Isabella. "But everyone's been on edge since then."

"Where is the professor?"

Isabella nodded upward. "In the greenhouse. Bundle up, it's not as warm as it should be."

Aurie threw on an extra layer and an Arcanium hoodie before heading to the stairwell. She ran into Xi along the way. When she passed him, he shied away from her as if she carried a communicable disease.

"Xi?"

He backed down the hallway, facing her, and when he reached the halfway point, he turned and sprinted into the next hall. Aurie thought about chasing him down, but decided that would only make him worse.

A freezing rain was tapping against the greenhouse. There was a strange humming that Aurie couldn't figure out until she saw the space heaters set up around the perimeter. Normally, they used magic to keep the vegetation humid and warm. The enchantments infused into the greenhouse seemed to be wearing off.

Professor Mali was sitting between the rows of cackleberry bushes. The bloodred fruits looked ready to ooze ichor, with white cracks forming in their bloated skins. They smelled like wet graves at midnight.

"How are you feeling, young lady?" asked the professor, putting Aurie on her back foot. She hadn't been expecting pleasantries from the normally grim-faced professor.

"Better than the rest of Arcanium, I think," said Aurie.

"And why is that?"

"Because I got to use magic in whatever place or time that was."

"Time travel is impossible," said the professor.

"Then what happened?"

Professor Mali absently stroked the long gray braid hanging over her shoulder. "I've been trying to figure that out. I don't have a good answer. It wasn't time travel, we can rule that out. And you didn't go anywhere. One moment you touched the Engine, and the next, you fell on your side with all your injuries."

"Could I have been teleported somewhere and back?" asked Aurie.

"And your body placed in the exact same position that you left in? That makes little sense," she admonished, then shook her head. "Magic is a strange beast, and we know so little about the Engine. The only thing I can surmise is that Semyon's life is being sped up, but you failed to give the Engine a proper outlet, so it created its own."

"It's not sentient," said Aurie.

"I never said that." The professor flashed a glare. "But a river constrained by a levee will find a way out. And magic isn't as simple as water. It looks for the lowest energy way to reach equilibrium. Satchel's Second Law," she added, as if it were a lesson in class.

When Aurie had first woken up, the professor had quizzed her about what had happened. Aurie had been working on theories of her own. "I thought the alternate reality might have come from Semyon's memory, but since he wasn't in it, and

Bannon Creed was, I didn't think that was it."

The way the professor looked at Aurie told her that she'd struck close to her guess.

"What you may or may not know is that the original patrons are closely linked by the charter. It's more than a document. It's a binding–an enchantment—that keeps them as close to each other as Invictus, Merlin rest his soul. There is much we do not know about what they shared in those early days."

"Did Semyon tell you?"

Mali shook her head, looking away. "Nothing directly. But teachers talk. We piece things together."

"What about the Riders? I did some research on them, but couldn't find what they were, or even if they were defeated," said Aurie.

"I'm not certain they are important. There were many dangers that existed then that do not exist now. It was the problem of their time."

"Then what was it? You've told me the things you think that didn't happen," said Aurie.

"Does it matter?" asked the professor with an uncharacteristic shrug. "If I had to make a bet, I'd say that it happened in either your mind or Semyon's, like a dreamstalking. Except you came out with the injures you obtained in that place. Which means that you can die there."

"I gathered that much," said Aurie.

"Energy equilibrium is a fundamental law of science and magic. Whatever happened satisfied the Engine because after you returned, the hum reduced to its previous state," said the professor.

"So science wants to kill me. Great."

"Technically, the Engine does, or Semyon, or the connection to the other patrons through the charter, or something else entirely."

Aurie looked outside the hazy glass of the greenhouse. The buildings were fuzzy and streaked, as the ice-rain ran down the sides.

"I have a feeling that it's not done with me."

Professor Mali rolled next to Aurie. "I'm afraid not. Already the Engine vibration is increasing. The mind-transfer didn't happen when I touched the Engine. It's keyed to you, and you alone."

"What if I don't touch it again?" asked Aurie.

"It would likely explode."

The professor was looking at her gravely.

"Now is the time, Professor, when you lecture me about how foolish my decision was to visit Oba and convince him to give me the Engine."

"I wish that your total punishment would be a thorough tongue-lashing, or a two-hour lecture that would bore holes in your head." She sighed into a grimace. "You may not have graduated yet, but you're an adult. You made your decision to get the Engine, and now, you must deal with the consequences."

"Me and everyone else in Arcanium. I might have killed them."

The professor gazed up at Aurie with supreme confidence. "Or you may have saved them. Only time will tell, but I have faith in you, Aurelia Silverthorne."

Aurie wandered to the edge and put her hand on the cold glass. She wished she had faith in herself, but it was getting hard to find, especially without Pi around.

"I miss you, sis."

15

The hike through the Undercity had taken nearly three hours. Jade led the way, followed by Pi, and then the others. The first half the journey kept them on the organized paths that connected the various settlements beneath the city of Invictus. The way was well marked and occasionally lit with faint blue magelights.

Then Jade led them into the wilderness, cutting through vast caverns filled with strange fungi that pulsed purple or waved tiny stalks in unseen winds. Pi kept her questions to herself, though she had many, like where Jade was leading them that would take them to the surface.

When Pi saw the obsidian arch nestled into the corner of the bleak cavern between two white marble statues of naked men, she exclaimed, "How do you know about the Garden Network?"

Jade spoke over her shoulder. "A girl's gotta have her secrets."

This answer didn't sit well with Pi. The Garden Network wasn't a subway station that anyone could use.

The statues were twice as tall as the obsidian arch. Sisi ran up to one and poked his genitals with her finger. "What's with Tweedle-Dee and Tweedle-Hung-Like-A-Goldfish?"

"It's best not to poke things, Sisi," said Jade. "What if that had been activated by touch?"

Sisi pulled her hand back as if she'd been burned. "I didn't think of that."

"Where does it take us?" asked Pi.

"I only know a couple of passwords," said Jade. "Assuming they haven't changed them."

This news surprised Pi. She'd thought the way to the surface was going to be a hidden staircase or an elevator like the one in Freeport Games. The idea that Jade knew passwords to the Garden Network changed Pi's impression of her.

Sasha stepped forward. "What are you two blathering about?"

"It's a portal," said Pi. "The patrons and those they trust use it to get around the city quickly. I've been through a couple."

"Holy shit," said Bethany, running her hand along the glassy black stone. "I'd heard rumors, but thought people were joking. Like when they send freshmen to get the elevator pass in a one-floor high school."

"I can get us into the fourth ward. The portal comes out in the back of the City Library. I'll take everyone one at a time once I make sure the coast is clear. So you'd better tell us where we're going from there, Pi."

"Right," said Pi, rubbing her hands together. "There's a bar in the fourth called the Smoke & Amber. It's a popular haunt of Coterie mages."

"I heard about that place," said Bethany.

"We need information," said Pi. "We're going to grab one of them and make them talk."

Jade held up a plastic spray bottle, the kind used by gardeners to water the leaves of delicate plants. "And this is going to make them want to never shut up."

Pi had worked out the details of the plan with Jade while they were in bed last week. It'd taken a few days to acquire the reagents. The mixture was a contact potion that would make the relevant information spill out of them, enhancing their memories until they couldn't stand not to talk about them. A few well-placed suggestions would make their captive babble like a talking brook about whatever subject they wanted.

The trip through the portal made Pi nauseous, but it wore off within minutes. Sasha's trip left the girl retching into a trash bin.

"I get motion sick easy," she said once she'd recovered.

The obsidian archway was in the back of the library in a locked room. Pi got them through the door. Outside, despite the late hour, the city was alive, or at least Pi had gotten used to the muted underground, which seemed to simultaneously silence sound and reflect it in mysterious ways. She'd forgotten that it was early December, and the air was chilly, but not enough that they'd need spells to keep warm.

The Smoke & Amber was two blocks away, pulsing and thumping with music. Pale smoke leaked out the bottom of the door, disappearing into the night sky. Pedestrians gave the mist a wide berth as they passed the establishment.

The seven women stopped in the alleyway behind the bar.

"So who wants to go in and lure someone out? It can't be me or Bethany."

To Pi's surprise, Jade added, "Not I," then added after a breath, "I had friends in Coterie."

Jade looked away when she said it, which suggested it was something she wasn't proud of. Pi decided to ask later, rather than in front of the others.

"I can go," said Yoko, with a cautious smile and a slight head nod.

"I've got to go then," said Sasha, looking unhappy about it. "'Cause Stone Arm sticks out and Sisi doesn't look like she's old enough. My only question is what do we do to get someone out?"

"That'll be something for you to figure out," said Pi. "Don't try any spells. They'll be sure to have protective enchantments, trinkets, and other warning devices that'll keep them safe. Attacking them in any way will bring unwanted attention. Mage bars like these like to keep their clients, which means a night of safe fun. We don't want to trip up their alarm systems either."

Sasha rolled her eyes. "Great. No spells. Find someone and lure them outside into the alleyway. Like maybe, hey, I'm a nice black girl who wants to talk to you out back. Wanna come with me and my sexy Japanese friend?"

"Yeah, whatever, try that," said Pi.

Sasha returned a dead look. "They probably won't even let me in."

"Hurry up," said Jade. "We need to get this done before someone wonders why we're hiding back here."

Before they went in, Pi pulled a handful of gold dust from a pocket and sprinkled it over Sasha and Yoko, murmuring a spell. The particles flashed as they drifted onto their hair and shoulders.

When Pi was finished, Sasha looked at the sparkling dust on her arm and said, "It looks like you rolled me in a vat of strippers."

"What does this do, Pi-san?" asked Yoko.

"The spell is shit, supposed to make you luckier, or better at being rich, like that prosperity gospel crap, but the reagents are expensive, so only the wealthy can afford to cast it."

"Sounds a bit self-selecting," said Sasha.

"As long as it keeps anyone from assuming you don't

belong," said Pi.

Sasha grabbed Yoko's hand. As they left, Pi heard Sasha say, "Let's grab someone and get the hell out, like quick. These places give me the heebie-jeebies."

While Sasha and Yoko were inside, the other five waited in the shadows. Pi crouched on her heels, feeling exposed above ground after weeks in the Undercity. She kept getting an itchy feeling between her shoulder blades like someone was watching. She knew it was practically impossible for anyone from the Cabal to know she'd returned above ground, but she kept expecting an attack to come as soon as she let her guard down.

To distract herself from her worried thoughts, Pi pulled out her cell phone and rubbed the ON button with her thumb, deciding whether or not to send a message to her sister. She caught Jade watching her, so she shoved the phone back into her pocket.

After an hour, the others started to get worried.

"Should we go in?" asked Bethany.

The others crowded around her for guidance. Pi saw the annoyed frown and arm-cross from Jade. She clearly thought of them as her followers. Pi hoped this wouldn't come between them. She hadn't had a girlfriend or boyfriend in a long time, and was really enjoying having a connection with Jade.

"Give it more time," said Pi. "Maybe it's taking time to get someone to leave. I wouldn't get worried yet."

After her little talk, Jade found her away from the others. Pi's eyes had adjusted to the darkness, so she saw the way Jade was biting her lower lip.

"Why haven't you messaged your sister yet?" asked Jade.

"What?"

The word slipped from Pi's lips. It was the last question she'd expected.

"I saw you fidgeting with your phone earlier. You should send her a note, let her know you're okay," said Jade.

Pi's face flushed warm. "I, uhm, thanks."

Jade leaned over and placed a soft kiss on Pi's cheek, squeezed her arm, and wandered away to give her privacy.

After collecting her thoughts, Pi turned on her phone, cursing its slowness. When the little bars filled in at the top left corner, she opened up the messaging app and typed in a quick note, letting Aurie know that she was alive and doing well. She didn't mention anything about Jade or the others, or that she was still messing with the Cabal. She didn't want her to worry.

After the message whisked away with a quiet bright noise, Pi stared expectantly at the phone, waiting for a response. But the time was 1:48 a.m., and Aurie was likely asleep.

Pi froze when she heard voices entering the alleyway, until she recognized Sasha's deep voice. The guy and girl with them were weaving back and forth, clearly intoxicated. The guy was wearing a fashionable white suit, and the girl a silvery flapper outfit. The four of them were laughing.

"Are we really going to have a foursome back here?" asked the guy in a slurred voice.

The voice was familiar, and in a nagging not-good way. Pi was on the other side of the alley, so she couldn't see them clearly.

"Hey, Sasha," said the girl, stumbling in place. "Who are all them?"

"Friends," said Sasha.

Before Pi got over to them, she recognized the girl's voice. Bree Bishop. She'd been in the same year as Pi in Coterie. Bree and Brock DuPont had tried to kill Ashley numerous times. A red-tinged rage washed through Pi's mind, but she had to push it back. Now wasn't the time for anger.

"Sorry, Ashley," she whispered.

The others crowded around the two mages. Jade stepped forward and sprayed the potion into their faces.

"What the hell was that?" asked Bree, starting to be annoyed, but clearly too drunk to do anything about it. "Is this a robbery or something? That might not be a good idea. We're mages, or at least I am. I could take the lot of you with my pinky tied behind my back. Or is it my arms tied behind my head? How does that go?"

Pi stepped in front of them. "Not a robbery. We're going to ask you some questions before you get to have your foursome."

"Oh, goody."

She'd been so focused on Bree, that she hadn't noticed who the guy was until she was staring straight at him. He was looking at her with a confused expression on his face. It was Alton Lockwood.

The last time she'd seen him, she and Aurie had turned the tables, using his vial of succubus tears to place a near-permanent enchantment on him. It was supposed to have made him forget he could cast magic, cause him pain if anyone saw him naked, and keep him from remembering them. Last she'd heard, he'd been sent away to his rich family.

"Merlin's tits."

He leaned forward, scrunching up his nose. "Do I know you?"

"Oh my god," said Bree, punching him in the arm. "That's that stupid twit who left Coterie to join Arcanium. Cake or Pie or something like that. Alton, honey, don't you remember her?"

He blinked and looked sad as he tried to remember. Pi held her breath as he spoke, afraid that they'd been able to fix his memory.

"No?"

Bree shook her head. "You're such a retard, Alton. If you weren't hung like an elephant and richer than a third-world country, I wouldn't put up with you."

Her comment brought chuckles from everyone except Bethany, who was staring at Alton as if he'd murdered her puppy. Pi was about to check on her, when Jade shook the bottle at Pi.

"This potion isn't supposed to be this good. What did you do to them?"

Yoko giggled behind a cupped hand. "She tried to put something in our drinks. I switched the glasses."

Pi focused on Bree. "Unintended effects from the mixing. I guess this is going to be a little easier than we thought. Can you tell us what Coterie's plans are for Arcanium?"

Bree tapped her electric blue fingernail against her lower lip, keeping her mouth open like a bass. "Uhm, Arcanium." She giggled. "Hall defenses are falling faster than Semyon can recover. The patrons have offered vast wealth and a pick of artifacts for whoever can take down that self-righteous prick Semyon. This is way better than those second-year games. Soon, they'll be weak enough, and that's when the real fun will begin."

A sob came from Bethany, momentarily distracting Pi. The girl was crying, but Pi put it out of her mind. She had more questions to ask.

"How soon? Do you know any specific plans?" asked Pi.

The distractions continued as Bethany was mumbling. Then Alton broke out in laughter as he seemed to notice Bethany for the first time.

"I know you," he said as Bree was explaining something about a secret way into Arcanium. Pi wanted to pay attention, but whatever was unfolding between Alton and Bethany had put up alarms in her head. "You're the dumb girl I ran out of

Coterie after I tricked you into touching that cursed Sumerian artifact. Oh yes, see-through guts girl."

He started laughing, pointing at her. The scent of faez warned Pi, but she couldn't react fast enough. Bethany blasted Alton with a force spell, hitting his defensive enchantments. The spell rebounded onto the group, scattering them like bowling pins.

Pi bit her tongue as she landed on the concrete. She spit the coppery-tasting blood out.

A siren was going off in the Smoke & Amber. Pi stumbled to her feet.

"Run, get out of here. Back to the portal," she said.

Two bouncers from the bar entered the alleyway. Pi knew she was too slow. They were going to use the Voice of Command. High-end bouncers were typically members of the Protectors.

To Pi's surprise, Jade pulled a ziplock bag of orange powder from her pocket, poured it in her hand, and blew it at them. A mini-tornado formed and whirled towards the bouncers, knocking them into the street and shattering the side window of a passing car. When Jade released the spell, she collapsed. Her eyes flickered black, and her face contorted with a quiet agony.

Before the bouncers could regroup, they abandoned Bree and Alton and ran the other way. A sudden ice storm formed overhead, raining fist-sized balls of hard ice onto them. Pi countered with an umbrella-shield, and so did Jade, but the others didn't fare so well. Their screams filled the alleyway as they were pummeled.

Pi spied the mage behind the spell at the other end, peeking around the corner. She sent a tightly focused force missile straight into his face, throwing him backwards and ending the ice storm.

Sisi and Nancy had been knocked out. Sasha grabbed Nancy, while Pi grabbed Sisi. Bethany had blood running from a gash in her forehead. They looked like they'd been through a meat grinder. No one ran straight as they headed to the City Library, only two blocks away.

Pi thought they might get away, but then a floating metal ball appeared above their heads. Tendrils of electricity shot out of it like from a Tesla electrical generator. When the first bolt hit Bethany, it seized up her legs and knocked her to the ground. Within moments the whole group of them were on the sidewalk, screams erupting as the metal ball shocked them. Pi launched a water spell, using lexology to collapse the liquid around the ball, shorting it out.

When they stumbled into the City Library a few minutes later, the librarian behind the counter stared at them with wide eyes as they marched up the marble stairs to the second floor, where the portal was located.

They were able to wake Sisi and Nancy before taking them through the portal. When they were on the other side, safely in the undercity, only then did they relax.

Before they traveled again, Pi moved amongst them, using her Aura Healer skills to assuage the worst of the damage. There were no broken bones at least, but there were at least three concussions, and Sasha might have torn her Achilles.

"I'm sorry," said Bethany in the quiet time after, when everyone was still breathing heavily. "I couldn't believe it was him. He took everything from me."

"For what it's worth," said Pi, "my sister and I had a serious run-in with him, and gave him a taste of his own medicine."

"It'll only feel better if he's dead," said Bethany grimly. "What did you do to him? He didn't seem quite right."

"Made him hate magic, and sex," said Pi. "But it looks like he's gotten some of that fixed. He didn't remember me, which is good. That was part of the enchantment."

"That was terrible," said Jade, wiping the dried blood from her jaw.

"Sorry, Jade," said Bethany. "I kinda lost my head."

"Not that. The spell work. We got our asses kicked. There was only one mage that got us in the alleyway, and that sentinel drone was probably an auto-defense for the bar. Those should have been trivial. If it hadn't been for me and Pi, the rest of you would be dead or in jail," said Jade.

Pi eyed Jade for signs that the aftereffects of her spell work were gone. She didn't know what had caused Jade's eyes to turn black.

"I think we need to do some training before we venture above ground again," said Pi. "Right now, we're a bunch of misfits."

Sasha coughed into her hand, then held it up to show blood. "It's like my own Rorschach test," she said, chuckling at her own gallows' humor. "And I think it says, at least this bunch of misfits isn't dead."

"You almost look like you enjoyed that," said Pi.

Sasha shrugged. "It was good to do something. I'm sick of hiding in the undercity. I felt like a real mage for once."

The others nodded their agreement. Jade gave her a secret smile.

"You're still a bunch of misfits," said Pi.

"Damn straight," said Jade. "We're the Misfits."

The name passed between them like a virus, bringing smiles to everyone's tired lips. A shiver of pleasure went down Pi's spine.

"Come on, Misfits," said Pi. "Time to go home. I've got homework to assign."

They left the portal for the Garden Network behind, marching into the darkness of the undercity. Pi pulled her cell phone out and checked to see if she'd gotten any messages from Aurie, but there were none. She turned it off, shoved the phone into her pocket, and hurried to catch up with the others.

Bree had mentioned a secret way into Arcanium. When Pi returned to Big Dave's Town she planned to climb the spiral staircase to the Goblin's Romp and send another message to Aurie to warn her. She thought about trying to talk with her sister in person, but after interrogating Bree Bishop, they'd be on the lookout for her.

At the present moment, Pi was more concerned about Jade. How did she know passwords to the Garden Network, and what happened to Jade after she made that mini-tornado?

"Hey, Jade," she said as she caught up.

Jade winked, a promise for later. "Hey, you." She raised an eyebrow. "What's on your mind?"

Pi pushed her thoughts away. "Nothing. Just thinking about what happened back there, and how we should have done it differently."

Jade nodded as if she understood, but there was something else in her dark gaze.

"I'm really glad you're with us," said Jade.

"Me too," said Pi.

But what wasn't Jade telling her?

16

Aurie knew the summons would come even before Tristen had arrived at her door. The vibration from the Engine could be felt throughout Arcanium. It'd started a few days ago, and rose quickly, until Aurie worried that it was going to explode. She'd tried to see Semyon, but Professor Mali had restricted access.

This had been for two reasons. The first was that she'd passed the information to the professor that there was a secret way into Arcanium that nobody knew about, and the second was the concern about the Engine. Aurie wasn't sure how credible the secret passage theory was, but if it was true, the Cabal could cause all sorts of havoc.

"Thanks for getting me," Aurie told Tristen as they walked down the hallway.

"I had a choice?" he asked. "Not like I have anything better to do."

"Are you, uhm, doing okay?" she asked, eyeing him for signs of faez madness or that he might be compromised by Cabal treachery.

"No, not really," he said, glumly. "But I'm doing better than most. Xi attacked Deshawn last night. Someone got him sedatives to calm him, but we can't keep him drugged until Semyon is fixed, can we?"

"We have to do what we must." She paused at the top of the staircase that went down to the waterfall. "This is my stop. Be safe."

"You too."

Tristen disappeared down the other way. Was he too calm? Aurie didn't know what might indicate if the Cabal had snuck in and charmed someone, but she felt like Pi would be way better at figuring it out.

When she reached Semyon's chamber it was radically different from before. The room looked like it was a massive science experiment, or a Rube Goldberg machine. Antennas and beeping black boxes were set up everywhere. Professor Longakers, in his tweed jacket, was typing at a computer while Professor Mali sat with the unconscious Semyon, who had little round pads attached to his forehead that connected to a host of machines. The runed brass cylinder rested on his chest.

The Engine whined for a moment, setting off a reaction in the sensors. Professor Longakers looked worried for a moment, then shook his head.

"I have a feeling I'm not going to like this," said Aurie.

"You have to go back in," said Mali.

The Engine felt like it was tugging on her. Invisible strings pulled her towards the bed, but she resisted.

"What am I going back to?"

Mali shared a glance with Longakers. "That's what we mean to find out. Is this a memory, or a trip to the astral plane? Or maybe an alternate reality. Whatever it is, we'll know."

Aurie stared at the brass cylinder.

"You knew you were going to have to go back."

"I know," said Aurie. "I started this, and I'm going to finish it."

But I really want Pi to be with me.

"Can I take someone else?" asked Aurie.

Both professors' heads bobbed up like gophers. "I suppose it's possible."

The whine increased in frequency, causing them to squint.

"Maybe next time. Seems like I should start."

Aurie reached towards the cylinder. Mali said, "Wait! We got you some period clothing and a few other items. They're in the bathroom."

"What if it's not the same time? Never mind. Better than these. I can always claim I'm a historical actor."

Aurie was relieved when she saw they'd given her pants. As much as she enjoyed a fancy dress, gallivanting in the past in a skirt that might get tangled up in a fight was less than appealing.

She felt like Paul Revere when she looked at herself in the mirror with the ponytail sticking out of the back, her jacket over top a billowing white shirt, and dark trousers.

"One last thing," said Professor Mali. "Whatever you do, don't tell anyone the truth about where you come from. If this place is a projection in Semyon's memory, then disturbing it might be dangerous. For all we know, this time and place has special meaning to him, so he's retreated back to it. Upsetting it might cause a reaction."

"A reaction. That's a nice way of describing death in a dreamland."

The professor gave her a sardonic look. "Good luck."

Aurie nodded and touched the cylinder.

She landed in a freshly tilled field, digging her fingers into the moist soil as she rode the waves of nausea that followed the translocation. After she got her bearings, Aurie checked her surroundings.

It was midafternoon, a cool spring day judging by the state of the field. A man was leading a plow horse on the other side, facing away, so he hadn't seen her appear suddenly. A light haze of smoke on the horizon indicated the direction of a larger town.

Before the farmer could notice that a brown girl wearing a coat and trousers had suddenly appeared in his field, she scurried into the woods. A group of biting flies attacked her as she struggled through the dense foliage. It took about twenty minutes, but she found her way to a dirt road.

The wheel tracks were deep. A pile of steaming horse manure attracted flies on the far side of the road. Aurie picked the direction that went towards the haze of smoke.

The sun was warm, bringing beads of sweat to her neck and forehead. Aurie wished they'd given her one of those tricorn hats she'd seen in the history books, but knew that they probably weren't as common as the pictures led people to believe.

After a couple of miles, she came upon a small town with stone buildings and an air of bustle to it. It wasn't the source of the smoke as that town was further away.

No one gave her a second glance as she tramped down the uneven dirt road towards the Blue Buckle Inn, which either was a result of her disguise or the nature of whatever reality she was participating in. She didn't quite know what the point of the place was, except as an outlet for the Engine's temporal energy.

As she pushed through the front door, wondering what the purpose of this place might be, she saw two familiar faces seated at a table.

A young, pock-faced Celesse D'Agastine with dirty blonde hair, wearing a peasant dress, sat across from a stern-faced

Priyanka Sai in a rich silken gown the color of the pale sky.

Aurie tried to check her reaction, but the young patrons caught it, snapping their heads in her direction. A frisson of faez hit the air. Aurie readied a spell, but did not unleash it, staring back at Celesse and Priyanka, until the innkeeper returned to the counter.

"Greetings, sir," he said. "May I help you?"

Aurie lowered her voice and nodded towards the table. "Looking for some friends."

"Wonderful. Ring the silver bell if you need attention."

Aurie approached the table. Celesse was a younger, more homely version of herself, though the fierceness of her gaze had not changed. Priyanka looked almost exactly the same. She appeared, at first glance, to be the older of the two, though it was hard to tell with magic.

"Who are you?" asked Priyanka, low and level, the threat carried between her clenched teeth.

"I know who you are," said Aurie, hearing the surprise in her own voice.

Aurie realized that Celesse had her hands beneath the table. She sensed they were working furiously in a spell, so she held her hands out. "Wait, don't do that. I'm here to talk." Then she added, hoping she had not guessed wrong about the nature of his friends, "I know B.C. He sent me."

Celesse's arms stopped twitching. Priyanka narrowed her gaze.

"You know us," said Priyanka in a thick Indian accent. "And that might be your undoing."

Voices approached from the stairwell. A man and woman in their twenties, wearing upper-class attire, strolled into the common area and stopped speaking when they saw the standoff. Their frowns stopped their conversation cold.

Priyanka's lips curled into a smile as she said, "Sit, friend.

It's been a while."

Aurie nodded towards the couple, putting on a fake smile, and took the seat opposite the two women, careful to keep her hands above the table. The couple resumed their conversation as they left the inn.

"Speak now, speak fast," said Priyanka in a low voice, the richness of her accent disappearing in the threat.

"Mayhap we shouldn't let her speak at all," said Celesse, glowering.

The country accent startled Aurie into staring. She blinked it away, turning her attention to Priyanka.

"Like I said, I'm a friend of B.C.'s. I fought the Rider with him."

Mention of the Rider brought the whites to their eyes.

"How do we know you're not the Rider?" asked Celesse. "Our friend is three days late, and you show up claiming to know him."

"Do you know what happened?" asked Priyanka.

Aurie felt the severity of their inspection, and knew that at any moment, the conversation could turn to action.

"I...I am like you," she said, pausing for effect. Both women nodded to acknowledge their hidden natures. "I met him by chance on the road. We traveled for a while together. He told me he was traveling to meet friends, and described you both."

"How long ago was this?" asked Celesse.

Aurie tried to estimate a plausible time that might have passed. The only gauge she had was the state of the fields. They'd been harvesting their crops in the village that had been attacked.

"Last fall."

As soon as the words left her lips, she knew she'd spoken wrong. A sudden seizure hit Aurie, freezing her in place. She tried to move her jaw, or fingers, or anything, but the spell had made her completely immobile. She hadn't even noticed that Priyanka had been casting a spell.

Priyanka looked to Celesse. "Let's bring her back to my room, it's on the end of the house. Carry her up to the room. You can do the thing, right?"

Celesse nodded, though she appeared to be holding back her frustration at the command. She pushed away from the table and made a few gestures at her waist. The spell was primitive, but Aurie recognized its lineage. The rounded knuckle-curl that one used to connect the spell to an individual was well known for being difficult because the finger didn't bend that way. Modern mages had adapted a less painful gesture.

After the first failed attempt, Priyanka glared at the younger woman, the muscles between her eyes knitting to a "V." The second try was punctuated with a few mumbled curses about goats and cocks. Upon the third, and successful, attempt, Celesse apologized to Priyanka. If there hadn't been an audience, Aurie was sure Priyanka would have backhanded Celesse for her mistakes.

Aurie was as rigid as a statue, but Celesse lifted her with ease, cradling her like a baby. When they reached the room, they tied Aurie to a chair. Priyanka pulled a small locked box from beneath her feather bed and opened it up, revealing a few glittering rocks, some vials of plant material, and a silver hook. Aurie's stomach did back flips when Priyanka pulled the hook from the box.

"What's that for?" asked Celesse, who looked uncomfortable.

"To make her talk."

Priyanka pried Aurie's mouth open, pulled out her tongue, and shoved the silver hook through the meat. The pain wasn't as terrible as she'd expected. It probably wasn't much different than having her tongue pierced, but there was a good reason why she'd never done that, since it interfered with enunciating spells.

Then Priyanka set the silver hook on the table and touched Aurie's mouth, whispering a releasing spell. Aurie really wished she could massage her jaw, as the locking spell had exhausted her muscles.

"You may talk, and nothing else. If you try any spells, I'll put my knife through your heart," she said. "Tell me you understand."

"I understand."

"Good," said Priyanka, sitting across from Aurie on a reversed chair. "Now, tell me. Who are you?"

"Aurelia Silverthorne."

"And how do you know B.C.?"

"I told you. I met him on the road."

Priyanka stood up quickly and grabbed the silvery hook, looking at it incredulously. "You're lying."

"I'm not, I swear."

"I know when people lie. Always. You didn't meet him on the road. But what I don't understand is how you were able to lie after this." She held up the hook. "It's always worked before. Let me try a different question. How do you know us?"

"It's complicated."

Priyanka yanked out her knife and slipped it under Aurie's jaw. The blade nicked her skin, bringing a bead of blood. Aurie held still, hoping not to incite her.

"Is she the Rider?" asked Celesse, holding herself still.

"I don't know. This whole game is too subtle for it, unless it was surprised when it entered the inn, and tried to talk its way out."

"What about the accent?" asked Celesse. "I've never heard

such a thing before."

"Nor I," said Priyanka.

Aurie wagged her eyebrows, trying to get Priyanka's attention so she could speak. The young patron frowned.

"You may talk, but I slice you open like a pig at the first wrong word."

Aurie swallowed. If Priyanka gutted her, she'd be dead back in her world. She tried to think of something that might convince them she wasn't dangerous, without explaining the truth, since the professor had told her not to upset the illusion.

"I'm a mage," said Aurie, "but I trained far from here. I know of you all because, well, reasons I cannot explain. But I came here to help. I swear. That's all I've got."

"Cuddy wallows," said Priyanka, slapping her hand on the table.

"I swear."

Priyanka nodded to Celesse. "Grab the chamber pot. I don't want the blood to get everywhere."

"No. Wait. Please," said Aurie, her mouth as dry as the summer wind. "I swear. Please don't."

The irony that she was begging a patron of the Cabal to save her, and thus, in turn, thwart the Cabal in their quest for the Halls, did not escape her.

Priyanka grabbed Aurie by the hair, pulling her head up to expose her neck. Celesse approached with the chamber pot, currently empty though reeking of old urine, not that it would matter to Aurie much longer.

"I know the others too," Aurie blurted out. "All five." And then when she remembered what Professor Mali had said, she added, "And who you're coming to see."

The knife moved closer to Aurie's neck. "Speak quickly."

"B.C. That's Bannon Creed. And Semyon Gray. Malden Anterist. You're Priyanka Sai. She's Celesse D'Agastine. And you're going to meet Invictus."

The two women shared glances. Priyanka tightened her grip on the knife but didn't pull it away.

"That's not my surname, but I like it," said Celesse. "Shame you'll have to die."

The knife hung in the air. Uncertainty roosted on Priyanka like a carrion bird.

"You know some interesting names, yet you've gotten some of the details incorrect. This makes me think you're a spy, or a Rider. Where did you learn those names?"

Aurie chewed her words before speaking, worried that the repetition of her excuse might get her killed. "It's complicated."

"Your life is about to become less complicated," replied Priyanka.

Heat and indecision rose through Aurie. What could she say that wouldn't earn the blade? It had to be truthful, yet vague enough not to cause a reaction.

When Priyanka moved the blade closer, Aurie blurted out, "I work for Invictus."

She meant to say Semyon, but changed her mind at the last moment in case he was nearby and could dispel her half-truth. Aurie figured that since everyone was connected to Invictus, that in a sense, everyone worked for him.

Priyanka paused. "He never mentioned an apprentice."

Aurie chose her words carefully. "I don't know what he told or didn't tell you. Like I said, I came from far away and I wasn't supposed to come here."

Celesse looked to Priyanka, who replied, "All truthful."

"Why did he send you?"

"He didn't. I came on my own. He'll probably be mad when he finds out, but I had to help, even if it meant disobeying him."

Priyanka narrowed her gaze, before giving a little nod. In

a liquid smooth motion, the knife disappeared, and then Aurie was released.

Aurie rubbed the end of her tongue where the hook had gone through. The wound had closed but there was a little dimple.

"What are we going to do with her?" asked Celesse.

"Let her come along," said Priyanka. "We could use the help in case something goes wrong."

"Just like that you trust her?" asked Celesse incredulously.

"She was truthful with me, and that's enough." Priyanka gave Celesse a cutting glance. "And you're lagging on your finger work. That was atrocious."

A blush stained Celesse's cheeks, a mixture of embarrassment and anger. The history of the Halls never mentioned that Celesse had been Priyanka's pupil.

Priyanka left the room, expecting them both to follow. Celesse pushed her in front, lip snarling with distrust. Priyanka marched up the street like a soldier.

"Where are we going?"

"A farm on the outside of town," said Priyanka. "There's a young woman we need to speak with."

"Is she—"

Priyanka shushed her, motioning for caution. Aurie had forgotten that in this time, magic was a thing to be feared and brought the danger of being lynched by a frightened populous.

Aurie spoke again, this time in a hoarse whisper. "Is she a mage?"

"Untrained if she is," said Priyanka. "A prime candidate to be taken."

"How did you find her?"

Priyanka produced a newspaper article from a hidden pocket in her dress. The paper was the *Downingtown Digest*. The article discussed miraculous recovery of a local boy after

166   Thomas K. Carpenter

being run over by a runaway wagon train. The girl, sixteen-year-old Abby Church, had saved her brother's life. The article praised the Lord for bringing his miracle to Downingtown.

"I see," said Aurie, handing back the paper. "Does this method find many...well, you know."

Priyanka nodded back to Celesse, who stuck her tongue out when she turned her head back.

"Usually it's the overactive imagination of the newspaper, but occasionally it pays off. We can only hope that we've reached her before the Rider."

"What is this Rider?"

Priyanka slowed, glancing at her disdainfully. "Invictus has not told you?"

Aurie shook her head.

"A deficit in your education. We do not entirely know the nature of this beast. Malden thinks it a shadow demon, though he sees demons in everything. His paranoia will be his undoing." Priyanka looked ready to spit as she spoke about Malden. "Bannon, on the other hand, says it's older and comes from this world. What we do know is that it thwarts us at every turn, battling us when we least expect it."

The farm was on the edge of town. A storm rumbled to the north, bringing dark clouds and a cool breeze, while the sun shone on their backs. It appeared for the moment that the rain was going to miss them.

As they approached the dirt road that led up to the one-story stone house, a man with a weathered expression and wearing dirty overalls walked his horse up to them.

"Greetings."

"Greetings, good sir," said Priyanka. "And praise the Lord for his bounty."

He eyed them suspiciously.

Priyanka gave him a curtsey. "We are from the Sisters of

the Poor. We heard about your daughter and came to ask a blessing from her."

The farmer frowned, deepening the wrinkles on his leathery face. He appeared uncomfortable with the idea of his daughter having religious significance.

"Please, sir," she said, "we've come quite some way. We won't stay long. Just a few minutes."

The mention of a brief visit took the rod from his shoulders. He nodded towards the barn on the leeside of the house. "Abby's feedin' the pigs."

The stench of livestock grew stronger as they approached. It didn't seem to bother Priyanka or Celesse, but for Aurie, who'd never been on a farm, the smell was so strong she had to swallow back bile.

Abby froze in mid-throw as they came around the corner. A pair of enormous pigs nudged the fence she was sitting on, demanding more feed be given, snorting and whining like toddlers.

A pit formed in Aurie's stomach based on the way Abby looked at them. She recognized the fear in the whites of her eyes. A frightened mage was not safe to approach.

"Greetings, Abby," said Priyanka in a loud voice, keeping a healthy distance. "We heard about your brother. Praise the Lord."

"Praise the Lord," responded Abby coolly, then her gaze darted towards the stone house. "Does my pa know you're speaking to me?"

"We asked his permission at the threshold of your property," replied Priyanka.

The girl kept looking back to the house as if she didn't believe it. Priyanka stepped close and spoke quietly.

"This miracle. Has a thing like this happened before?"

Abby looked everywhere but at Priyanka. Then she shook

her head, a tight, fearful answer.

"Are thee certain?" asked Priyanka. "Have you ever had fire appear suddenly in your hand, or objects move across the room without you touching them?"

Abby's eyes widened with understanding. She knew what they were speaking about, that much was clear to Aurie, but she was more surprised when the girl declined again.

"Do not fear, girl," said Priyanka. "We're like you. We can teach you, keep you safe."

Priyanka held her hand out, palm facing upward. A candle-sized flame appeared at the center, dancing in the valley of her hand. Abby stared at it in wonder as the flame hopped from palm to fingertip, and fingertip to palm. Aurie sensed the girl's concerns resolved by Priyanka's display, and she'd just leaned forward to offer her support when a pig squealed in alarm.

She turned to find Mr. Church in mid-swing, a hefty maul flying at her face. Aurie brought her hands up to block, bones breaking as the maul head made contact her fingers. The maul missed her face by a hair.

Aurie collapsed to the ground, cradling her mangled hands against her chest, screaming. Abby's father advanced on the others, eyes wild and feral, the maul swinging through the air like a chain.

Celesse fumbled her spell, the force bolt evaporating like a popped balloon. She cursed and tried again, backing up as she gestured, until she hit the fence. Abby's father brought the maul overhead. Celesse abandoned her spell work, crossed her hands above her head, and waited for the maul to crush her skull.

The blow never landed, as Priyanka threw a knife that sliced through Mr. Church's shirt, spraying blood in a wide arc. He dropped the maul, made fists of his hands until flame burst outward, and tackled Priyanka.

The sudden display of magic stunned Aurie. She had thought the daughter had been the source of the healing magic.

Priyanka didn't get her spell up in time, and he knocked her to the ground, pummeling her with molten fists. Burning wool and flesh filled the air.

Aurie struggled to her feet, unbalanced by the pain. She screamed at Celesse, who was staring in horror at what Mr. Church was doing to Priyanka.

"Do something! Cast a spell! Anything!"

Understanding registered on her shocked face, until she nodded. She fumbled the first attempt at a force spell. The second fired, knocking the father off Priyanka, who was smoldering.

As Mr. Church climbed to his feet, Priyanka leapt up, a curved blade in her hand, and slit his throat. The flames in his fists consumed him like a living torch. As the heat rushed outward, Aurie tried to run away, tripping over the maul and landing hard on her broken hands.

On her stomach, she screamed until she realized that she was no longer lying in the upturned pasture, and Mr. Church wasn't about to turn into a nova five feet away. She was back in Semyon's room. She looked at her fingers. The right forefinger was bent at a ninety-degree angle, while the third and fourth looked like dog food. Her left hand was only slightly better, swollen like a mitt. At least two bones in her hand had snapped from the impact.

Professor Longakers was at her side, shoving a potion down her throat that made the pain disappear almost instantly.

Aurie rolled onto her back, resting her hands on her chest as she sobbed. The smell of burnt flesh still filled her nostrils.

"What happened?" asked Professor Mali. "You smell like pig shit."

"The Rider. We were attacked."

"Who?"

"Me, Celesse D'Agastine, and Priyanka Sai," said Aurie, through breaths.

Professor Longakers examined her hands without touching them. "I'll give Dr. Fairlight a call. She should be able to fix this."

He helped her up and into a chair, then left to make the call.

"Did you figure it out?" asked Aurie.

"Partially," Professor Mali said, rubbing her chin. "It's definitely a place in his mind, like a dreamstalking spell, and based on what happened to you the last two times, it appears anything that occurs in the dream, occurs in real life."

"We already knew that," said Aurie. "Why am I seeing the patrons when they were young? And what's this with the Rider? I haven't seen Semyon. Is this his subconscious at work?"

The professor shook her head vehemently. "I don't know, Aurelia. But we have a lot of data now. Maybe we can figure out it."

"Have you ever heard of the Rider? From Semyon? Or read about it?"

"No."

"There's got to be a clue there. I think he's trying to tell us something," said Aurie.

"Doubtful," said the professor. "Semyon is in a very bad state. I cannot imagine that his mind is active enough that he can communicate."

"I'm not saying that he is directly, but maybe indirectly."

"And what does that mean? Or do for us?" she asked sternly.

Aurie carefully laid her mangled hands in her lap. "I don't know. But I'll find out. I need to know what it is before I go back in."

"About that," said the professor grimly. "It's not working."

"What's not working?"

"The time dilation. It's not going fast enough. Based on the changes from when the vibrations reduced, I was able to estimate how long it would be until he was healed."

"And?"

"Around twenty years," said Professor Mali.

"Twenty years? We won't last twenty days!"

"Then we're going to have to find a better solution," she said, then stared at Semyon's unconscious face with a thousand thoughts passing across her eyes.

17

The striped cat was bright blue like a blueberry Slurpee, creeping across the cavern floor with wide, exaggerated eyes, delicately placing one paw before the other. It minced around the stalactite, hunched forward like a racecar, ready to pounce on a cross-legged Bethany, who was facing the other way, practicing her finger work, going through the Five Elements in succession.

Pi put her hand on Yoko's shoulder and whispered so she didn't warn Bethany about the electric blue spectral cat.

"Now, make it sprint past, then turn and face her, as if it's about to do battle."

Yoko giggled, and her hands danced as if she were holding marionettes, which wasn't too far from the truth, as the spell connected her hands to the illusion. Pi didn't know where Yoko had learned it, but her illusions were some of the best she'd ever seen.

The bright blue cat leapt past Bethany, who squeaked in surprise, climbed to her feet, and summoned a shimmering ball of water between her hands.

As the cat bent forward, Bethany turned her head towards them. "Enough with the illusions, Yoko. I was in the middle of a good practice session."

"Sorry," said Yoko, wrinkling her nose in apology.

"Blame me," said Pi. "I told her to do it."

"How did you know illusion?" asked Yoko.

The ball of water popped like a balloon, sending droplets across the cavern wall. Bethany put her hands on her hips as her neck went translucent, revealing her muscles rippling as she swallowed. "It was a blue cat, and you forgot the tail. You might want to think about making real looking illusions next time, not that anime stuff."

Yoko was pained by the rebuke. Pi put a reassuring hand on her. "She's right. The creatures are skillfully created, but no one's going to believe a neon blue cat that looks like it fell out of an Alice in Wonderland book."

Yoko made a little noise in her throat as she closed her eyes and bobbed her head. Pi hated giving that feedback because she knew Yoko was harder on herself than anyone else.

"Would you like to try something else? Maybe we can work on something more normal?" asked Pi.

Yoko shook her head and scurried off in tight little steps as if she were wearing a kimono.

"I suck at this," Pi said to no one in particular.

"Not true," said Jade, coming up from behind. "You're actually pretty damn good at teaching. It's just that she has a serious Miyazaki fetish. It's why she never passed the trials. She kept trying to get creative, but all they care about are solutions to the problems. You don't get points for cleverness."

Jade had pulled her hair back into a ponytail, except for one strand that had escaped and was dangling before her right eye, the green tip tickling her upper lip. Pi reached out and tucked the strand behind her ear as she stared back.

"How long have you been watching?"

Jade ran her fingers across Pi's exposed shoulder, bringing chills, gooseflesh, and memories of the previous night.

"Long enough to be jealous of you touching Yoko," said Jade.

"I'm sorry, I really wasn't meaning anything by it," said Pi, right away.

Jade held her hands up. Her eyes were wide with apology. "Ignore me. I didn't mean that. I was being flirty, but as you can tell, I'm really bad at it."

As they moved close, Bethany made an exaggerated coughing sound. "At least give me a chance to leave before you get all gooey."

"We're not gooey," said Pi.

"Sappy, probably, but definitely not gooey," added Jade with a smirk.

After Bethany left them, Pi asked, "What's up? Your lip is twitching at the corner, which means you have something to ask me."

Jade's hand went to her mouth. "Really? God, I need to work on that."

Pi swatted her hand away. "No, please. No. It's cute. It means you're a little nervous about it. You present as so tough, but it's nice to know you're not always a hard-ass."

"So..." began Jade with an eye roll, "when are we going back up? It's almost February."

Pi knew Jade was trying to act sweet about her question, as if this were something she was only "wondering" about, but the hard edge to her gaze said the opposite. She could tell Jade had been chafing at their lack of progress.

"They're not ready."

"You're not pushing them," said Jade.

"I don't want them to get hurt. Faez madness is a real thing. I don't like the idea of them using magic without a patron."

Jade stepped away, crossing her arms. "I don't know why you believe that bullshit. It's a con to get people to sign up to the Halls. I can show you the truth if you'd just go with me and read those articles I was telling you about."

"You can put anything on the internet," said Pi.

"Exactly! They want you to believe, to keep you chained to them," said Jade.

"I'm not chained."

Jade threw her hands up. "And you've never told me why."

"Nor you about why you knew the passwords to the Garden Network."

"I have trust issues."

Pi crossed her arms. "I couldn't tell."

"Can we get back to the real subject? When are we going back up?" asked Jade.

"They're not ready yet."

"They're ready enough," said Jade. "We should hit Coterie."

"Whoa, you're getting a little crazy there. The Obelisk is wickedly defended, even more than Arcanium, and I know."

There was a weight on Jade, pushing her down. Pi could see something bad had happened in her past. She wished Jade would tell her about it so maybe she could work through it, but now was not that time.

"What if we do a test run?" asked Pi. "Something that causes some damage, but doesn't stretch their abilities too much."

Jade seemed to sense that she'd pushed too hard, and she glanced away, water in her dark eyes. She mouthed her agreement, turned, and left without another word.

With Jade gone, Pi searched her conflicted feelings. She liked Jade, a lot. The sex was great, and their connection made her feel like she'd known her a long time, but the Halls had hurt her, and she'd never recovered.

Pi caught up to Bethany, who'd headed back to the island. She found her at the rowboat, pushing it into the water. The skin along her arms went translucent, showing all the way down to the bone before returning to healthy pink skin.

"Need a ride?" asked Bethany, pausing with the boat half in the water and half in the sand.

"I need to head to Big Dave's Town, but I wanted to ask you a few questions."

Bethany glanced around. "I take it these questions aren't to help you make a shopping list."

"It's Jade," said Pi. "What happened to her? Before, I mean."

Bethany bit her lower lip. "I don't think that's my place to tell you. If she wanted you to know, you'd know."

"Does everyone but me know what happened?"

"No, and I wouldn't be asking around. Jade gets pretty sensitive about this subject." Her gaze darted around. "You don't want to make her mad."

"What the hell is that supposed to mean?"

Bethany pushed off and leapt in. The rowboat glided through the water. Bethany grabbed the oars as she settled onto the middle seat.

"Thanks for the help earlier," said Bethany. "My fire elements are way faster now. I was totally doing that wrong."

Pi frowned. "You're welcome. And if anyone asks, I'll be back tomorrow, or the day after. I need to run some errands."

She left the cavern, heavy with thoughts. Pi wasn't taking them anywhere near Coterie until she learned more about what had happened to Jade. Plus, it would give her an excuse to talk to Aurie and see how things were going with Semyon and Arcanium. Pi knew her sister would love the chance to do some research. Pi hoped that whatever they found wouldn't damage her relationship with Jade.

18

The empty spaces between the rows in the main library seemed particularly lonely to Aurie. During the first few months after Semyon's injury, the place had teemed with students desperate to make use of their time without magic. In every nook, there was someone whispering spells, sans faez, practicing their elocution. The place had the feel of a backstage before a play, where the actors rehearsed their lines in nervous anticipation. These days the library was like a morgue with only the Biblioscribe as her companion.

Aurie was returning a book to the rows, a thick tome called *Colonial Creatures*, about the beasties that mages of that age had encountered. Despite the title, the text had been rubbish, which was typical of the older books, since superstition and fear clouded scientific analysis of the creatures. Rare was the volume that could be trusted at face value.

She'd been trying to find information about the Riders, the creatures that hounded the young patrons in Semyon's dream state, but there was nothing that remotely resembled the abilities those creatures employed. It was almost like they'd never existed, or learned to hide in the populous.

The stacks were dimly lit, as the magelights that operated

in the library needed a rejuvenation of faez, which was in short supply these days. Aurie walked through the rows, lost in thought as she mulled over her next question to the Biblioscribe. She'd exhausted her current lines of research about the Rider, and considered spending time on the other item she'd been investigating, her sister's girlfriend, Jade Umbra.

Aurie ran right into someone rounding the corner. She dropped *Colonial Creatures* and knelt to pick it up as the other person fled down the stacks. She saw long dark hair.

"Wait! Come back!"

With book under arm, Aurie chased the dark-haired girl around the corner. When the girl showed no sign of slowing, Aurie took a guess as to her identity.

"Isabella! Wait! I know where your room is!"

This slowed her.

Aurie caught up to Isabella. The petite girl clutched an over-sized book in her arms. Wild-eyed, she glanced every which way, as if she were about to be descended upon by murderous crows.

"I didn't know anyone was in the library."

Aurie patted her arm. "It's okay, you're allowed."

"I...yeah, that's right. I am allowed. Why was I worried about that?" asked Isabella with a nervous laugh.

The lack of magic had put a strain on Arcanium. Everyone was getting a little fried. Aurie knew that the professors had been discussing letting the worst students use a little bit of faez, as they didn't think a small amount would hurt Semyon, but no one knew how much was too much, so they'd decided against it.

"Whoa.   *Night Haunts and Deadly Apparitions, a Summoning.* That's some pretty heavy reading," said Aurie, poking the spine with her forefinger.

Isabella looked away. "It passes the time."

"How's Deshawn? I haven't seen you two together much," said Aurie.

Isabella twitched and fidgeted. "You know, with everything, it's hard to...well, be together."

Aurie sensed how much being in another person's presence was bothering Isabella, which under normal conditions would have been suspicious, but inability to use magic had turned everyone into a serious introvert.

"I don't want to hold you here," said Aurie. "Anyway, it was good to see you. I'll see you at the formal."

Isabella scurried away, leaving Aurie as the lone soul in the library. Her next order of business was Jade Umbra. Aurie checked both the library and the internet for information about Pi's girlfriend, but came up blank. She tried to do a search for the name Jade only, in case the last name was a fake, cross-referencing with the lists of students in the Hundred Halls, but that was a dead end too. Even when she checked against the applicants who'd failed the trials and never made it into the Halls, she found nothing.

Aurie concluded her search, assuming that Jade Umbra was a fake name, and sent a text to her sister that she'd receive the next time she was within range of a cell tower. She headed back to her room to get ready for the Spring Formal.

Back in the fall, when the idea for the formal had been hatched, it'd seemed like a good idea, a break from the monotony, something to look forward to. But as the months had rolled on with no sign of improvement from Semyon, a certain dread hung over the Spring Formal like industrial smog.

Aurie wasn't even sure anyone would show up. Perhaps everyone would hide in their rooms. But she wasn't going to let that creeping malaise bring her down. Aurie put on a flimsy black dress that felt like she was wearing a handkerchief and gave it a spin, noting the way the bottom half flared up.

The pair of enchanted silvery high heels that she'd ordered off the internet claimed to be the most comfortable heels ever made, and after putting them on, she found it hard to disagree. Aurie didn't have much practice walking in them, but felt less like the newborn giraffe she'd expected, and more like a woman attending a star-studded gala.

When Aurie arrived in the Grand Chamber in the west wing, her heart dropped. The decorations were the cheap stuff found at the dollar store, and the space, normally impressive, seemed tawdry. Only a few students milled around the edges while a soulful R&B song played over the speakers.

Aurie looked for Isabella, who was supposed to be in charge, but she was nowhere to be found. She did find Deshawn standing off to the side with his hands in his pockets.

"You look handsome," she said.

He wore an expertly fitted suit with a dark purple shirt and black tie.

"Thanks," he said. "Wish this place looked as good as I do."

"Yeah, this wasn't what I was expecting."

He frowned. "Izzy sort of forgot that this was even happening. I had to order this stuff last second." He shrugged. "Not that it's going to matter. Doesn't look like anyone's showing up."

They stood and chatted for a while, and to their surprise, the other members of Arcanium started rolling in. Even the professors attended.

Professor Longakers wore his normal tweed jacket, but accented it with a bow tie covered in golden dollar signs. Professor Moonie sported a '70s style tuxedo with a frilly shirt and flared pants. Only Professor Mali wasn't in attendance, but everyone knew where she was.

What started off as somber, turned into a real dance party. When Isabella didn't show up, Aurie dragged Deshawn onto the floor. Before long, her calves hurt, but she kept going, afraid to stop and return to the dismal reality that haunted Arcanium. She shared face-splitting smiles with her fellow students as she gyrated across the floor.

Aurie was dancing with a group of girls from third year when screams erupted on the far side of the Grand Chamber. At first, Aurie mistook the noise for genuine excitement, then she realized it was naked fear.

Stomping through the middle of the dance floor, scattering students in its wake, was a towering creature that looked like a mean Buddha with tentacles coming out of its belly. Jacob Finders, a second year that had frozen in place, got caught by a pair of tentacles and was torn in half, guts spilling onto the wooden floor in a wet splash.

Under normal circumstances, a creature of this nature would be trivial for a room full of Arcanium students and teachers, but without magic, Aurie feared it would be a slaughter.

Before the creature could snatch up a fallen Xi Chu, Aurie blasted it with truth magic, knocking it backwards. The tentacled beastie screamed in rage, stomping forward. Forgetting that she was wearing high heels, she tried to run and slipped on the blood-soaked floor.

Professor Longakers threw a vial at the tentacle grasping at Aurie. The acid sizzled across the mucus-laden flesh of the beastie. It roared in response, giving Aurie a chance to scurry out of the way.

As it recovered and raged forward, Deshawn blasted it with a bolt of force magic, stunning it in place.

"Deshawn, no!"

He looked back, holding his hands out. "We have to. It'll kill us all."

A group of students, mostly fourth and fifth years, and the attending professors formed a ring around the beastie. Everyone who remained had a weapon or trinket that didn't require faez, but collectively they were still no match.

Xi Chu whistled a sling overhead, smiting the creature with a glowing rock that smashed into its huge blue eyes before reappearing in his hand to be reloaded.

"We're only making it madder," shouted Aurie.

Professor Longakers threw another acid vial. "It's a summoned creature. Does anyone recognize it?"

No one answered.

Everyone was coming to terms with the idea that they had a traitor in their midst.

Aurie saw a figure peeking around the far doorway, where the creature had entered the room. Even though she couldn't see her face, she knew who it was, and what had to be done.

"Hold it here," said Aurie. "I have an idea."

She ran out of the Grand Chamber. She could reach the other side if she went through the kitchens and the storage area. Aurie heard screams and the thump of impact through the walls.

Isabella tried to run the moment Aurie saw her. She fired truth magic at her feet, tumbling her to the ground. Aurie dove on top of her, pinning her to the floor.

"Why did you do that? Why did you summon that creature?"

Isabella looked back star-eyed, her mouth open slightly. When she saw the faint blue stain on her tongue, Aurie had guesses as to the nature of the betrayal.

"Where is the tome?" asked Aurie as she shook her. "Where is it?"

Either the girl was in shock, or she was forbidden from saying anything. Aurie climbed off the stunned girl, looking for signs of the beastie. There were claw marks on the wall. She followed them to an empty conference room, where the professors probably met for administrative meetings with Semyon. The table had been pushed against the wall, and a salt circle surrounded by flickering candles was in its place.

Aurie found the tome discarded to the side. She furiously paged through the book, looking for a description of the tentacled beastie. She found the summoning spell midway, the corner of the page bent from use. An order sheet had been shoved into the book's spine.

It appeared that Isabella had ordered a potion from the internet that soothed the aching mage. Aurie had no doubt that this company was owned by Celesse through a proxy, and had substituted the potion with something that had made her suggestible. Aurie wondered if they'd find instructions, or messages in her room, or emails.

Aurie set the order sheet aside and studied the text. Nothing would matter if she couldn't send the creature back to wherever it'd come from. The creature was called a Cthulhu-beast due to its similarity to the legend, though the text claimed no actual relation. To release the creature back to its plane of existence, Aurie needed a freshly slaughtered lamb, something called Hen of the Woods, and a handful of salt.

"Where the fuck am I going to find the first two?"

Aurie scooped up the salt from the circle and went back to the kitchen, hoping she could find the materials she needed there. The battle continued in the Grand Chamber. She hoped they were still keeping it contained.

She found a hunk of beef in the freezer. She poked the frozen meat with a fingernail. "You'll have to do. Now if I could only figure out what Hen of the Woods is."

Her skimpy dress didn't have room for a cell phone, so Aurie ran back to Isabella, who had her head bent between her legs, sobbing.

"Give me your cell phone."

Isabella looked up, eyes red from rubbing. She handed it over.

"Type in your password, I need it."

After a quick series of taps, Aurie brought up a browser and put Hen of the Woods in.

"Mushrooms?" she exclaimed when she saw the description.

Aurie threw the phone back in Isabella's lap, telling her, "You stay here until this is finished."

Isabella nodded obediently.

Aurie found some Hen of the Woods in the kitchen, grabbed the package of frozen beef, and ran back to the Grand Chamber. There were at least three motionless bodies when she returned. Deshawn was holding his right arm against his body as if it was broken. Professor Longakers was out of acid vials, and was using a chair like a lion tamer.

Aurie threw herself onto the ground, flipping open the book to the bent page. She lifted the package of frozen beef, whispering lies to it, telling the meat that it was really lamb, freshly killed with a curved knife. When warm blood leaked from the white wax paper, she knew it'd worked.

The meat went into a small circle of salt. Then she arranged the fanlike mushrooms at four corners of the circle.

As the words of the spell flowed from her lips, the rush of faez sent shivers of pleasure through her aching body.

"I thought you said not to use magic," Deshawn shouted over the battle.

Aurie couldn't answer She was in the middle of the spell and couldn't pause, or create more problems.

The beastie sensed it was being sent away and surged forward. A tentacle came flying at her head, only knocked away at the last second by a chair-wielding Professor Longakers. His bravery was rewarded by a second tentacle that knocked him backwards against the wall. He groaned in pain.

As the Cthulhu-beast marched forward, ignoring the attempts of the others to slow it down, Aurie finished the spell. The creature cried out as the summoning energies reversed course, throwing it back to wherever it had come from, ending with a satisfying pop.

With the creature gone, Aurie went straight to Deshawn. He was grimacing as he held his right arm awkwardly.

"It was Isabella. She was drugged with a potion. I'll explain later, but go take care of her. Make sure she doesn't hurt herself or try to run."

Deshawn was joined by Xi, who had survived mostly unscathed. They left through the far door, avoiding the mess of blood and mucus that had been splattered across the dance floor.

With the creature gone, the other students returned. Calls were made to the Aura Healers. Once Aurie knew that those alive would be cared for, she went straight to Semyon's room. She had to know if the use of magic had hurt him.

When she arrived, Professor Mali stared back grimly. "What happened?"

"Is he okay? I had to use magic."

"What? Why?"

Aurie quickly explained. The professor nodded the whole time.

"He jerked a few times. At first, I thought he was waking up, then I suspected what was really going on," said the professor.

"I'm sorry, it was the only thing that would stop that

creature."

The professor nodded. "It looks like everything is fine down here. No harm done. You stay here with Semyon. I need to go up and survey the damage."

Aurie's heart was beating in her chest like a frightened jackrabbit. She paced around the room, coming back to check on Semyon repeatedly, thinking that her spell had done more than Professor Mali had let on, but after she calmed down, she realized he was fine. They'd survived the incident.

But how much longer could they hold out? There was no way they could keep the Cabal out for twenty years. Celesse and the other patrons would find new ways to infiltrate Arcanium, if they didn't just make an all-out attack when the defenses weakened enough.

There was always the option of transferring their patronage to Celesse, and that was probably the secondary purpose of the attack, to remind them how perilous their situation was. Aurie still hadn't told anyone about the offer that the Alchemist patron had made, and now, after so much had happened, she feared that if she did, they would abandon Semyon.

"I'm not ready to give up," she told the soul-torn patron. "If I give up on you, then the Halls are finished. But is it fair of me to tie the rest of them to that decision?"

No answer came, not that she was expecting one.

"Can't you heal faster?" she asked, beating her fist lightly on the edge of the bed.

Then she remembered that there was a way for him to heal faster, but it was fraught with danger. The Engine of Temporal Manipulation could be sped up, but she wasn't sure she was strong enough to withstand the effects.

The Engine was sitting on a shelf behind Semyon's head, humming with eldritch energy, not yet vibrating enough that she would have to enter the dream state of Semyon, but close enough that she knew it was soon.

Aurie had the knowledge on how to turn it up. With a heavy heart, she traced the runes activating the brass cylinder. When they glowed with a terrible yellowish purpose, Aurie swiped her hand a third of the way across the tube, and the first three runes turned translucent with light.

Immediately, the vibration picked up until it was a tooth-rattling ache. She stared at Semyon Gray, lips white as she squeezed them together.

She didn't know how long it would be until she would have to go back in, but it would be soon. Soon.

Aurie was afraid she wouldn't be strong enough this time.

19

Everyone survived the Garden Network without puking. The Misfits were getting used to traveling. This was their fifth excursion, and the last three had gone much better than the first, when they'd triggered the defenses of the Smoke & Amber.

The City Library was desolate at 3 a.m., and lacked the security measures that might normally cause problems. Pi didn't take any chances, placing see-me-not enchantments on the rooms before they passed through them.

Nancy and Sasha carried an olive green army box, complete with military font reading "Magical Munitions" and "DANGER - NO FAEZ." Normally, the box would be too heavy for them, but they'd bulked themselves up with strength spells that made thcm look like they were about to enter a bodybuilding contest.

"Isn't this a little conspicuous?" asked Jade. "I mean, we're wandering through the streets with a box that clearly looks stolen and dangerous. We could have MWAT down here if someone calls."

"Remember those pins I told you to put on?" Jade nodded. "For anyone not wearing one, that box reads like gibberish. And if someone opens the box without one, it looks like it's filled with dance clothes."

Yoko brightened up. "So we dance crew? So sweet!"

They walked the eight blocks to the Protector Hall. For the rest of the city, it was the dead of night, but without a sun to modulate their sleep/wake cycles, this was their current middle of the day.

"I forget how much I miss being above ground," said Bethany.

"I hate it. Too much empty space, too many things that could fall," said Sisi, glancing suspiciously at the skyscrapers.

Before they arrived at their destination, Jade pulled Pi aside. Her forehead was hunched with concern.

"I hope we're not doing another prank," said Jade in a low voice.

"Those weren't pranks, they were training. And they were fun. The Misfits need a little fun. Being down in that cave all the time is depressing," said Pi.

"They were stupid."

"Enchanting half the city's pigeon population to shit on Coterie's Obelisk was anything but stupid. It looked like a giant turd-sicle. Coterie thrives on its reputation, and that prank reached every perspective student in the world. Plus, it looked like a prank from another Hall, which should keep them distracted."

"You're still trying to save Arcanium," said Jade, shaking her head. "And the Halls."

"I don't have to apologize," said Pi. "But will you trust me on this one? This'll be good. You'll see."

After a smile and a kiss, Jade joined the others, leaving Pi to walk behind them alone. It wasn't that she didn't hate the Hundred Halls for what they'd allowed the original patrons to get away with, it was that she feared what would happen without them, not to mention that her sister would get hurt because of their collapse.

Though she wouldn't admit it to Jade, she had been steering them away from real attacks on the Cabal. Not only because they weren't up to it training-wise, but because Pi didn't completely trust Jade, who'd never been forthcoming about her past and why she hated the Hundred Halls. Unfortunately, Aurie had come up with nothing about Jade, only that her name was either made up or she'd removed all traces of her history from the internet. Which left Pi wondering what could have happened to make Jade hate the Hundred Halls with such passion.

The others weren't as absolute in their disgust. Pi assumed that all of them would join the Halls if they still had the opportunity. But they also respected Jade, and would follow her if she led them against the university.

They stopped in a park about two blocks away from Protector Hall. The building looked like a modern version of the Alamo, or a military penitentiary. It was quarter to four, and already lights bloomed inside the concrete armory.

"Augh," said Bethany, "they're probably getting them up for latrine inspection or something. Why would anyone join Protectors?"

Sasha's head turned so fast her afro bounced and swayed. "Some people like discipline and service."

"You wanted to be in Protectors?" asked Bethany, clearly aghast.

"It wasn't my first pick, but had I passed the trials, and they offered, I would have accepted."

"Crap-on-a-stick," said Bethany, shaking her head. "You think you know people."

"My brothers and I like to go camping, play war in the forest. They were bigger and stronger, but I outthought them. Always kicked their asses when it came to strategy. I considered joining the Arcane Service Division after Protectors."

"Quiet now," said Pi, waving them into a circle. "Here's the plan. We're going to set up these munitions around the Protector Hall. I've sent you the spell that will set the trigger on your phones. Remember that it's a hard 'r' on the third word. That's super important, or the trigger will be delayed. Also, don't point them too low, or they'll shoot past the fence line and hit the neighbors. We don't want to start any fires in the city."

The box contained large military-grade fireworks that she'd acquired from Big Dave. Instead of being in a colorful package with an interesting name like Firecat Surprise, or Fountain of Faeries, each firework had a serial number printed onto its olive green covering.

After the fireworks were handed out, Jade poked Pi in the arm. "Don't I get any?"

"We've got a special job."

"I hope so. Otherwise, this trip is going to be for nothing."

Pi ignored the comment, handing Jade a plastic shopping bag filled with white tablets.

"What are these?"

"Skunk pills," replied Pi as they headed up the street.

"Will they make them turn into skunks?"

"Kinda."

Before they got within range of their target, Pi handed Jade a kitty mask.

"What enchantments are on these?"

Pi shrugged. "Nothing. Works as good as a spell."

Jade narrowed her eyes suspiciously before slipping it onto her face. After they were both masked, Jade asked, "Aren't you going to put some no-see-me's on us?"

"Hell, no. Protector Hall is covered in defenses. The more you magic up, the harder it'll come down on you. We're going in naked."

"You've got to be kidding me," said Jade. "They're going to know who we are."

"I thought you wanted to be a rebel."

"I don't want to have a criminal record," said Jade.

"You mean, you're all anti-Halls, but you won't take any risks?"

"I'd take a risk if we were actually doing something. This is bogus. We might as well be throwing toilet paper in their trees," said Jade.

When they got within fifty feet, Pi handed Jade a slingshot from her backpack.

"Put the pills in these, and fire them over the wall. They're chemical, not alchemical, so there will be no triggers."

As carefully as they could, they fired the pills over the wall to land in the courtyard that surrounded the Hall. Inside, the place was awakening, so Pi hurried them so they wouldn't get caught. After the two bags were empty, they headed back to the park.

Everyone returned without incident, and except for Jade, they seemed excited to see what they had wrought.

Pi pulled a switch from her backpack. She set it on the ground, and hovering over it, she cast the connecting spell to the munitions. When she was certain it'd worked, Pi held it out for the others.

"Someone want to do the honors?"

Before anyone could say a word, Sisi stepped forward and slapped the chrome switch into the "ON" position, and for a brief moment, Pi thought it wasn't going to work.

She really didn't know what to expect from the fireworks. They were meant to mimic the spells and missiles that would get used in a war, so troops could train under close-to-real conditions.

Pi remembered footage of reporters during the first

Congolese war as magically guided missiles rained down on the antiaircraft stations, sending white-flash plumes of smoke high into the sky. The shock-wave blast rattled the microphones and cameras, and the rat-a-tat-tat of machine-gun fire was loud in the distance. For about five minutes, their magical fireworks mimicked that battle, with streamers of fireblast spitting over the Hall.

Within a minute, the courtyards were filled with Protector students manning the defense. Pi couldn't hear if the pills had worked until the wind shifted and a whiff of skunk reached them in the park, followed by a chorus of retching and gut splatter.

Bethany, who was standing nearest the Hall, gagged and immediately ran back towards the rest of them. "Oh, that's awful."

"Shit, that's terrible," said Nancy, pinching her nose.

"That's worse than shit," said Sasha. "Think about those sorry suckers, trapped in that, hoping to god someone knows a smell dampening spell."

A host of sirens and helicopters were descending on the region. Smoke and stench rose from the Protector Hall in a gray cloud.

"We should get out of here," said Pi. "Cavalry's incoming."

"Walk, don't run," said Jade sternly.

They strolled back towards the City Library, linked arm in arm. A couple of fire trucks and police cars sped past. They happily waved, and made drunken stumbles, as if they were returning from the bars.

By the time they reached the portal, everyone had giddy grins, except for Jade, who was sullen. Pi had hoped that this prank might lighten her mood, but it only seemed to have made things worse based on the pulsing of her clenched jaw.

20

The whiplash of returning to the present time gave Aurie a headache, but it was much better than the broken bones and burnt flesh she'd received on previous visits. Dr. Fairlight had repaired each without comment, but it was getting difficult to keep the truth from getting out.

"How long were you there?" asked Professor Mali from her command post, surrounded by sensors and computers, her face up lit with screen glow. Behind her, Professor Longakers was typing furiously on his computer, humming the latest hip-hop chart topper.

"Six hours," said Aurie. "Then it got a little dicey, so I scrammed."

"Was it the same time and place?" asked the professor.

"More or less, though I think this time might have been earlier than the others. I seem to jump around the time line, never straying too far."

"There must be some reason," mused Professor Mali, stroking the long gray braid hanging over her shoulder.

The low whine coming from the Engine was less than when Aurie had gone in, but based on the lack of real change, it appeared her visit hadn't dissipated the energy enough.

"The return spell?" asked Professor Longakers.

She'd been using a modified dreamstalking spell to get out of Semyon's memory. She sighed and gave him the news. "Better this time. I'm not sure the last word is the best. There was still an hour delay, which was fine, I wasn't being chased by a mob this time, but you never know what the next visit will bring."

The professor tapped on his lower lip, eyes glittering with thought. "I'll give it my undivided attention. We cannot have our glorious psychonaut getting run down by colonial ruffians."

"Thanks, Prof."

He winked and returned to his typing.

"We've only seen a sixteen percent reduction in the Engine energy," said Professor Mali. "I'm afraid you're not affecting it enough."

"I can't stay in much longer. No matter what I do, events conspire to bring me to battle. It's like his subconscious doesn't want me there," said Aurie.

"That would be consistent with the dreamstalking spell."

"Are we ready to bring others into the Engine?" asked Aurie. "Maybe having more people will convert it faster."

"Can you ensure their safety?"

"Come on, Professor. You know the answer to that one. We need to start trying new things. Bringing people in should increase the conversion, and at the very least, it'll give them a chance to use faez. Not being able to use magic is really messing with everyone. It's like they're constipated."

The professor's lips squeezed tight, then she gave a slight nod of acceptance. "I suppose we don't have much choice, though we must be careful. We don't know if the rules for using faez in the dream state is the same for you, since you're connected to the Engine, as it is for anyone you bring in."

"So that means we have, what, nineteen years and three

"Joanne," said Professor Chopra, tutting his finger at her, "she's violated our trust."

Aurie eyed the exit longingly. "I prepared. It was dangerous, but as you can see, I got out safely."

Professor Mali glanced back at the crowd. "I take it you had coconspirators, which is beside the point. The real question is why you did not bring this information forward."

"You're not seriously considering this, are you?" asked Aurie.

"She brought danger into the school," said Professor Chopra.

"Alain, please. Let me handle this," said Professor Mali.

Chopra crossed his arms and frowned as if he'd been asked to eat a spoonful of sewage.

Professor Mali flared her nostrils, giving Chopra a side-eye. "We must evaluate all options. Even if they are distasteful. It's my duty to you and your fellow students, as much as it is to our patron, Semyon Gray. He would want me to consider this."

"Then those assholes will have control of the Hundred Halls!"

"Might I remind you that if something tragic happens here, not only will they have control of the Halls, but everyone will likely be deceased or lost to faez madness. Don't you think that's something that should be decided by everyone involved, not by a lone student who must think very highly of herself?"

Aurie opened her mouth to speak, but nothing came out. She couldn't even think of a response that wouldn't sound self-serving or naive. And maybe they were right. She should have brought it up, but she didn't want to be manipulated by Celesse.

A part of her wanted to be angry, since she was the one risking her life in Semyon's mind, trying to figure out how to use the Engine to speed up his healing. But they didn't know about that.

She wiped a tear from the corner of her eye with a thumb.

"I...I don't know what to say. I'm sorry. I thought I was doing the right thing. I screwed up. Big time."

The lines in their faces softened.

"What are we going to do, Professor?" asked Deshawn.

Professor Mali thought for a moment. "Since this affects all of you, there shall be a vote. Majority wins. This is an all or nothing deal. If we accept, then we invite Celesse to take everyone into Alchemists. If we decline, then we're on our own, now and forever."

"I don't think she should get a vote," said Professor Chopra.

"Everyone gets a vote," said Mali.

Aurie opened her mouth to bring up the Engine and the progress they were making, but the professor shot her a glance, a reminder that she'd agreed to confidentiality about the dangerous artifact. Aurie almost wished Pi was there, because she knew that her sister would violate that promise in a heartbeat.

"When will we vote?" someone asked.

"We can't wait much longer," said Professor Mali. "You have until tomorrow night. On Friday at 4 p.m., we will take the vote. Secret ballot. Is everyone in agreement? Speak up if you disagree."

Much to Aurie's disappointment, no one spoke up. There was going to be a vote. The crowd filtered out of the Map Room, leaving only a small group. Isabella tried to come talk to her, but Aurie marched out of the room.

She'd done everything she could to save Arcanium, but it wasn't going to matter. She'd seen it in their eyes. Nearly everyone would vote to join Alchemists. Soon, they would be no more, and the Cabal would have the Hundred Halls.

21

Jade had left a message on her door for Pi to meet in her apartment above the Devil's Lipstick. Pi knew it wasn't a hook-up request, or anything fun like that. Jade had left notes before—they'd been long, meandering messages in flowery scrawl that had clearly been planned out in advance.

This one said, "I need to see you right away —Jade," which felt as cold and impersonal as a request to see the boss, which was pretty much how Pi felt as she approached the bleached white door at the top of the stairs, then hovered her knuckles above the wood.

Her feelings for Jade were as complicated and exciting as a rocket ship. Whenever Jade touched her, her skin tingled with anticipation. Kissing was like soaring through the clouds on a magic carpet. Every time she pulled away, she almost felt like she was going to plummet to the ground, the difference was so severe.

But Jade was a little broken, and full of secrets. Pi wasn't naive enough to think that she should know all of Jade's inner desires, since she'd kept a lot from her in return, but the event that was driving Jade to hate the Hundred Halls so much seemed like something she should have told her by now.

Which made this visit even harder, because Pi had all but decided to break up with Jade and return to the city of Invictus. She'd been planning on telling Jade, even before the note.

After Pi had received a message from Aurie about the vote, and the lack of progress with the Engine, she knew it was over for Arcanium, which meant Pi didn't have a reason to hide in the Undercity any longer. Once she saw her sister, Pi planned to leave the city and find a new life somewhere else that wouldn't contain so much drama.

Pi rubbed her temples. She really didn't want to have this conversation with Jade. What she really wanted to do was tackle her into the bed, strip off her clothes, and spend the night drowning in kisses. But that was the easy way out.

Before she could lose her nerve, Pi banged on the door with her fist.

"Come in."

Pi pushed her way into the tiny apartment, which was little more than a bedroom with a cubby and a hotplate. Jade had the look of a doctor about to deliver bad news. There was a bottle of whiskey and two glasses on the table next to the bed.

"Planning on letting me down easy or hard?" asked Pi.

"Was it that obvious?"

"There were no little x's or o's at the end of the note, and it was about as personal as bulk mail."

Jade closed her eyes softly for a moment. "I'm sorry. I threw away the first three versions. I figured it was better to tell you in person."

"Do I get to know why?" asked Pi.

"Does it matter?"

Pi nodded. "It does."

Jade grabbed the bottle of whiskey, motioned for Pi to

sit on the lime green folding chair across from the table, and poured both glasses brimming full.

They clinked their glasses, and Pi took a sip. The whiskey burned like lava on the way down.

"Oh, god, what is that? Turpentine?" asked Pi.

Jade had a sour look. "Is it bad? I'm not a whiskey drinker. But I asked Delilah for something to soothe a breakup."

"Break up," repeated Pi, taking another painful sip.

"You knew that's what I meant, right?"

Pi nodded. "Yeah, but saying it out loud made it more real."

"You're not mad, are you?"

Despite the roughness of the whiskey, Pi took another long draw, grimacing the whole way down. The drink warmed her middle and brought heat to her face. She felt a little dizzy and had to steady herself before answering.

"Yes," said Pi. "I think I am mad."

She was a little surprised that she'd just come out and said it, but maybe it was the whiskey talking.

"Why?" asked Jade, leaning forward, studying Pi intently.

"You were closed off to me," said Pi. "Whatever happened before that caused you to hate the Halls so much, that you won't tell bothers me. Maybe that's what really makes me mad, that I still don't know."

Jade nodded knowingly.

"What about you? Why?"

"Because you act like you know better for me," said Jade. "You tell me those things in bed, making me feel special, then treat me like I don't know what I'm doing when it comes to the Halls. I want to tell you about what happened, but I really wanted you to trust me without knowing. If we can't have that, then it's hard to have a real relationship."

Pi leaned back in the folding chair, which rocked on a bad

leg. "This is the calmest breakup I've ever had. Either you've drugged me, or this is what being an adult means, reasoned discussions, not shoe throwing, screaming fights."

Jade held her glass out. "To being an adult."

"To being an adult."

Pi gulped the last of the whiskey and slammed the glass down on the table, rattling the ice. She'd have a headache later, but she didn't care.

Without asking, Jade poured another draught.

"So what will you do now?"

"Even before you invited me here, I was planning on leaving the city," said Pi, surprising herself with her honesty.

Jade raised an eyebrow. "What changed?"

"I got a message from my sister. The students in Arcanium are going to pledge themselves to Celesse. Arcanium is done, and the Halls will be controlled by the Cabal. I don't want to stay around to see what's going to happen."

Jade seemed genuinely shocked by the news. She poured more whiskey into her glass and took a drink, staring at it for a long moment.

"What about your sister?"

"She'll be alright. At least Celesse isn't so bad. Aurie's a great student. She can learn anywhere, and Celesse isn't about to throw away a resource like that. Aurie will come out on top, it'll just be under a different system than I'd hoped."

"I don't understand. Why would they do that? What's happened to Semyon Gray?" asked Jade.

The answer came easily to Pi's lips, because why hold back on the truth now? Pi explained what had happened, starting with the soul thief, leading to the Engine and Aurie's quest to fix him, and ending with the current situation. Jade listened with rapture.

"I had no idea your sister was so resourceful," said Jade.

"We both can be," replied Pi, a little miffed that Jade hadn't included her in the compliment.

"That's a lot to think about," said Jade, who seemed to vibrate with new thoughts.

The world swam around Pi. "Hmmm...maybe I shouldn't have drank so much. That stuff is strong."

"Would you like to stay the night?" asked Jade, tongue teasing the bottom of her teeth. "One last time?"

Heat bloomed into Pi's face. "Very much so."

Jade beckoned her over. Pi ran her fingers across the purple flowers on Jade's tattooed arm. "So pretty."

Jade cupped her face. "So are you."

The kiss was wet, and put water in Pi's knees. She wobbled, and Jade spun her around, pushing her onto the bed and climbing on top. Jade pinned Pi's hands above her head.

"Meeting you has been the best thing that ever happened to me," said Jade, right before she jammed her lips against Pi's, silencing the question that rose up in response.

Before long, Pi wasn't seeing anything but the inside of her eyelids. It was like falling into a delirious pool of warm milk, when time and space didn't have meaning anymore. She was, for all intents and purposes, not even a body, just a quivering thought at the end of Jade's fingernails, not caring what the empty alchemy flask that rolled out from under the bed had contained before she had arrived.

22

The result seemed a foregone conclusion to Aurie, even before the final vote had been cast. The bin sat next to the Biblioscribe, a repurposed letter box. Aurie had written on the blank sheet of paper: "ARCANIUM" in clear block letters so no one could misunderstand, not that Alchemists was a close homonym or anything. After she'd folded it in half and placed it into the slot, she'd caught the guilty glances of Isabella and Tristen, who were in line behind her. They looked away, shame staining their cheeks bright red.

But she didn't hate them for their decision. In fact, she found herself nervous, and twitchy, because there was one out left, if she was willing to take it, but it would either end in her death or come up short of the goal.

She hadn't slept all night. While the other students clustered in various areas of Arcanium, arguing about the decision placed in their path, Aurie had been chewing her fingernails, trying to decide if she was crazy, desperate, or both.

There was a bit of dislocation to her thoughts as well, because this kind of decision was something Pi would make. Normally, Aurie relied on the mechanism of structure to win the day, but with Semyon's incapacitation, the normal rules had been thrown out. There were no more adults left to make the hard decisions, or at least that's what she told herself.

After casting her vote, Aurie marched out of the library, right past Professor Chopra, who stared at her flatly. Only Deshawn had the courage to meet her gaze, which she assumed was only because he had voted to remain.

Aurie headed straight to Semyon's quarters. Professor Longakers was on sentry duty, wearing oversized headphones that he'd dug out of the 1970s. They were connected to his laptop through a squiggly wire.

"I'll stay and watch," said Aurie. "You can go vote now."

He set the headphones down gingerly. "We both know what the result is going to be."

"I know. But I think it's important that we vote, even if it's for the losing side. That way we can say we made the decision together," said Aurie.

Professor Longakers considered her words for a moment, before nodding in agreement. "Well said, Aurelia. I will go and vote then. You have the captain's chair."

As he left, the professor put his hand on the blanket over Semyon's foot and gave it a squeeze. Aurie could tell the professor was fighting back tears.

With the professor gone, Aurie approached the Temporal Engine. It hummed softly, almost respectfully, as if even the artifact knew that its duty was about to end, one way or another.

She hesitated with her hand over the runes. Once she performed the ritual, there was no going back. It was likely it wasn't even going to work. Based on their earlier experiments, they'd figured it would take eight years and four months on the current setting to fix Semyon. Since they hadn't tested the Engine on higher settings, they had no idea if increasing it would affect the transfer rate linearly or exponentially, or if it would just blow up.

"Only one way to find out," she said.

Aurie cleared her head. Once she increased the settings, things were going to get dicey fast. She performed the ritual smoothly, the runes lighting up as she touched them in the proper order.

When she swiped her finger across the length of the brass tube, bringing a warm glow to the room, and immediately setting the Engine to vibrate, Aurie felt strangely at peace.

"What did you do?" asked Deshawn, who'd just stumbled into the room. He was cupping his hands over his ears.

"Giving us a way out, I hope," said Aurie, squinting as the frequency increased. The whine was sharp, right at the edge of hearing. She wouldn't have long before she had to enter Semyon's memories.

"Go tell Professor Mali what I've done. Tell her I'm sorry, and I hope it works out," she said. "Also, when Celesse shows up, delay her for as long as you can, give me a chance to make this right."

"I don't understand," he said, grimacing. "What are you doing?"

"I can't explain, and even if I wanted to, there's not enough time," said Aurie, which made her laugh, because that was exactly what she was trying to do, create enough time.

"I don't know what you're talking about, but good luck with whatever it is you're about to do."

"Go on, Deshawn. I got this. I'll see you on the other side."

Her cryptic words seemed to worry him as he ran out of the room.

Aurie took a big breath as if she were about to dive into deep waters. She had no regrets, only a wish that she could see her sister one last time before she entered the Engine. And as if her thoughts had summoned her, Aurie realized someone else was standing in the room, someone in a magical leather jacket that Aurie knew so well. And then she heard a gun click.

23

From a foot away from Pi's left ear, a drum was beating in 2:4 time. It felt like a hippo had wandered into the room and plopped its buttocks on her head, because when she tried to sit up and figure out what was making the noise, she struggled to lift her head from the pillow.

"Oh, god, please make it stop."

Pi swiped her hand out, attempting to silence the drumming, and she impaled her hand on the corner of the bedside desk. She cradled it to her chest, contemplating an appropriate spell to annihilate the noise-maker that had invaded the room.

Eventually she opened one eye enough to ascertain that it was an alarm clock sitting on the table, the second hand ticking with a soldier's precision and a demolition expert's volume. Pi army-crawled over to the edge, reached out, and knocked the alarm clock onto the floor. This did not make the ticking go away, forcing Pi to continue her mission.

As she reached over the edge, gravity took hold and yanked her onto the floor, face-first. She landed in a back-bending pose that briefly looked like an advanced yoga technique until she collapsed, naked and injured, on the floor.

The offending alarm clock was next to her face, hammering at Pi's eardrums like a rock concert.

"You're an annoying little shit, aren't you?" she asked the alarm clock as she slapped around the edges, searching for the OFF button.

Around the time her palm turned the clock to snooze, Pi realized there were a pair of empty vials beneath the bed. Their existence brought into clarity that Pi felt way worse than a couple of glasses of whiskey, and that Jade was no longer in the apartment.

But she couldn't do anything with a Class A hangover stomp-kicking through her head. Using a spell that came from Ashley, Pi scrawled a faez-imbued rune into midair, then when the faint web of the spell collapsed around her skull, she pinched her fingers against her forehead, squeezing and tugging—the agony of the hangover condensed to that moment, bringing a low moan from the back of her throat—until a brown slug slipped from her knotted forehead. Once it was out, she flicked it onto the wall, where it made a sickening slap. The mucusy creation started crawling towards the door.

"That was unpleasant."

With her wits returned, Pi examined the two vials beneath the bed. Each had a smattering of liquid clinging to the glass. She uncorked them in turn, sniffing like a wine sommelier, and identified them as the same potions they'd given to Bree and Alton outside the Smoke & Amber to loosen their tongues.

"Merlin's tits. No wonder I couldn't keep my mouth shut last night."

But it didn't explain how Jade had slipped the potions into the whiskey drink, until Pi opened the small refrigerator in the corner, finding faint blue ice cubes in half the tray.

Upon further review, Pi found her magical leather jacket missing, which had, among other items, her old Arcanium pin.

Jade's interest in the happenings of Arcanium, and especially Semyon Gray, became dreadfully clear. Pi recovered her clothing, which had been scattered around the room like a bomb explosion.

During Pi's search, she came across a piece of paper with a phone number and red lipstick on the edge. The name on the paper read "Bree Bishop."

The pieces came together quickly for Pi. Bree had mentioned the Cabal had a way into Arcanium. After hearing about the creature Isabella had summoned during the Spring Formal, Pi had thought the danger past. But it appeared there was still another way, and Jade had slept with Bree to find out.

Pi couldn't decide which betrayal hurt more. Being used to get into Arcanium, or that Jade had been with Bree Bishop of all people. A red-tinged rage echoed through Pi's mind, a remnant of Bree's misdeeds against Ashley.

But Pi pushed those emotions away to concentrate on the next step: how would Jade get in? The Arcanium pin was like knowing a code, but not which door to enter. Pi searched the room for more clues to the method of entry, but only found a handful of dried kelp in the bottom of a candy tin.

"I'm a fool," said Pi as she hastily threw her clothes on, then she ran out the door. She had to get to Arcanium, but Jade had a head start and access to the Garden Network.

How could I have trusted her?

The knowledge that she'd been used made Pi feel like a lovesick preteen with a mad crush on a pop star. She'd ignored her gut feelings not to trust Jade, because she'd liked her. Jade had buried her past for a reason. Despite not knowing the truth, her goal was clear enough: the end of the Hundred Halls. And Pi had given her the tools necessary to do the job.

Pi broke into a jog, heading towards the spiral staircase that led to the Goblin's Romp.

"Pi! Wait up!"

It was Bethany. She was wearing a dark hoodie and long jeans to hide her translucent skin.

"What are you doing in town?" asked Pi.

"I was looking for Jade."

Pi put her hand on Bethany's arm. "What's wrong?"

"I think she stole my bracelet. It was the only trinket I own. She was asking about it the other day, and now it's gone," said Bethany.

"What does it do?" asked Pi, squeezing Bethany's arm.

"It's nothing fancy. I was a terrible swimmer as a child, and my parents got it for me. If you get into trouble, it lets you breathe water for a few minutes. Long enough to survive until someone can rescue you."

The purpose of the dried kelp in the candy tin became clear to Pi. She knew how Jade was going to get into Arcanium, and it would take her right into Semyon's apartment. She was going to use the moat, which connected to the pool beneath the school. The creature in the water should be sufficient to protect that entrance, but clearly Jade had figured out a way past.

"What's wrong?" asked Bethany. "Did I say something?"

"No. But I know what Jade is doing now. She'd going to end the Hundred Halls, once and for all." Pi speared Bethany in her gaze. "Can you tell me why Jade hates the Halls so much? I need to know. This is important."

"I suppose it doesn't matter now," said Bethany, who was clearly working through Jade's betrayal. "There was someone she was close to that was a member of Coterie, a girlfriend maybe, but before my time. I don't know much, this is just from the little things that Jade said from time to time, but I think this someone was an assistant to the Coterie patron. I think. That's all I know."

"Is Jade Umbra even her real name?"

Bethany lifted one shoulder in a half-shrug while squinting as if her answer were pure speculation. "Probably? Considering her secretive nature. I mean, Umbra is pretty on the nose."

Pi felt like an idiot as soon as Bethany reminded her about Jade's last name. Umbra. Which meant shadow.

"Thanks, Bethany. I have to go," said Pi, running towards the west side of Big Dave's Town.

"What are you doing?" shouted Bethany.

"I have to stop her," replied Pi. "I have to keep Jade from bringing down the Halls."

Bethany said something afterwards, but Pi was too far away to hear. She was already so far behind. It was probably too late, but she had to try.

The only question was how she was going to get in without being noticed. She was already not welcome in Arcanium, which meant the defenses would consider her a threat, not counting the Cabal students that were likely posted around the Hall.

It took too long for Pi to reach the fifth ward, where Arcanium was located. She left the Red Line, pushed out the train doors as soon as they opened, and ran towards the towering castle that looked nearby, but was still a couple of blocks away.

The sky was filled with big, fluffy white clouds, and the brightness of the day made Pi squint until her eyes adjusted. The streets were packed with tourists snapping pictures on their cell phones. She passed a gaggle of kids carrying plastic light-up versions of the Spire as they pointed them at each other and made noises as if they were space guns.

She approached Arcanium from the south side, the opposite direction from the bridge that led to the main entrance. She hoped to get someone's attention at a window so they might let her in, or at least to warn them. She was jogging to a stop, when she saw a group of mages climb out of a black SUV.

The identity of the mage in the tailored all-white suit was unmistakable—Alton Lockwood—as was the identity of the one in a gray suit with a black-and-white striped tie, but not because of his clothes, but because the last time she'd seen Sunil, his lifeless eyes were staring back up at her. Four more male mages climbed out of the vehicle and spread out into a line.

"Surprised to see me?" asked Sunil.

The words stumbled out of Pi's lips. "You can't come back from the dead."

"Lucky for me, I wasn't dead. Close, but no cee-gar. The fine doctors at Golden Willow healed me. A damn miracle if you ask me, though it took months of recovery."

Her gaze flicked over to Alton, who was concentrating on her as if she were a complex math problem.

"We met in Golden Willow. Sunil tells me that I hate you. I don't remember the reason, but what you did to him is enough for me," said Alton, pulling a wand from his pocket.

The binding she'd placed on him years ago should have kept him from using magic, but a trinket could be activated with only a tiny amount of faez. If he was recovered enough to be able to speak to her, then he could probably use the wand.

"How did you know I was coming?" asked Pi as she scanned the area for an escape route. If she'd been prepared, she would have felt more comfortable facing off with six mages, but she'd been busy trying to work out a way inside Arcanium.

"I figured out how you were tracking us down," said Sunil. "Cybermagics are pretty new, so I wasn't aware of their capabilities until I had a long talk with Dustin Davies."

"He's not my friend," said Pi.

Sunil shrugged. "Either way, he's dead, but not before he informed the rest of his friends that hacking your betters is not a good way to remain a viable Hall. In the future, they will do what they're told."

Pi hadn't liked Dustin Davies, but she felt bad that he was dead because of her. A fate it seemed she was likely to soon share.

The standoff was coming to a close, she sensed. Their fingers itched with spells. Pi knew she was only going to have one chance.

The shield she threw up deflected the first attack—a hailstorm of ghostly daggers—but the second and third were angled high, and over her barrier, as if they'd guessed what she was going to do from past battles.

Pi conjured a shield, courtesy of her Daring Maid soul, and knocked the majority of the falling weapons away, but a handful went through her, sending waves of agony through her limbs. They did no physical damage, but wracked her body with pain.

Distracted by the first three attacks, she did not see Alton Lockwood wave his wand, which elicited a warbling song from the slender stick, and turning the concrete around her boots to mud, until they'd sunk overtop, trapping her in place.

Sunil followed it up with a privacy barrier at either end of the street that would keep anyone from seeing what was happening to her.

Pi tried to work a counterspell that would vibrate the concrete into dust, but a second volley of ghostly daggers flew over the barrier. As each one zipped through her body, not damaging it but feeling as if she had been speared through the middle, she coughed out a scream, each cut short by the next impact until she was reduced to blind agony.

24

The gun was huge. It looked big enough to blow a hole in a concrete wall.

"You must be Jade."

Jade nodded, moving to the end of the bed, but keeping the gun trained on Aurie. Jade was wearing Pi's leather jacket and her hair was sopping wet.

The Engine whined like a symphony of strings scratching their way across the high registers. The vibration rattled Aurie's gut and made the corners of Jade's eyes squeeze together. There wasn't a lot of time before the buildup of energy in the Engine had to be dealt with.

Aurie could see why her sister had fallen for Jade. She was strikingly beautiful, the kind of girl that could be the cover model on a hardcore biker magazine. The flowery tattoos on her dark skin softened the image, but Aurie saw something else, a familiar darkness in the eyes, full of rage and fear.

"You came in through the moat," said Aurie, trying to engage Jade so she didn't pull the trigger before someone else could arrive. "I assume you borrowed Pi's jacket to protect the gun from the water. But how'd you get past the Watcher?"

"Those idiots in Coterie figured it out," said Jade, her gaze dancing around the room, trying to figure out where the noise was coming from. "I just stole it from them."

Aurie was standing to the side of Semyon. She was only two steps away from Jade, but that might as well have been a mile considering how easy it would be to pull the trigger. If a mage was prepared, guns were trivial to disarm or ward against, but Aurie wasn't prepared, which meant both she and Semyon were likely going to die.

"Is my sister okay?"

Aurie broke out into a cold sweat, until Jade screwed up her face. "You're her *sister*? Aurelia?"

"Yeah. Is she okay?" Aurie asked cautiously.

"Shit, yeah. I guess I should have seen the resemblance. She's okay. Probably mad as hell, but she's not hurt," said Jade, a little frown at the corner of her lip. "Don't do anything that makes me shoot you. I came for him, not for you."

"If you kill him, everyone in Arcanium will die."

Jade seemed to consider this, not as something new to discover, but as a choice she'd already made but pushed away the consequences.

"Yeah," she said regretfully. "I'm sorry. But this has been a long time coming."

Aurie went cold again, and not because she might die. *A long time coming.* When Jade had first come in the room, hot with anger, ready to pull the trigger, Auric had seen something in her gaze, a familiar hate.

The Rider.

She wasn't about to lament the bad luck that it'd gotten to this point. Whatever the patrons and Invictus had done centuries ago hadn't banished the creature. It also meant that she wasn't likely going to convince it not to kill Semyon, though it had shown some affection for her sister.

Jade pointed the gun at Semyon's head. His unconscious

form was like a mummy in a sarcophagus: eyes closed, lips slightly apart. The beep of the medical instruments was slowly being drowned out by the Temporal Engine as if the whine were rising waters of sound.

Aurie saw this as her only chance to stop Jade. If she lunged over the bed, she might be able to knock the gun away, or at least force Jade to shoot her instead, then maybe if another Arcanium member heard it, they could stop her.

She hesitated, only because getting shot was not going to be pleasant, and probably fatal. But if she didn't, everything she cared about would fall apart. *This is going to hurt.*

The muscles in Jade's hand started to tense.

Aurie lunged forward, reaching out to grab the gun.

The barrel swung towards her.

A cacophonous sound filled the room.

Aurie was punched in the shoulder, pushing her away from the gun.

Before Jade could bring it around for another shot, Aurie slapped her hand out towards the Engine, and pushing through the pain in her shoulder, she touched Jade's arm at the same time.

The world revolved around her.

They landed on a dirt road in the middle of two lines of trees. Aurie collapsed onto her knees, hand over the bloody wound in her shoulder, warm blood running between her fingers.

Jade wheeled the gun around, looking for Semyon.

"What in the fuckity-fuck just happened? Where did you send us? How did you teleport us like that?" Jade cried out. She brought the gun around to Aurie. "Send us back, right now, or I swear to whatever Creator you pray to, I'll put a bullet in your head."

Aurie was dizzy. She wasn't sure if the bullet had gone all

the way through, but it felt like her whole shoulder was on fire.

"I can't, and even if I could, I wouldn't. Shooting me won't fix the problem, and would likely make things worse, since you don't know how this place works."

Jade wiped her forehead with the back of her hand, swiping at a few gnats that had descended upon her. The sky was a pale blue, and the sun hovered over the edge of the trees, bringing a punishing heat upon them.

Eventually Jade pointed the gun back to Aurie. "Maybe I'll shoot you and find out. What have I got to lose?"

"Everything if you want out of here."

"Dammit." Jade stomped her foot in the dirt.

Aurie thought about keeping Jade in the dark about where they were, but she wanted to live, and not knowing might lead Jade to pull the trigger.

"I can explain if you let me fix this," said Aurie, grimacing.

"I thought you couldn't do magic, or you'd hurt your patron."

"I can here because we're in Semyon's head."

Jade spun around, head craning in all directions as if she could see the inside of his skull beyond the clouds.

"You'd better start fucking explaining," she said.

Aurie wouldn't be able to fix the damage completely, but she could at least close the hole in her shoulder. As sweat rolled down her arms, she leaned over and scooped up some dirt, forming it into a ball, which was challenging because she needed both hands, so she manipulated the dirt near her waist. Once it was roughly the size of a golf ball, she held it in her right hand, the side with her injured shoulder, and manipulated the spell with her left. She wasn't as ambidextrous as her sister, so getting the fingerings correct was difficult, but she managed. As the dirt glowed with faez, she slapped it against the wound, crying out from the impact.

Almost immediately, the dirt ball spread out, closing the wound and stopping the blood loss. The spell dampened the pain only slightly, so she had to keep from using her right arm.

When Aurie turned back to Jade, she caught a raw expression which made her wonder if she was truly a Rider. There was solace and regret in the rounding of her eyes. Or maybe like the patrons, the Rider had changed over the centuries.

"Explain."

Aurie tilted her head. The sound of horses reached her ears. "First, let's get off the road. We don't want to be seen right now."

They moved into a copse of trees and hunched down in the grass. Jade kept the gun pointed at Aurie.

"We're inside Semyon's dreams, much like a dreamstalking spell. But different. The Temporal Engine speeds up this place, so we experience a considerable amount of time in comparison to what's going on outside. For example, neither you nor I have probably hit the floor by now. If we were able to return to our bodies, we'd be in mid-fall."

The sounds of horses grew nearer. They were pulling a carriage. Peeking through the trees, Aurie couldn't see them yet, but it sounded like there was more than one.

"Like a dreamstalking spell," said Aurie, "it's unwise to let the dreamer know you're inside his mind. Because anything that happens to you here, happens to you outside. And in this case, it's much worse because of the time dilation between here and outside. We have to survive here until someone can pull us out or the energy of the Engine has dissipated enough that it'll kick us out."

This wasn't the complete truth. Aurie knew a spell to get out, but she needed at least a couple of minutes to cast it, and then another hour for it to take effect. If she could get away from Jade, then she could strand her inside of Semyon's mind. This would not only give her a chance to survive the gunshot, but help with the Engine transference.

The crunch of horse hooves grew louder. A line of soldiers on horses was headed their way. They wore the red jackets and white pants of the English army. There were three carriages behind the first line of horses.

Under her breath, Jade said, "What time period is this?"

"Mid 1700s," said Aurie softly, wondering if the Rider inside Jade would remember.

When the horses and carriages stopped, Aurie and Jade crouched lower. She was trying to hear the conversation when a half-dozen soldiers came around the trees, pointing muskets in their direction.

"By the queen's order, you are under arrest."

For a moment, Aurie thought Jade was going to resist, but then she stood and held up her hands. Aurie joined her. A solider removed the gun from Jade's hand, and they were led back onto the road.

The lead soldier leaned into the nearest carriage, handing over the pistol. "We captured some rebels, Colonel. One of them had a small rifle, make of which I've never seen before."

Aurie eyed the way behind her, wondering if she could make it to the woods before someone fired on her. If she could get past the tree line, she could use some magic to put distance between her and the soldiers, but then the chase would be on, and Semyon's subconscious would be alerted to their presence. For now, it was better to stay inconspicuous, she decided.

The carriage door swung open, and the colonel stepped out. He had dark skin that stuck out against the white crossed sashes on his chest.

When he rounded the door, Aurie sucked a breath in through her teeth in shock. It was Semyon Gray.

25

The concrete had trapped Pi up to her ankles, keeping her from falling to her knees in agony as they strafed her with ghostly daggers. She could do nothing to stop them. Pi screamed until she was hoarse, her voice sounding like loose pebbles in a tin can.

Then through tear-soaked eyes, she watched as Alton and Sunil, along with four other mages, approached.

"If she moves a muscle, kill her," Sunil said to the others.

Alton strolled near, a curious expression on his face. "I wish I could remember what it is that you did to me. I wonder if this revenge goes far enough, or should we make you suffer even more?"

"I spurned you because you have a small dick," said Pi.

The slap came like a thunderclap. The left side of her face stung.

As blood trickled out of her nose, she said, "It's amazing how such a small thing can drive you to rage." She chuckled under her breath at her joke, waiting for the next blow.

But they were not paying attention to her. The six of them had their heads up, looking down the street towards the privacy barrier.

Pi was halfway through the spell when the first explosion rang overhead, scattering Sunil and his ilk. Pi managed to turn the concrete to dust before Alton remembered she was still there. He fired his wand, but she deflected it with a ghostly shield, sprinting into an alleyway.

"Die, you pig!" screamed Bethany, blasting force bolts at Alton.

The Misfits burst through the barrier. The battle was engaged, and with six against six, there was little time for fancy spell work. Quick fingers summoned the Five Elements, leaving the air crackling with energy.

Sasha pounded them with earth magic, stones that grew into boulders as they soared down the street. Bethany fired force magic at Alton, unerringly, one after the other, like an automatic weapon. Nancy and Yoko twisted their fire and ice, which burst through counters and turned the air to steam, while Sisi moved like a supernatural creature, collapsing air pockets, causing thunderclaps that punished them sonically.

Lurking from her alleyway, Pi flanked the enemy mages, firing solar spears into their midst, forcing them to retreat. Once the first mage went down, Sunil and the others broke and ran, abandoning the fallen one and their SUV.

The Misfits cheered when they were gone.

"That was amazing," said Nancy, breathlessly. "I want to do that again."

They high-fived and hugged, except for Bethany, who was standing off to the side, crying.

"What's wrong? Are you injured?" asked Pi, checking the semi-translucent girl for blood.

"No. I almost had him. I made the spell just like you taught, but it wasn't enough. One of the other mages blocked it, and he got away," said Bethany.

"Alton?"

She nodded, using two fingers to wipe the tears flooding down the valleys on either side of her nose.

"You did great," said Pi. "If it weren't for you coming here, I'd be dead right now. We'll get Alton eventually, I swear to you, but today's not that day." She turned to the others. "At a later date I'm taking you all out for gourmet cupcakes in thanks, but for now I need your help again."

"We're in," said Sasha. "Bethany told us what happened."

The others added their grim nods, which warmed her heart. She almost felt sorry for Jade.

"She went in here, I think," said Pi when they reached the edge of the moat. The water, which was normally crystal clear, was brackish, covered in dead leaves, soft drink bottles, and colorful food wrappers.

"Why don't you go in the front door?" asked Nancy.

"I'm not welcome anymore, and those weren't the only Cabal goons around. I need to get in there fast before we get attacked again." Everyone looked around. "And I don't think I have much time. I might be too late."

"What do you need us to do?" asked Yoko.

"Who can hold their breath the longest?" asked Pi.

After a quick poll, Sasha raised her hand. "I used to hold my breath in grade school when I got bored. I can hold it for about two minutes. Do you need me to go in?"

"I know a spell," said Pi. "You'll be holding your breath for me, but out here. That'll give me a little bit longer to find my way in."

"Isn't there a guardian in the water?"

Pi's stomach tightened like a rope had been cinched. "Unfortunately, yes. I'm just going to have to hope that it still remembers me."

"And if it doesn't?" asked Yoko.

"Then I'm afraid you're not getting any gourmet cupcakes."

Nervous laughter passed through the group. This was what happened when you made real friends, she realized. She'd had it briefly with Ashley, but now she was just an echo in her head. Pi wished she could have this forever.

"I know this is a long shot, but anyone have a fish scale for a transference spell? I'm going to need help swimming through that quick enough. The place I need to get to is on the other side of Arcanium, and I don't know how far the tunnels go."

The girls patted their jackets and pockets.

"No? I guess I'll have to make do."

Sisi pulled out a tiny coin purse made of a soft gray fur. "Will baby seal work?"

"Yes, but—wait...I don't want to know," said Pi, taking the purse as Sisi gave a wild-eyed grin that would have been appropriate for a serial killer.

Using a pocketknife she borrowed from Sasha, Pi scraped fur from the coin purse, then she rubbed it on her hands in a warming motion while chanting the transference spell. When she was finished, she swallowed the fur dry, which choked her until she cleared it past the back of her throat.

After connecting her breath to Sasha's, Pi stripped down to her sports bra and panties and dove into the chilly water in search of the underwater tunnel. She knew there were multiple entrances around the moat, but had never bothered to learn where they were.

Pi kicked along the bottom, keeping her hand against the pockmarked concrete. She found the entrance after about a minute, and kicked up to the surface to reconnect with Sasha and apply magelight on her hands before continuing.

The glow revealed the murk in the water, motes of dirt and air pollution that had settled in the moat. She swam straight down into the tunnel, dodging around a plastic spork that swirled up from the deep. After a good fifty-foot swim straight down, it turned to a ninety-degree angle, heading towards the center of Arcanium.

Her hopes that it was a straight shot ended when she reached the T. She'd been in the water about a minute and was getting nervous. *Left is right, and right is wrong,* she sung in her head. She swam left, kicking off the wall for speed, kicking hard past rotted leaves and tiny fish that scurried away from her light. The passage split again, but she took the right this time, heading back towards the center.

When she reached a vast underwater chamber, Pi grew worried because Sasha's air was gone and she was relying on her own. With no time, Pi darted forward, swimming hard and at a slight upward angle, which used up her air faster.

Her chest burned as she swam, kicking and stroking, hoping to hear the waterfall cascading into the pool to give her an idea of where she was, but there was nothing but her frenzied heartbeat in her ears, drumming away like a rock concert.

When a massive dark shape slipped beneath her, Pi almost opened her mouth in surprise, letting out a bubble of precious air.

The Watcher had found her.

A tentacle thicker than her waist grabbed her by the chest and yanked her deeper into the water. The sudden pull released the remaining air in her lungs, turning her chest into a wildfire.

The Watcher dragged her deeper into the water, swiftly undoing her passage. Even if it released her, she knew she would drown before reaching air.

But it was not releasing her. She wished it would flex its muscles and crush her like a tin can, ending her misery, but it was determined to make her drown.

Pi tried to use Five Elements, but the thick water, her lack of air, and the giant tentacle around her chest kept her fingers from making the correct shapes.

Black dots started forming in her eyes. In moments, she knew she would open her mouth, and the water would rush in, silencing her forever.

Is this what it feels like to die?

Her heartbeat was thunderous, growing louder like an onrushing train. The last bubble of air slipped from her lips, the agony in her chest overcoming her will to fight. The water rushed past her lips, into her lungs.

The knifelike pain to her chest annihilated her thoughts. The world was almost black.

Then she was slammed onto the hard floor outside the pool. Water crashed around her, forming a patina of mist.

She still couldn't breathe. Water was in her lungs. The spots were forming a black curtain, slowly shutting her out from the world until the tentacle rose from the water and slammed her in the stomach. The water shot out of her lungs in a geyser, a brackish vomit that felt like she was having her lungs sandpapered.

The tentacle hit her a second time and more water gurgled from her lips, enough that she could cough and sputter the remainder as she crawled forward on her hands and knees.

Pi wanted to curl into a ball, but the tentacle pushed her towards the apartment, like a dog's master reminding it where home was.

"I'm going," she rasped, spitting out more water.

As she climbed to her feet, the tentacle slipped back into the pool.

Pi stumbled into the room to find Professor Longakers holding a bloody rag to Aurie's shoulder. Jade lay on the other side of the gurney where Semyon slept. Pi's ears were full of water, but she could feel the whine from the Engine in her chest.

"Miss Pythia," said the professor, going wide-eyed at her near nakedness. "What are you doing here? How did you get in?"

Pi banged on her chest, trying to get the water out. "A story for later. Has Aurie been shot?"

"Badly."

"Let me see her," said Pi, pushing the professor out of the way. She wasn't recovered enough for a proper healing spell, but she stopped the bleeding and placed an antibiotic enchantment on the wound.

While she was fixing Aurie, the professor told her what was happening, some of which she already knew.

"So Celesse is in Arcanium, and she's coming down here to make the transfer. Aurie and Jade are stuck inside Semyon's head, and the Temporal Engine is trending towards a dramatic end, which will be the opposite of pleasant."

He nodded. "Yes, you've got the rub of it. Even with the two of them in there, it's not dissipating the energy enough. And with the time dilation, they probably don't realize how much time is passing here. On previous visits, Aurie awoke within a minute. She's been out for an hour already."

"Can you get me in?" asked Pi.

He considered it. "I suppose so. We haven't tried the spell yet, but it should work."

"Teach me."

"First, you need clothes," said the professor. "In the bathroom, there are period clothes that Aurie normally wore."

Pi stumbled in, threw them on, and returned.

"The spell, the spell."

He taught it to her, and she leaned over to put her hand on Aurie's head, until the professor nodded at Semyon.

"Quickly," he said. "I don't know what Celesse is going to do when she arrives. She will likely make the transfer anyway. If you're in his head when that happens, then you're all dead."

"Then don't let her."

"I'll try," he said, though he didn't look confident. Without magic, the students of Arcanium were at the mercy of Celesse D'Agastine. They'd let the fox into the hen house.

The spell was nothing more than a pair of runes drawn onto the side of Semyon's head with a paint marker. As her fingertips brushed the glowing purple runes, the world flipped upside down.

26

The goaler pushed the clay bowl through the cage into Aurie's eager hands. The wagon rattled across the dirt road, splashing the lumpy gray, foul-smelling paste onto her wrist, and she eagerly sucked it off, ignoring the dried blood from where the chains had rubbed her raw.

"Do you have to watch me eat?" she asked the soldier sitting behind her cage with the musket stuck against her head.

"Stop talking," he said, bumping her in the shoulder with the muzzle.

Aurie spooned the gruel into her mouth, thankful that a cloud bank hid the punishing sun, and for her mother's darker skin tone, which protected her from being burnt. If it'd been Pi in the cage, with their dad's lighter Irish skin, she would have been as bright as a tomato by now. Of course, Aurie thought, Pi would have never allowed herself to be captured.

The British company was headed to Philadelphia, which they would reach in two more days. The wagon following her contained an almost comatose Jade. She was alive, but after getting knocked out with a rifle butt, she'd spent the rest of the time curled up in the bottom of the cage.

At least she hadn't used magic. Semyon had given the soldiers orders to shoot them if they even waggled their fingers. They were being taken to Philadelphia to be hanged as witches.

Aurie had no idea how he knew that they could do magic, but it was the first thing he'd said. It was entirely possible that his subconscious knew who she really was. At least they hadn't been attacked by any Riders.

Using her fingers, Aurie ate the gruel, which she noted rhymed with cruel. She hummed a song about the Cruel Gruel under her breath until the soldier tapped her on the back of the head with the musket.

Afterwards, she rubbed her fingers across the black iron bars, wishing for rust to scrape off with her fingernails. She knew a spell that would blast the lock open, but she needed flecks of rust. Her imprisonment had been foiled by well-oiled bars.

They reached a small town near dusk, when the fireflies flooded the fields, the crickets were in full symphony, and she could almost enjoy the world's beauty. The only two-story brick building in the town had been given over to Colonel Semyon Gray.

Their cages were carried into the garden in back. Two soldiers guarded each cage, while a lieutenant stood back and watched the soldiers for inattention.

Aurie bided her time with ideas on how she might escape. She was certain she could convince the lock that it was really open using mendacy, but she needed time and a distinct lack of muskets to accomplish that task. Truth magic might blast one soldier, but not the other, let alone the second pair around Jade's cage. Coordinating an escape with her was out of the question since they weren't allowed to talk and Jade was lying in the bottom of her cage in the fetal position.

The biggest issue was that time was passing outside of

Semyon's mind.   Aurie assumed that her gunshot wound had been healed to a certain extent. It still ached, but blood stopped leaking from her dirtball bandage. But that wasn't the real danger. For all she knew, Celesse was in the room, preparing to transfer the students, which would strand her and Jade in Semyon's mind as he died.

"At ease, gentlemen," said Colonel Semyon, who had strolled into the garden from the back of the house. He was wearing his red coat and white pants. His bushy mustache turned his mouth into a permanent frown. "Lieutenant Bristle. You and your men may take your tea."

"Sire, are you certain?   You said these women were witches, and dangerous."

"Both true, Lieutenant. But trust that I can handle myself. They're looking as energetic as a flea-bitten dog, at any rate. I don't think they'll stir any trouble."

Aurie studied Semyon when he faced the cages, looking for signs that he knew who she was. If his subconscious mind realized she wasn't a figment of his dreamstate, he would try to get her out by any means possible.

She could hear Jade stirring in the other cage, clanging her feet against the bars and cursing under her breath.

Semyon smoothed his mustache down with his forefinger and thumb. He seemed to be considering what to say. She was surprised by the hardness of his gaze as it contrasted with his youthful demeanor, a stark difference to the older version with kind eyes she knew in her world. But this was a different time, even if it were part of his memories, and he was a different person.

"Where did you learn your foul arts?" he asked.

"Not at your stupid school," said Jade.

"Hush, you idiot," said Aurie, banging her hand against the cage, hoping that Jade would remember not to provoke him. Or maybe she remembered and didn't care, which was worse.

"Curious you mention a school, since I said nothing of the sort."

"She's addlebrained, speaks nonsense on a daily basis," said Aurie. "Why, just the other day she was mumbling about why ponies with wings don't visit her anymore."

"You have a serpent's tongue, trying to deceive me. But I will not be swayed," barked Semyon.

His attitude wounded Aurie, who looked upon him as a mentor. Dream or no dream, it was hard to hear that from him.

"I ask again, women of the arts. Where did you learn your foul abilities? Would you rather be burned at the stake or receive a quick snap of the neck? The choice is up to you. Cooperate and I will be merciful."

Aurie sunk against the back of the cage. She'd fight before allowing herself to be burned alive, but that would only bring the full force of Semyon's subconscious against them. Speaking to him was like tap dancing in a minefield. If she said the wrong thing, she'd trigger him, and get them both killed.

"We are not without our resources," said Aurie, hoping to remain cryptic enough, "but we are not witches."

"Then what are you? I've examined your pistol at great length. Fired it upon a small tree, only to find it is like a cannon. By what witchery did you make such a thing?" he said.

"We didn't make it," said Jade. "I bought it from a—"

"Jade!"

"Merchant," she finished.

He glared at her. "Why did you interrupt her thusly?"

"I didn't want her to tell you the source," said Aurie.

"You're a soldier. You like weapons. We could provide more like that one if you promised not to kill us."

"The law is clear. Witches and warlocks must be purged."

Aurie pushed against the front of the cage. "What about you? Shouldn't you be purged too?"

"I don't know what you're talking about. I am her Majesty's greatest hunter of foulspawn," he said with such earnestness that it gave her pause.

In those years, had he not known that he was of the ability? It seemed hard to believe, but this version of him seemed to believe it. She was skilled in mendancy and knew a lie when she saw it, and he was being truthful. What about the others? Bannon had mentioned he was going to see friends. And Priyanka and Celesse had been waiting for Bannon. They had to be going to see the other two, Semyon and Malden. Or at least that's what she'd thought.

"What about your friends?" Aurie asked cautiously.

"I have no friends but the saber, the musket, and the queen's honor," said Semyon, lifting his chin and pulling back his shoulders.

As far as she could tell, also truthful. She needed more information.

"What about Malden Anterist?" she asked.

Colonel Semyon Gray flinched. "Why do you speak of the mayor?"

"Mayor?" asked Aurie, suddenly concerned.

"Mayor Anterist of the good city of Philadelphia," he said. "It is on his grounds that you shall swing by the neck until dead. There is word that he harbors your kind in his city, and I wish to make an example in plain view to flush the rats from the sewers, so to say."

Questions about Bannon, Celesse, and Priyanka were swallowed back. Nothing of this sort had been in the histories.

If it were anyone else's dream, she might have questioned it, but since it was Semyon's, how could she not believe that he'd been a mage hunter?

This left her reeling, with no idea of the way forward. How had Invictus brought these diverse mages together? Semyon Gray, a hunter of mages. Priyanka Sai, a mentor to a young Celesse. Bannon Creed, a well-meaning traveler. Malden Anterist, the mayor of Philadelphia.

Aurie had always assumed that they'd come together in fellowship, to drag wizardry out of the dark ages and give young mages a chance to explore their craft rather than be hunted like dogs.

In her deep introspection, she'd forgotten about Colonel Semyon, who watched her with particular interest. Had she not been staring directly at him, she might not have seen the white sash across his chest suddenly yellow with age and curl at the edges. It was the Temporal Engine at work, and it marked the hastening of their demise.

"You have a question lurking on your devilish tongue," he said.

"I...I'm tired. Being kept in a cage is not pleasant."

"It is not meant to be," he said briskly, then stepped closer, the hard line of his mouth softening. "You would be better off confessing to your crimes. Burning at the stake is most unpleasant. At this point, there's nothing you can do. The queen's law is clear about witches. I would at least like to learn more about you before your time must come to an end."

There was conflict in his gaze. Aurie saw within him a desperate plea that he not be forced to burn her, and deep concern, as if part of him knew the truth about himself. Was this what informed him? Drove him towards books and knowledge to drown out ignorance and superstition? Of the major patrons, he was the most hands-on, teaching his students directly, while the others had outsourced that to their professors. Some embers of guilt must still smolder in his soul.

"Your answer?" he asked.

"There's nothing I can say."

Semyon moved to Jade's cage. "And you? Will you repent?"

Jade spit on him through the bars. The spit landed on his jaw, and he wiped it off unceremoniously. He marched out of the garden, and before Aurie could find mischief, the soldiers returned to their posts.

Later, when the moon had risen, Aurie asked one of the guards for the remains of his apple, which he was about to toss into the bushes. The mealy flesh of the apple had been devoured, leaving only a fat core and a worm-holed hunk on one side.

"Soldier, please. I'm starving. I'll take the rest of that."

The dusty-haired soldier looked at the apple, checked back with the lieutenant, who was nodding asleep, and shrugged as he tossed it through the bars.

"My thanks," said Aurie, cradling it greedily between her hands.

She brought it to her lips to nibble the remaining apple flesh from the core, only to find what only moments before had been nearly ripe, become an ancient dried core with three black seeds being squeezed out.

She silently cursed the sudden aging of the apple core before she could eat the good parts. But that had only been one reason she'd wanted the apple. The other had been for the seeds, which prepared properly contained cyanide, which she could use for a number of spells. Aurie plucked the three seeds from the mummified core and tossed the remainder into the bottom of the cage.

The seeds were an opportunity, but she wasn't sure if she was going to have enough time. Other items in Semyon's dream were rapidly aging, like a blackberry bush in the garden which had gone through the seasons in about ten seconds while she watched. This meant the energy from the Temporal Engine wasn't dissipating, and Aurie was the only person who could turn it back down, but she was stuck inside Semyon's dream.

Covertly, Aurie lifted the apple seeds to her mouth and slipped them—one, two, three—past her lips, swallowing them whole like baby aspirin. She wasn't sure how long it was going to take for her stomach acid to activate the amygdaline and turn it into cyanide, but she gave it a couple of minutes, before sticking her finger down her throat.

At the first gag, a soldier banged on the cage with his musket. "Hey, stop that. What are you doing?"

Aurie ignored him and shoved the finger deeper.

"I'll shoot you. I'll shoot you," said the soldier, pulling back the hammer on the musket.

Aurie kept shoving until her stomach rolled like a wave, and the horrible gut-churning release came. She vomited onto the floor of the cage, the splatter forcing the soldiers to jump back.

To silence their fears, Aurie feigned slumping over on her side as if she'd passed out. The lieutenant joined them as they poked her with their fingers like a wild animal, testing her to see if she was alive. After a few minutes of discussion about whether or not they should let the colonel know what happened, they decided that they didn't want to face his wrath for waking him at this time of night.

Once they were away from the cage, Aurie felt around the bottom of the cage for the bile-covered seeds, secreting them in her palm for later use. Only then did she allow herself a bit of sleep. If they were going to escape, it needed to be tomorrow before they reached Philadelphia.

27

The British had sixty infantry, twelve mounted officers, four supply wagons, and two cages containing Pi's sister and her ex-girlfriend. The odds would have been in Pi's favor, except for one crucial factor that she'd only uncovered while she was scouting them as they crossed a bridge on the winding Schuylkill River—and that was the presence of Semyon Gray in what appeared to be an officer's uniform.

Professor Longakers had warned her as to the nature of the dreamstate, and that alerting Semyon to the intruders in his mind would only bring calamity. What was a small company of soldiers would quickly grow out of control as his subconscious brought in reinforcements.

But if she didn't act soon, the wagons would reach Philadelphia, and there were additional British barracks in the city, which would only make their escape more difficult.

The peasant dress she was currently wearing hung loosely on her frame since the clothes she wore into the dream had been fitted for Aurie. Pi hated that she couldn't alter reality like a normal dreamstate, but Semyon's unconsciousness was not typical, and did not follow the regular rules.

She cupped her hand against the sun, considering her

options, and saw a whole line of trees on the opposite side of the road turn their leaves: first autumnal coloring as if paint had been poured over them, then crisping brown, before falling onto the earth and blowing away as dust.

It was the third major instance of rapid aging she'd seen since she entered the dreamstate, which meant she was running out of time.

The British company rumbled along the dirt road that ran parallel to the river, kicking up dust that was carried away over the fields by the warm wind. At this point, there was no use delaying any further, but yet she did. Why was that?

Pi felt like there was something she was missing. Before she'd entered, Professor Longakers had explained what had happened to Aurie on previous visits. He didn't explain the reason that each one had been to this general place and time, which left Pi wondering. Why this moment? Why here? Was this Semyon's subconscious returning to an important time randomly, or was this him directing the dreams to tell them something that would help them in the present time?

The pieces whirled in her head, never staying in one place for long. It was an itch at the back of her brain that she couldn't scratch.

"There has to be a reason," she whispered as the wind ruffled her dress. "But for now, I just need to get them free."

Pi lingered on the word them, thinking about Jade and if she deserved pity. After all, she'd shot Aurie and tried to kill her friends and destroy the Halls.

"Get Aurie, maybe Jade, and get the hell out of here while not getting murdered in Semyon's dream. Check."

Her plan was to hit them hard, and get away fast. Aurie knew the spell to escape the dream. She hoped her sister could cast it on the fly, because they weren't going to get a chance to hunker down.

The one-on-many battles with the Cabal during the year had trained her for this moment. Pi didn't have to think about what enchantments to layer, and how to infuse her body with speed and strength. Those spells came to her fingers and tongue like notes to a skilled pianist.

She lacked some reagents, and focuses that would otherwise make her spells more potent, but she'd learned to be resourceful in the Undercity.

Before long she was sprinting up the river on the south side, skirt tied to her waist so her legs would have room to pump. She felt like a racehorse, her bare feet kicking up soil behind her in a rooster spray, beads of sweat collecting on her upper lip until she wiped them away with the back of her hand.

She caught up to and passed the British company, keeping far enough south that they would not spy her, then turned a narrow section of the Schuylkill to ice, to scamper across before the pieces dissolved back into the slow-moving water.

Pi dropped to her knees in the middle of the road in the path of the company and started digging with her bare hands, quickly scooping out chunks of hard packed dirt like a badger creating its home. When she was finished, Pi had created a person-sized hole in the road.

After climbing into the hole, she pulled dirt back in, covering her body, then cast a slow-acting hardening spell on the soil before pulling the rest over her face. For air, she'd stolen a whisking mat from the inside of a barn and fashioned it into a tube, which stuck out from the dirt mound.

As the dirt hardened around her, Pi reviewed the ways that her plan was entirely ludicrous: the soldiers might step on the breathing tube, jamming it into her mouth, the wagon could veer out of the tracks and crush her, a horse might break through the soil and impale her gut, Semyon might detect her presence, or there might be too many of them when she emerged.

This gave her a bit of panic, until she calmed her breathing by imagining the world's best hug that Aurie would give her when they finally got out of this mess. The soil was cool and soothing at least, like a suffocating spa treatment.

The rumble of marching hobnailed boots, stomping ironshod horse hooves, and rolling wagon wheels shook her cocoon in the road. As the first of the soldiers walked over her, barely moving the covering above her, she relaxed. The spell was doing its work.

The hard part was figuring out what part of the company had passed over her, so she could emerge beneath a wagon. There were about thirty troops before the mounted officers, then Semyon's wagon, then the two cages in wagons, followed by supply wagons, and then another thirty soldiers.

The last of the soldiers passed over, and Pi tensed up, expecting horse hooves, when everything went quiet. The British company, for some inexplicable reason, had stopped. If they were speaking, Pi was too deep into the road to hear them.

The longer it was quiet, the more she panicked. Why would they have stopped there, in that exact spot, unless they had detected her?

She imagined Semyon lining up dozens of soldiers with muskets prepared and pointed at the spot of upturned soil in the middle of the road. There were so many clues she'd left to her existence. They surely had figured it out and were preparing to ambush her when she emerged.

Pi readied herself to burst from the earth, spells slinging in all directions. She would only get one chance. She had prepared herself to withstand musket shot, but the combined firing of dozens of soldiers would be too much to stop.

She tensed her muscles, ready to break out, when the marching resumed. Her foot had poked through. Pi waited, expecting them to stop again. A horse stepped on her midsection, which knocked the air from her lungs, but otherwise did no damage.

When she figured the cavalry had passed, Pi broke the covering over her face to find the fitted dark wood of a carriage sliding over top. Pi sprung from the soil like an ancient, nimble mummy, covered in sweat and dirt, and placed herself directly ahead of the horses leading the wagons, keeping out of sight of the driver, who was napping on his seat, letting the horses plod along behind the carriage.

Pi swung up onto the bench, placed her hands around the driver's nodding head, and made the Five Elements spell for electricity, shocking him at his temples and knocking him out to slump to the side.

She could have outright killed him since he was only a figment of Semyon's dream, but taking someone's life—even imaginary—without good reason was a step too far.

The soldier in the wagon with his musket pointed into Aurie's cage didn't see what happened to the driver, so she quietly performed the same trick. The soldier leaned to the side like a drunk after a hard night.

The cage containing her sister had provided cover for her deeds, so no one had been alerted to the rescue. Pi hopped into the back.

"Aurie."

Her sister jumped, spinning around in the small cage, first wide-eyed with terror at her dirt-smeared form, then recognition dawned. "You're here!"

"Of course I'm here. You were in trouble," said Pi.

They squeezed each other's hands.

"Can you get out—" Pi started to ask, when a shout of

alarm went up from the driver in the wagon behind.

A moment later, a musket blast careened off the cage bars.

"Ow, I'm shot!"

Pi sent a spray of superheated water at the wagon behind, trying not to hit Jade's cage. The soldier and driver screamed, the latter falling off as he stumbled around the bench. She grabbed the reins and veered the wagon into the field.

Aurie burst from the cage, sending a billowing blast of truth magic to knock over a group of soldiers running after them.

"Keep 'em off us!" Pi yelled to her sister.

"What about Jade?"

Pi glanced back to the British company, which had been stirred up like a hornet's nest. Soldiers in red coats, more than she remembered from before, were lining up to fire. The officers had charged after them on their horses, swinging sabers above their heads. Going back to rescue Jade would be suicide, not to mention stupid, considering what she'd done.

"Merlin's tits," said Pi as she yanked on the reins, dragging the horses to make a wide circle. As she plowed back towards the British, musket balls zipping past her head, Pi stood on the bench with the reins held in her teeth, and with no time for nuanced magics, she fired force bolts at the British soldiers.

Musket balls slammed into her chest, and though the enchantments protected her from serious harm, they still felt like getting hit with paintball guns from point-blank range. As they rushed towards the other caged wagon, Jade emerged, blasting soldiers from her position.

With Aurie and Jade providing covering fire, Pi drove the wagon past the other, slowing long enough for Jade to leap into the back, then Pi turned down the road, heading away from the company.

As their wagon thundered down the road, bouncing and

bumping, nearly out of control, Aurie yelled to her from the back.

"Jade's been shot!"

"Come up here, take my spot."

As they were making the transfer, a nearby patch of ground exploded, sending stinging soil against their unprotected faces.

Behind them, cannons had been lined up, and were firing. They hadn't been there moments before.

"What the hell!"

Aurie settled onto the seat and whipped the reins. "It's Semyon's subconscious. It knows we're here."

"I know, but, fuck, cannons. Really?"

"Jade first. Then cannons."

A lot passed in their glance. Aurie knew that her and Jade's relationship was complicated. The shooting in Semyon's room hadn't helped.

Before dealing with Jade, Pi created a barrier that would stop the smaller projectiles. Without runes or anchoring materials, the shield would likely disintegrate at the first major hit, but she didn't want to worry about musket fire while she examined and fixed the wound.

More officers on horseback had materialized and were chasing the wagon, but Pi ignored them and focused on Jade. The dark-haired woman was lying in the bottom of the wagon, propped against the cage, blood oozing through her hands pressed against her stomach.

"That's not good," said Pi, kneeling in front of Jade, whose eyes were white, her normally dark skin almost pale.

"You might need to work on your bedside manner," said Jade, her lower lip quivering.

"You might need to work on not killing my sister and my friends," said Pi as she pulled back Jade's hands, examining the pulsing wound.

Jade closed her eyes. "If you let me die, I'll understand."

"I'm not letting you die," said Pi. "Lucky for you, I know a few things about healing, though this is pretty bad. If you really lived in this time you'd be a goner."

Tears bloomed into Jade's eyes. "I'm...I'm...I don't deserve this."

"Shut up and let me work," said Pi, trying to figure out how to stop the bleeding. The middle of a battle was a terrible time to work, and the constant bumping wasn't helping Jade, so Pi did the only thing she knew how to do that would work in this situation, and that was to cast a stasis spell on the wound. The blood stopped flowing out of the wound. Then Pi used the coat from the fallen soldier in their wagon, tore some bandages, and wrapped them around Jade's middle, putting antiseptic enchantments on it to keep her from getting infected.

"Pi!" yelled Aurie from the front.

"What?"

"Pythia! Come quick. This is not good."

Summoned by the invocation of her full name, Pi scurried to the front, leaving Jade to recover. She thought there might be more soldiers or cannons, but they'd left those behind. Instead, there were four figures standing on the ridge ahead. They were still about half a mile away, but the wagon was closing the distance.

"Is that who I think?"

"The other four patrons," said Aurie coolly. "And I don't think they're here to be the welcoming committee."

"How can that be them?" asked Pi.

"It's not them, but Semyon's memories, though they are connected in some way, because I learned things about the others that Semyon wouldn't have known otherwise."

Combined with her earlier suspicions about the nature of

this place, Pi had an idea.

"Let's get out of here," said Pi. "You know the exit spell."

Aurie shook her head. "I need time. The spell is quick, but it takes an hour to take effect."

"An hour? Professor Longakers didn't say that. Is there a way to speed it up?"

Aurie pushed her hand into her greasy, dirty hair. She looked like she was trying out for the part of a colonial witch with her crazed expression.

"Maybe. But Longakers hadn't figured it out. He said a bit of lexology might work."

"Then do that," said Pi, taking the reins. "Speed it up."

"I could just as easily make it take a day, or longer," said Aurie.

"An hour? A day? What's the difference? We won't survive twenty minutes."

Her sister climbed in back and started the spell.

Pi stared ahead at the four figures standing on the ridge, facing them. She sensed the gathering faez like the pressure dropping before a storm. They weren't a greeting committee. They were a death squad.

She yanked the reins, turning the wagon north on a dirt road that passed between two farms.

"Hurry up, Aurie," she whispered to herself, not wanting to disturb her sister. "Hurry up."

28

Shivers of faez sped through Aurie as the last word of the return spell left her lips. Being locked up in a cage without a way to use magic had left her stiff and agitated, but a little release of faez had gone a long way, even under the current circumstances.

"When the spell triggers," Aurie said to Pi and Jade, "a ghostly rope will appear, hanging down like a bell ringer. Grab it and you'll get yanked back into reality."

Pi had chunks of dirt stuck in her hair, and her white peasant dress was stained brown and red. She looked like the survivor of a budget horror movie. She whipped the reins as she glanced back over her shoulder. "How long?"

Aurie lifted one shoulder, squinting. "I wish I knew. Just be ready. It could be in a minute, it could be in three hours."

She gave the surrounding fields a once-over. There was no one in sight, though she assumed they weren't far. The horses pulling their wagon weren't going to keep the pace in the heat. But while they had a break, Aurie planned to get some answers.

"Who are you, Jade Umbra?" asked Aurie, crouched down before the nut-brown girl with the flowery sleeve of tattoos.

Jade looked worn down from captivity. Her eyes had dark rings around them. Her lips had lost their sure lines.

"I'm sorry I shot you," said Jade.

"That's not what I asked. I asked who you really are. Why do you hate the Halls so much?"

The softness in her face gained rigidness as if steel girders had been shoved into place. She shifted, wincing from the wound in her gut.

"The Halls have taken everything from me," said Jade, glaring in defiance as she held her arms around her stomach.

"Are you a Rider?" asked Aurie.

Pi's head snapped around. "What's going on, sis?"

Jade didn't answer. She seemed confused by the question. "I don't understand."

"On my previous visits, I encountered a being called a Rider that can attach itself to other people and get them to do what it wants. It's attacked me on two separate occasions. I think that's what Semyon's trying to warn us about. These Riders were an early foe of the patrons, and they banded together to fight them. As far as I know, you're a Rider, returned to finish the job."

"I don't know what you're talking about," said Jade, meeting her gaze.

Aurie studied her expression for clues. If it was a lie, it was a skilled one.

"That's why Jade's trying to take down the Halls," Aurie explained to her sister. "Because it's not really her, but this creature."

"I'm not so sure," yelled Pi from the front. "Don't you think I would have known?"

"I don't know," said Aurie. "I couldn't find anything about them. But why else would Semyon bring me to this time and place? It has to be about the Riders. Which means they're a grave danger to our reality. Otherwise, why bother?"

"I get what you're saying," said Pi. "I have the same thoughts about the significance of this time and place. But I don't know about Jade."

"Are you two just going to talk about me while I'm sitting here?" said Jade, frowning.

"Why yes, we are, until you come clean with what's really going on, and even then, I'm not sure I can trust you," said Aurie, grabbing onto the side of the wagon as they hit a big bump.

Jade grimaced, then panted in exhaustion.

Aurie sighed at the wounded girl. "Let me help you with that. Pi stopped the bleeding, but I can reduce the pain. At least so it's not so awful."

"Why would you do that if you think I'm the enemy?" asked Jade.

"Maybe I'm not sure if you're the enemy, and even if you are, it's not right to make you suffer."

After the spell finished, Jade looked on the verge of tears.

"What's wrong? Is it not working?"

"It's working," said Jade. "But it's hard to explain what's going on. But I will, because of, well, I've screwed everything up so far, and" —she gathered herself, taking in a quivering breath— "I see what you two have and it makes me ache. You see, I hate the Halls because I had a sister once. Older. She joined Coterie. She was a top student, assistant to the patron when he decided he didn't want her anymore, had her killed. How can he do that? Just decide that someone isn't worth keeping around and take them away from me? She was my sister. I loved her. I miss her."

The weight of what had happened to Jade came down on Aurie. If Pi had died because of the Halls, how would that have made her feel? Would it have changed her? She knew if it'd happened the other way around, Pi could have easily turned out like Jade.

"What was her name?" asked Aurie, so softly she wasn't sure Jade had heard it over the rattling wagon.

Jade blinked in thought. "Adler." She hung her head in remembrance.

In that noisy silence, Pi glanced back and mouthed the question: "Telling truth?"

As far as Aurie could tell, Jade hadn't lied. Aurie nodded, which released the tension from her sister's forehead and shoulders.

Aurie crouched down and handed Jade a water pouch they'd taken from the soldier she'd tossed over the side. Jade drank from it greedily, water spilling across her chin.

"What the balls?" exclaimed Pi from the front.

"Soldiers?" asked Aurie, glancing behind them.

"No."

"Patrons?"

"It's hard to explain. Come see."

As soon as Aurie looked over the front bench, the breath was stolen from her lungs. "Mercy..."

The wagon was cresting a hill, giving them a view of the landscape ahead. It looked like the world had been melted down, a vast desolation. Fields were as barren as a desert. Jutting blackened stumps stuck up from the earth like rusty pipes.

"The Engine," said Aurie.

"We haven't fixed anything yet," said Pi, pulling on the reins until the wagon skidded to a stop.

Gusts of wind created dust devils in the dead fields, whirling like living things. Aurie could taste the aridness, like decanting a mummy's bones.

"Celesse is still out there. About to take control of

Arcanium," said Aurie absently, reminding them of the hidden danger facing them. "If we don't get out soon."

Jade struggled to her feet and leaned against the bench, gasping at the view.

"Why aren't they chasing us?" asked Jade.

"I don't know," said Aurie.

A soft chime rung, and three ghostly ropes appeared in the air before them.

"Our rides have arrived," said Aurie, reaching out.

Pi knocked the dirt from her face, glancing suspiciously at the rope. "I'm not going back."

"What?"

"You see that." Pi stretched her arm towards the desolation. "The Engine is trending towards explosion, and we have no idea what a time bomb will do in Invictus. That energy needs to be dissipated. Longakers said you were coming here and using magic, and that was reducing it."

"Yeah, but our battle back there didn't make a dent in the change," said Aurie.

"Because we haven't used enough," said Pi. "But I have an idea of how I can use more."

"And that is?" asked Aurie.

Pi raised an eyebrow in Jade's direction, who noticed and said, "Yeah, I get it. You don't trust me."

"Why would I? You acted like you loved me, stole my jacket and pin, and tried to kill my sister."

"I still love you," said Jade.

"That's not something you say, it's something you show. You showed me who you really are," said Pi. "I feel bad about your sister, but that's no reason to take it out on the rest of the world."

While they were talking, Aurie watched as the dead zone crept towards them, grass yellowing and wilting, before shrinking into dust. The desolation moved like a living thing. It made Aurie's stomach crawl.

"Hey, you two. We don't have time. This place is falling apart," said Aurie. "Are we leaving or staying?"

"I'm staying," said Pi steadfastly. "You go, stop Celesse from taking Arcanium. I'll stay and figure this out."

"You don't have to do this," said Aurie. "You're only in danger if you stay. You could leave. The Engine or the collapse of the Halls won't affect you."

"No way, sis. You couldn't convince me to leave even if I was on fire."

Her sister's love made her chest ache.

"I'm staying, too," said Jade.

"No. I can't trust you," said Pi, turning on her.

"You need help. You can't take on an army by yourself," said Jade.

Pi shook her head. "You'll only slow me down."

Jade crossed her arms. "I'm not going back. I have to make this up to you. Like you said, you can't talk about love, you have to show it. Well, I'm showing it."

Pi looked at Jade like an older sister saddled with a tag-along younger sibling. Whatever feelings her sister had had for Jade, they'd been annihilated by the betrayal.

"I guess I can't stop you from staying, but if you get in my way, I will make you pay," said Pi.

Aurie gave Jade her fiercest expression and pointed towards the sky with a forefinger. "Remember, I'll be up there with your body. You do anything to my sister and I will feed you to hungry sharks."

Jade looked on the verge of tears. "I'll be good. I want to help."

"Before I go, Pi. I made these." Aurie handed the three apple seeds over. "I believe the arsenic is active. You should be able to put them to use."

"I know a few spells," said Pi, shoving them into a pocket on her dress.

Aurie pulled her sister in for a long hug, fingers digging past the crust of dirt on her dress, squeezing until her eyes hurt.

"Dooset daram."

"Dooset daram."

29

"Tell me why you stayed," said Pi, from behind the bench as they rushed back towards Philadelphia, leaving the desolation behind. Jade was at the reins, holding them with one hand while the other was clutched around her stomach. The wagon bumped along the road, dust billowing from the iron-clad wheels. The smell of fire was in the air, and Pi didn't think it was from a chimney.

"I told you why I stayed."

"I don't believe you," said Pi.

"I understand. I don't deserve your trust," said Jade. "I'm sorry. I guess my hatred for the Halls, for taking my sister, blinded me to what I had with you. I saw an opportunity to get back at them."

"I don't believe that's the only reason you stayed," said Pi forcefully.

When Jade shook her head, choking back a sob, Pi felt the villain.

"What was your sister like?" asked Pi, trying to change the subject.

Jade blinked heavily, mouth opening like a fish out of water.

"Your sister, Adler, what was she like?"

After a time, Jade responded. "She was a lot like yours, tall and smart and beautiful. I miss her."

Pi tried to gauge the truth, but she didn't have Aurie's ability to spot lies. Not that it was infallible. Pi didn't trust Jade not to betray her at some point and didn't plan to give her an opportunity.

The road led them back to the Schuylkill River. Jade pulled on the reins when they saw the barricades set against them. Bonfires had been built along the road. The fields on both sides of the river contained a host of British infantry, cavalry, and cannons.

"Are you sure we have to get to Philadelphia?" asked Jade.

"I'm not going into the city, but we have to go past it to get where I want to go."

"Where?"

"I'm not telling you."

Pi needed to use magic, and a lot of it, or the Engine would explode. She didn't have the capacity, but she knew a place that did. Whether or not it would work inside the dreamstate, she didn't know, but she hoped the connection between the patrons and the city would facilitate the transfer.

"Give me a moment to construct a shield," said Pi. "Then we're going to hit that line like a battering ram."

Using a belt knife from the soldier, Pi carved runes into the wagon, anchoring points for her shield. The barrier was Daring Maid spell work modified with lexology and reinforced with dangerous magics from Coterie. The whole setup was a house of cards. If one part fell, the whole barrier would collapse around them, killing them both, but she didn't have much choice if she wanted to withstand cannon fire and hailstorm of musket shot.

"Where are the patrons?" asked Jade.

Pi admired the shimmering shield around the horses and wagon, built like the prow of a ship, or a cowcatcher on the front of a train.

"I see Semyon, but not the others. I have a feeling we'll find out if we get through this. Aim for the side without Semyon."

As they began their charge, Pi tried hard not to tense up. She filled the shield with as much faez as she could muster. A metallic haze sheened into existence. The first musket balls reflected like hail on a tin roof. Cannon blasts thudded, ricocheting into the earth. As the British cavalry charged, sabers raised, Pi found herself screaming, voice amplified by the enchantments threading through her body.

She closed her eyes upon the impact, horses and men flying in all directions, ignoring their screams to maintain the shield. The second impact, crashing through the barrier on the dirt road, turned wagons into deadly man-sized splinters, shattered iron cannons, and pulped soldiers like thrown tomatoes.

The runes carved into the wood sides of the wagon caught fire in the blowback. Pi stumbled around the careening wagon, smashing her shoulder against the iron cage, putting out the fires with her hands, leaving blisters on her palms and fingertips. She cooled them with her breath, then checked behind them to see the line of soldiers—those that had not been destroyed in the impact—coming down the road in pursuit like a horde of angry hornets.

"The shield's gone," said Jade.

"It had its use," said Pi, gripping the back of the bench, leaning forward into the wind.

The road winded along the river, curling away when the terrain became uneven, but always coming back to the waterway. Fishermen on boats threw nets into the murky water, oblivious to the pursuit.

When they neared a wooden bridge wide enough to fit two passing wagons, Pi instructed Jade to turn away from the city. A nearby wooden cottage rotted to mush as they thundered up the road.

"How do you know we won't be blocked by the desolation?" asked Jade.

"Don't worry about it. Keep going."

The truth was that she didn't know, but hoped that Semyon's psyche was trying to tell them the solution. If the way was blocked then she knew they were on their own.

Pi was leaning down to grab the water pouch when the patrons attacked.

Priyanka leapt over a stacked stone wall, forcing Jade to duck under a fan of flying daggers. Celesse rolled from behind a copse, distracting Pi with a fireball that had to be countered with a collapsing orb of water.

As the wagon careened to the left side of the road, Bannon Creed lumbered from behind an illusionary wall that matched the verdant field, wearing his ghostly armor and shield, wielding a massive shimmering broadsword that sliced through the legs of the horses, killing them instantly.

Untethered, the wagon jumped the bodies, heading towards the rock wall. In the moments before being thrown, Pi noticed a fourth figure, who had likely been maintaining the illusionary wall that Bannon had hidden behind, appear. She assumed he was Malden Anterist, but had no time to satisfy her curiosity as she flew out of the wagon.

Her spell-aided reflexes allowed her to roll into a fighting position the moment she hit. Jade was not so lucky, landing awkwardly in the soft soil.

The four patrons collapsed towards Pi. She reflected the next batch of flying daggers, not at Priyanka, who she knew would expect it, but at Celesse, who at this point was the weakest of the four. Celesse screamed as one impacted her shoulder and another went into her left thigh. She collapsed to her knees and cried out as she wrestled the blade out of her thigh.

Before Bannon or Priyanka could reach Pi, she pulled the apple seeds from her pocket, spat faez onto them until they ignited into a smoldering fire, then cupped her hand and blew through the tube, sending a billowing poisonous smoke at them. The pair were forced to go around the cloud.

This gave Pi a chance to grab Jade by the shoulders and pull her upright. Jade grimaced but looked ready for action.

"Back to back. We can beat them."

Pi's fingers flew through the Five Elements like a concert pianist. Bannon fought through the spells using his ghostly shield for cover, while Priyanka nimbly dodged, throwing a never-ending stream of daggers from a sheath.

"I've got this," said Pi. "Take care of Malden."

"That's the Coterie patron?"

"Yes!"

Pi snuck a glance at the man approaching from the road. She couldn't make much out. He was waving his hands in big circles, summoning the wind that rose around him like a cloak, sending dust and clumps of grass bouncing across the field.

"Stop him, Jade. If he finishes that spell, we're toast!"

Pi superheated the air around Bannon until he retreated, keeping Priyanka busy with an earthen snake that was trying to constrict around her legs.

When Pi sensed no faez coming from Jade, she turned to look, right as Jade smacked her with a spar of the wagon across the forehead. The world spun around Pi until she landed on her back.

From above her through a fog, she heard Jade say, "Thank you for saving me! She's a Rider and she made me drive that wagon for her. She wants to destroy your world!"

Pi fought through the fog to refute the betrayal. Her lips smacked together, but she couldn't muster a word. Unconsciousness came like a flood, carrying her into oblivion.

30

Semyon Gray's quarters were crowded with unfamiliar legs as Aurie returned to her body from beneath a table where wires ran across the room to sensors on her patron. She recognized Celesse's upper crust New York accent amid the fervor, along with Professor Mali, who was shouting like a Marine drill sergeant. Above it all, the whine of the Temporal Engine had become an ear-shattering pulse. The computers on the tables were red-lining with alarm, and the faez in the air was so thick, it choked her like smog.

"You cannot make the transfer!" yelled Professor Mali. "You'll kill those three young women."

"It's not my intent, Joanne, but if you don't allow me to take control of your students and fix the Engine, there won't be a school to worry about."

"Please, we have to give them more time," said the professor, desperation in her tone, yelling over the whine.

"You know there isn't time left to give."

Before another word could be spoken, Aurie crawled from beneath the table. Heads spun towards her when she appeared. Both Arcanium professors were in the room, along with Celesse and three mages from Alchemists she didn't recognize.

"See, she's out. I can begin now."

Celesse had a bookish look with her hair pulled high, stylish dark rimmed glasses and a librarian's aesthetic, if that librarian walked the runways of Paris. She was dressed for the part of savior.

"My sister is still in there," said Aurie, grimacing as the pain in her shoulder reminded her that she'd been shot earlier. It appeared by the sheen of bright blood that the worst of the damage had been delayed by a slow spell.

"Then get her out," said Celesse. "And whoever that other girl is too."

"She shot me," said Aurie, yelling to make herself heard. "She wanted to take the Halls down. I pulled her in there to keep her from killing Semyon."

Professor Mali gave her a look, but Aurie couldn't explain.

Celesse cleared her throat. "Well then, I guess we don't have to worry about her. Fetch your sister and then we'll be done with this. Quickly, before this artifact kills us." She snapped her fingers twice to indicate her impatience.

"I can't," said Aurie, throwing herself between Celesse D'Agastine and the gurney that contained Semyon Gray. "She's trying to fix the Engine. Give her time. Please."

"We don't have time," said Celesse. "If you can't get her, then we die. I'm sorry, Ms. Silverthorne. Please move."

"Is it that bad?" Aurie asked her professors.

Professor Longakers looked up from his computer screen, shaking his head. "I'm afraid we're in catastrophic territory. It could blow any time."

Professor Mali wouldn't make eye contact when Aurie looked to her for support.

"Stop delaying, Ms. Silverthorne," said Celesse sternly. "You know it's the right thing to do. Better one die than many."

"You can stop it?" asked Aurie.

"Of course I can, if I am your patron. The connection will pass from him to me, which means you'll be linked to me, thus giving me a measure of control. It won't be pretty, but I can deal with the excess of energy. You were foolish to speed it up without the knowledge required to control it. Let me put things to right."

Aurie kept herself in front of Semyon. There was no way she could stop Celesse or her three mages, but she couldn't let them kill her sister. If she'd only known that Celesse could have fixed it, she would have had Pi come out of the Engine with her. Joining Alchemists wasn't as bad as losing her sister.

The warning from Professor Mali came back in that instant, the request to stay away from the Temporal Engine. Aurie had thought she could handle it when she'd visited the ancient mage Oba. She didn't want to give up, not on Arcanium, not on the Halls, and especially not on her sister.

The truth was plain for her to see: had she not gotten the Engine, Pi wouldn't be stuck, about to be winked out of existence when Celesse pulled the plug on Semyon.

"You know it's the right thing," said Celesse, who flinched, touching her arm and then her leg as if something had bitten her. She glanced askance at Semyon before returning her gaze to Aurie. "Hurry, before it's too late."

Aurie hoped for support from Professor Mali, but she grimaced, acknowledging the dire situation.

As Aurie stepped to the side, the Engine dropped in pitch for a moment, warbling like a motor with sugar in the tank.

"It's working! It's working! See, she's fixing it," said Aurie, returning to her previous spot.

The whine still hurt her ears, but it'd lessened a hair. Enough that she could notice, anyway.

Everyone looked back to Professor Longakers. "It did

reduce the build up a little, a fraction of a percent. Maybe we have a few more minutes of time at best."

"Please," said Aurie. "Give her a chance. She can do it. She's my sister. Nothing's going to stop her."

Celesse almost looked ready to agree until one of her mages pointed to Pi's body on the floor. Blood pooled in her closed eyes, running down her cheeks. Her forehead had been split wide open, and the skin on her arms bubbled and blackened as if she was being roasted alive.

"Something got her," said one of the mages.

"I think they're killing her."

To make matters worse, the Engine increased in frequency, leaving everyone with their hands cupped over their ears. Aurie almost expected every piece of glass in the room to shatter.

"Aurie! Get out of the way!" yelled Professor Mali. "There's no more time!"

The mages with Celesse weren't waiting. They stepped forward to move her, whether she wanted to or not. Aurie looked down at her broken and burnt sister. She didn't even know if Pi was breathing anymore, but feared to check, or give Celesse a chance at Semyon.

How could she let everyone die so she could save her sister? She knew her parents would have forgiven her. They would have told her to step out of the way, let the transfer happen to save the students of Arcanium. But it was *her* sister. The bright-eyed fierce cub who never took no for an answer. The sister who put the ointment on her feet when she accidently turned the floor stove-hot trying to improve their imaginary "Floor is Lava" game. The best friend who never bragged about her ability, even though she was better than her older sister at everything. The person who made her ache with fever just at the thought of losing her.

"No," said Aurie, preparing herself for battle. "I'm not

moving. I'm not giving up on Pi. Never ever. You'll have to kill me if you want to destroy Semyon and my sister and ruin Arcanium and the Halls."

Celesse looked almost disappointed that it would have to come to violence, but she seemed ready, giving her three mages a heavy nod.

"Quickly now. Before we die in a temporal explosion."

31

There was a lot to say about the quality of pain as Pi lay in the pebble-strewn grass under a sweltering blue sky, receiving crackling bolts of electricity from the outstretched fingers of Priyanka Sai. She realized there were levels of pain she'd never considered until that moment.

The flesh on her left arm had cracked open like a pig on a spit after the flesh had been charred until the fat burst forth. Pi realized that the fat from her arm smelled almost as sweet as bacon, bringing laughing tears.

"See," said Bannon. "She's a Rider. Mad as they come."

"Water," said Pi, gasping like a fish on dry land. "Please."

The hoarse screams and the quivering bolts of electricity had sucked the moisture from her mouth and throat. Water seemed more of a priority than escaping or lessening the pain, which at this point was like having a knife dug into her bone.

"Where is Malden?" asked Celesse in her Southern accent, clearly distressed. "He should be back with that girl by now. Two Riders in one place. Unusual."

Bannon had kept his ghostly shield and sword, standing over Pi as if he planned to behead her at any moment.

"This one is more powerful than the others," said Bannon.

"We should kill it and be done. If it gets away, he'll be quite unhappy."

"Hush," said Priyanka, the corners of her lips curling downward. "Not everything can be solved with a sword or your fist. Violence is a tool, not a result."

Pi lay on her side, staring at the blackened flesh of her right arm, wondering if death was preferable to this pained existence. At the moment, living was winning, but she felt her resolve waning.

The only thing keeping her going was that failure meant disaster for Aurie too. Damn them all if they thought she was going to give up when her sister's life was in danger.

Pi tried to move her fingers in a spell, but the damage to her muscles and tendons had left her right arm inoperable. The fingers only twitched when she tried to move them. With her dry mouth, she didn't think she could use the Voice.

Using her knees and one arm, Pi started crawling towards the road. The four patrons had horses on the other side of the cottage. If she could only get to them...and if the three patrons ignored her...and if she could actually climb onto the horse... if...

"She's a resilient one," said Priyanka, standing over Pi. "I almost feel bad about what we had to do."

"Why do they keep attacking us?" asked Celesse.

"In this case, we were the ones who attacked," said Priyanka dryly.

"This I know," said Celesse indignantly. "I am aware of what we did. I mean the others. Rare has been the chance to turn the tables, but I don't feel right about what we've done."

Pi felt Bannon's presence move away.

"British cavalry are coming," he said from up the road.

"Curse him. Colonel Gray shows up everywhere," said Priyanka.

Pi had managed to work herself into a shaky-legged crouch position. She felt like a mouse being toyed with by a pack of feral felines.

"What do we do with her?" asked Celesse.

"We should kill it," said Bannon.

"I'm not sure," said Priyanka. "She seems different."

"We should let her go," said Celesse. "For all we know, she's like us. But we didn't give her a chance."

"If she's a Rider..." said Bannon.

"I have a better idea," said Priyanka. "We'll leave her for the colonel. He dislikes the Riders as much as we, and even if he doesn't, he'll hang her for a witch. And I'd prefer not to stay around for additional debate."

"Agreed," said Celesse.

Bannon growled. "This decision will come to haunt us. Mark my words. But for now I will go with the consensus."

As Pi wobbled on her bent legs, the three patrons ran to their horses on the other side of the cottage. She glanced to the west, seeing only the dust cloud of incoming cavalry from her position, but knowing her time was short.

She tried to stand, but the strength in her legs had been robbed by the lightning. Pi made a half-step then collapsed, landing hard on her right arm, turning her vision crimson from the pain.

When she came to, she was no further to the cottage, and the British cavalry was closer. If she could only get to the fourth horse, the one Malden had left, she might escape.

"Here, horsy," she whispered. "Water. I need water."

Pi crawled towards the broken wagon. The distance was only a few meters, but it felt like a marathon. When she reached the timbers, she moved them out of the way to find a ripped water pouch spilling its precious cargo into the dirt. Pi leaned down and sucked at the muddy water, taking in bugs and mud, but feeling her tongue unstick from the roof of her mouth.

With her throat lubricated, Pi attempted the Voice on the remaining horse, hoping it would work on an animal as easily as it did on humans.

"Come here."

The first attempt cracked her voice.

Pi swallowed. Tried again.

"Horse. Come here."

This time her voice carried across the distance. The horse's ears perked up, but otherwise the mount stayed in its spot and went back to chewing grass.

Pi was about to try a third time when a fit of coughing brought her to her side. When she was finished, she didn't have the energy to climb to her knees and call the horse again. The use of the Voice had drained her.

When the tromp of a hoof near her head startled her, she thought the British had arrived. But then she realized Malden's horse had come as called. This gave her a spark. She climbed to her feet, laborious and slow, grabbing onto the stirrups for leverage. Pulling herself up the side of the horse was like climbing Mount Everest, but she managed on the first try, flopping herself over.

The British officers on horseback were less than a football field away. Pi had never ridden a horse in her life, and when she nudged it towards the road, it took off at a back-breaking trot that nearly caused her to black out when the impact shook her burnt arms.

To Pi's surprise, the black horse—sensing pursuit—took off down the road, forcing her to grab the reins and hold on. She felt like a spring broken loose and dangling from a whirling clockwork.

There was no way she was going to outrun the cavalry in

her condition, but she spurred the horse to go faster, hitting the saddlebags with her heel. Leaning to the side to bring her left arm across her body, she dug into the leather pouch, bringing forth a glass vial with a vile looking brown liquid in it.

Using her teeth, she unstoppered it, giving the mixture a sniff. Mint. Maybe the breath of a hellhound. There was a fifty-fifty chance that the potion might heal her, or at least improve her in some way. On the bad side, she'd probably not survive drinking it.

Without another thought, Pi threw the liquid into the back of her throat. It burned like minty hot sauce, which made her gag and almost toss it right back up. When it hit her stomach it was like a wildfire had been lit inside her. Actual smoke puffed from her lips, and before she'd finished a second breath, she felt like an Olympic athlete about to sprint the hundred-meter dash.

Pi grabbed the reins firmly and gave them a flick, sending her mount into a sprint. The black horse shimmered in the afternoon sun, muscles flexing, mane whipping against Pi's hands as she rode away from the British.

The pain in her right arm was distant, but she knew the damage was extensive, and she'd pay later, but she didn't have time. The road traversed a series of hills which she took at full gallop. After about a half hour, she sensed the elixir wearing off and slowed, fearing a rebound effect.

The potion had given her excellent reflexes, so she held onto the horse with her thighs and used the temporary flexibility of her fingers to heal her arm enough that she would be capable of using it after the potion had worn off.

Free from pursuit, Pi worried about the time desolation blocking her from her destination, but as she neared, she sensed that her way would be clear.

She didn't know exactly where she needed to go, especially

without a GPS phone to tell her the location, but as she trotted down the road, she felt a slight pulling to the left. She followed her instincts when she found a dirt road that headed into the forest and rode for another five hours, breaking off into the wilderness when the road turned to undergrowth. She hadn't hit the Delaware River, so she knew she hadn't gone too far.

The wells of power grew stronger as she neared the location that would eventually become the city of Invictus. Without the modern metropolis built up and layered with faez, it was easier to sense the wells. Before it was like trying to use a compass in an MRI machine.

When she sensed that she was within a mile of the source of power, she kicked the haunches of her mount, spurring it forward. Halfway there, she spied a cottage on the other side of a small lake, and immediately, she knew who lived there without thinking about it.

The detour would take another half hour to wind around, not including the time spent if the occupant actually lived at that destination. Aurie and the rest of Arcanium needed her to dissipate the energy in the Temporal Engine, but here was an opportunity she couldn't pass up, even if it wasn't the real person, and only a figment made up of Semyon's and the other patrons' memories.

Pi pulled on the reins, turning the horse towards the cottage. There was no smoke coming from the chimney, but it was summer, so she hadn't expected it, but if no one was home, she was going to feel foolish.

Hopping off the horse, Pi jogged to the door. As she lifted her hand to knock, a deep voice said, "Come in, traveler."

The power in his voice shook her, even from beyond the door. It was like hearing the granite bedrock of the earth speak.

She pushed through the door, pulling up short when her

gaze fell upon him. Invictus.

"Greetings," he said, eyes sparkling with deep knowledge, like vast underground caves piled with books. For a moment, as his gaze shifted across her, her limbs trembled. She sensed his power, like standing next to a blast furnace and desiring to move away.

He was seated at a table, carving a hunk of bone with a paring knife. A pile of pale, curled bone-slivers had collected at the edge of the table.

Invictus was not much different than what she'd seen in pictures or shows, except that his wavy shoulder-length black hair had a healthy luster. He was shorter than she'd expected. For some reason, she'd always thought he was a towering figure, but she guessed that Aurie might almost be as tall. His warm, nut-brown skin tones suggested many origins.

"Hello...I mean, greetings," she said, glancing around the room at the many objects in the cluttered cottage.

There were, of course, the requisite books and tomes with silvery symbols, or other names she read at a glance: *The Maharal of Prague*, *Alphabet of the Magi*, *On the Value of Games*, *The Diary of Farmer Weathersky*, *The Magician and his Pupil*. Shoved into shelves and empty spaces were treasures such as a desiccated mummy hand missing the pinky finger, a geode in the shape of a skull with its tongue sticking out, an azure glass ball containing a billowing gas, empty vials in the shape of pyramids, a row of alchemy reagents (or cooking spices, she couldn't tell), a puddle of sunlight that oozed around the corner of the room, and other curiosities she had no time to investigate.

"You've come because of the wells, haven't you?" he asked, eyebrow raised into a magnificent arch.

"I...uhm, yes."

His expression fell flat. "Then why did you stop here?"

She glanced at the door, wondering if she'd made a mistake in coming. What if he didn't let her leave?

"I...I wanted to ask permission," she said, feeling like she'd entered a part of Semyon's memory with different rules, "and ask a question."

His lips spread into a smile that unlocked her breath. "A wise choice, the first part. Tell me, why do you need the wells? Do not lie to me, or I'll know." Without taking his eyes from her, he knocked another chip from the bone with his knife. If she squinted, the carving appeared to be a feline with ears pinned back clutching a sword. The cat-knight was perched on a base. She saw other figures on a shelf in the back of the room that suggested he was carving a chess set.

She had no idea if telling this figment of Semyon's imagination the real truth would create problems, but she couldn't exactly lie to him either.

"I need to save my friends," said Pi, "and I need to use the wells to do it. It's hard to explain much more than that without giving away secrets I'm not allowed to talk about."

"You can tell me or I will not answer your question," said Invictus.

Pi hesitated, and he flicked the end of his knife towards the door, and it slammed shut, then he went back to carving. She had a sinking feeling that the bone he was carving was not animal.

"I can't tell you, or it'll trigger a curse. Look, I know we don't know each other, or at least that you don't know me, but I know you. I know some people you know as well. Malden Anterist, Celesse D'Agastine, Priyanka Sai, Bannon Creed, and Semyon Gray. I even know why you know them. You want to bring them together to form a school of magic, though I have no idea how, because Semyon is a witch-hunter, and the rest of them are battling Riders, and they don't seem to like each other at all, which I guess, now that I think about it, is unsurprising."

The soft call of a cat came from the room behind the one they were in, though Pi could not see the animal. It appeared that space was a kitchen, of sorts.

"Excuse me," he said, setting his knife and carving onto the table before fetching a bowl from a shelf and setting it onto the floor. A tabby cat darted forward and shoved its face directly into the bowl, noisily eating while flicking its tail. Invictus stroked his hand across the cat's back before returning to the table.

"What do you want to know?" he asked.

"How did you get them to work together?" she asked, thinking about Aurie's description of previous visits and her own interactions with them. "At times, they seem like best friends, at other, mortal enemies. I have witnessed their schemes and backstabbing, yet they have come together for bigger things. Why?"

"It appears you know them better than I expected. It is true, they are a contradiction."

"They're a dysfunctional family, if you ask me," said Pi.

A hint of mirth perched itself on Invictus' lips. He snorted softly. "Dysfunctional family. This is truer than anything I have ever heard before."

"Then how did you do it?" she asked. "How did you get them to work together?"

If she could figure this out, maybe she could fix what had been happening in the Hundred Halls. The thought of which gave her a stab of irony, since she of all people had been the Halls' biggest critic.

"Knowing that might spoil the fun, though I can tell you that you can't force someone to be something they're not," said Invictus.

The arguments poised on her lips evaporated. Not only because time was short, and she'd wasted too much already, but she cursed her naiveté that this memory of Invictus might know the answer, when of course it wouldn't since this wasn't the real him. A cryptic answer was all she would receive no matter how much she pressed him. Shame at wasting time for her curiosity while more important events were in the balance brought heat to her face.

"I have to go," she said, hoping he would not bar her way.

He nodded with his eyes towards the door, and it clicked open. The weight of her burden returned.

She opened her mouth to say her farewell, but noticed he'd returned to his carving, completely ignoring her. She was, in a way, a figment to him, as much as he was to her.

Pi pushed through the door, relieved when she saw her mount was chewing on a fern by the path to the cottage, then she heard Invictus speak, his words sending shivers down her spine:

"When the error of the quarterarch you shall know, then through the thresholds you shall flow."

The soul fragment from Oculus woke briefly in her head, indicating the words had the force of prophecy behind them. Before she could turn and ask about the nature of his statement, the door slammed shut, the finality of it shaking dust from the rafters of the porch.

"I have to go," she reminded herself.

His cryptic words would have to be a mystery for another time. For now, she needed to fix the Temporal Engine, or there would be no time to return to.

The air was fresh and clean, except that which she desired. Pi smelled her way to the well of power, following the sharpness of faez, like a bloodhound on the hunt. The black steed galloped through the trees, leaping small ravines and fallen logs.

When she reached the spring-fed pond, she knew it was the source of the faez. Moss-covered rocks surrounded the western edge, where the sun cast itself upon it, but did not reflect against the water's surface. The pond seemed to exist in the forest without actually being a part of it. Pi crouched down to get a closer look at the water, expecting to see a mirrored surface, but the water reflected nothing, only a pale blankness like a canvas yet unpainted. She dipped her fingers into the bone-chillingly cool water, and upon that touch, sensed the influence of faez, like a low-level electrical current in the water.

The water was bubbling from the cluster of boulders, so Pi moved towards it. A tiny purple-tailed lizard scurried away when she approached on foot. As she climbed over the rocks, careful with her steps due to the slickness of the moss, she realized the pond itself was not the source, but a symptom. The spring bubbled up from deep in the earth because the faez had burrowed its way up, forging a path for the water.

Unspent faez lingered in the air. The closer she was to the hole in the earth, the stronger the magic. At the center of the boulders, there was a hole that went into the ground. She felt like she was standing near a gas leak. Pi was dizzy with power.

She also sensed it was nowhere near the levels that existed in her world, which meant they'd excavated the wells, bringing more power, but also danger. No one knew where faez came from, or why certain people could channel it, but that it existed was undeniable.

Pi pushed her mind to silence, focusing on the soul fragments, conjuring them to the forefront of her mind. If she was going to utilize the well, she needed more souls to channel it. She hoped that with thirteen of them, and the never-ending source of faez from the well, she could disperse the energy in the Temporal Engine enough to make her reality safe.

She lifted her arms to the sky, preparing a salvo of concentrated elements, when an arrow went right through her shoulder, the point sticking from her chest.

Pi collapsed onto the rocks, slipping hard to land against the boulders. Her feet dunked into the ice-cold water.

Not five meters from her location, Jade aimed another arrow at Pi.

"Twitch a fingernail and I'll impale you. You're not faster than an arrow," said Jade, shifting closer.

Pi coughed, blood splattering against her half-burnt hand. The arrow had gone through her shoulder and nicked her lung. She sensed the growing warmth through her chest.

"Why?" asked Pi, struggling even with one word.

"Don't you see?" said Jade, almost shouting as she moved closer. "They're ruining it. They always ruin it. Look at how beautiful this place is, and now there's steel and concrete and shit piled over top. We have to stop it. *I* have to stop it. And that starts now."

"What about Adler?" Pi asked, wheezing.

Jade blinked, didn't seem to understand until Pi added, "Your sister?"

"Of course, my sister. Her too. I will avenge what they did to her," said Jade, glancing behind her as if she expected someone to be lurking there.

"You're going to hurt people," said Pi, fighting through the pain to speak. "You're going to hurt my sister."

Jade released the tension in the bowstring. Her knotted forehead with fraught with pain. "Don't you see? None of this is right. I'm helping you. Helping your sister. Freeing you from all of this."

"Death? You put an arrow into my shoulder. I'd hardly call that freedom. You're trying to kill us. You're mad," said Pi, and then when she repeated it a second time, she realized that was the root of it. "You're mad as a hatter, Jade Umbra."

"Don't say that," growled Jade, pulling the bowstring again. The arrowhead was pointed right at her heart.

There was no denying it now. Pi realized the truth, the truth that should have been evident all along. She'd been warning Jade about faez madness since the very beginning, but she'd thought it was a conspiracy by the patrons, to keep them subjugated to the Hundred Halls.

Pi wondered if Jade even had a sister or if she'd been influenced by her surroundings. How long had Jade been in the Undercity practicing with magic, slowly driving herself insane? Guilt tickled at her thoughts, reminding Pi that she'd had a part in this.

The worst thing about faez madness was that it was incurable, and unreconcilable. There was no reasoning with someone who had developed it. Pi's mistake was that she hadn't seen it earlier. As she thought back to her and Jade's relationship, she realized there were clues, but she'd been blinded by her feelings for Jade and her mistrust of the Hundred Halls.

The worst part was that it removed the maliciousness of Jade's behavior. Pi could forgive her now, even with that arrow notched to kill, because she knew it wasn't really her. Which made it more difficult. It was hard to hurt someone when you loved them.

"Jade," said Pi, coughing. "Can we go back to what we had before? Let's forget the Halls, forget the Misfits, and run away from Invictus, just you and I."

Jade's eyes were oscillating between narrowing and widening. "You're trying to trick me."

"Jade. When have I ever done that?" asked Pi, every word an agony. "You were the one that tricked me into drinking that potion, and stole my pin and jacket, and shot my sister.

I just wanted to stay in the Undercity with you, read books, explore the deepest places. Maybe we could be adventurers, learn the history of what transpired in those dark places, find the artifacts lost."

The tip of the arrow dipped as Pi spoke, until it was pointed at the ground. Pi thought she was making progress until she noticed the trees on the other side of the pond dissolving into dust. She was out of time, the desolation had reached her.

Jade, who'd been slowing, turning introspective, suddenly followed the line of Pi's gaze, turning back towards the destruction of Semyon's mental landscape.

"You lie! You're trying to trick me!"

Pi used the brief window before Jade could bring the bow around to fire a force bolt from her fingertips. Her intent had only been to knock Jade out, but the presence of vast amounts of unspent faez turned the simple bolt into a cruise missile. In the blink of an eye, Jade was thrown into the collapsing trees like a doll from a catapult.

"Jade, no!" coughed Pi, then realizing she had no time for mourning—not even time enough to cast the return spell— she opened her conduit to the well, and collapsing against the boulders with an arrow sticking through her shoulder, she sent her magic straight into the sky.

And while the power surged through her—she felt a god.

32

The three mages moved on Aurie. She stood with her back against the gurney that held Semyon Gray while the monitors beeped frantically with alarm and the Temporal Engine wailed in its death throes.

Celesse was working through a spell, drawing pictograms in the air, golden sparks erupting from her fingertip, the spray dancing off the tables and wires.

Before the first mage could reach Aurie, Professor Mali stuck her foot out, tripping him to crash headfirst into a table with a heavy monitor on top. The two mages behind the first tried to keep the device from landing on him.

As the chaos whirled around Aurie, she spotted the gun Jade had shot her with. It had gotten knocked beneath the table. Aurie scrambled to her knees and, coming up with it pointed at Celesse, screamed over the Engine's teeth-rattling vibration, "Stop or I'll kill her!"

There was a good chance that Celesse had protections against bullets, but the wild-eyed glance from the golden-haired patron revealed that detail might have been missed before coming to Arcanium, or at the very least, she wasn't ready to test them.

Everyone froze.

Celesse's unfinished spell faded away like summer fireworks.

Aurie had no plan, except to keep them from killing Semyon, and by way of transference, her sister.

There was a good thirty seconds of staring, occasional shifting of the eyes, and the oppressive beeping of the equipment. The standoff lasted until Professor Longakers shouted, "It's working. The Engine is receding!"

Aurie had been so focused on Celesse and the Alchemist mages she hadn't realized the whine was coming down like an airplane landing. Her eardrums no longer felt like they were being pounded into oblivion, though they still rung as if she'd been at a heavy metal concert for twenty-four hours.

"This doesn't change anything. Arcanium voted, I get control. This Hall is mine," said Celesse, pointing at her chest. She motioned to her mages, who were climbing to their feet. "Take her. The bullet won't get through my protections. Her bluff is meaningless."

Before Aurie could point the weapon at the three mages, one of them pulled a wand from a pocket and made her hands cramp into claws, forcing her to drop the gun. They had her in their grasp before she could do anything to stop them, slapping magic-dampening manacles on her wrists, pulling a gag over her mouth to keep her from using verumancy.

They dragged her away from Semyon, letting Celesse approach. She stepped over the fallen equipment, gave a respectful nod to the two professors, and placed her hand on Semyon's chest.

"I'm sorry, old friend. I wish there was another way. If I don't do this, the others will move against you with force. In the end, it's best I take your students. The Hundred Halls will be no more, but at least I can make them safe."

Celesse brushed her fingertips against his forehead in a loving manner before taking a deep breath and settling her palms on his temples.

As Celesse chanted softly, the spell weaving through the air like a wistful song, Aurie struggled against her bonds. How could they make her watch? Part of her begged that they'd just kill her, rather than make her be witness to her sister's death.

Aurie searched the room for Pi's body, but the chaos had knocked things out of place, and she couldn't see her anymore. She kicked the mage holding her, struggled against his grip, but the other two grabbed her, keeping Aurie locked down. She shouted against the gag, tried to spit it out as she felt the spell coming to its conclusion.

No! Dooset daram! I didn't get to say goodbye!

Tears filled her eyes, turning the room into a watery tomb. Aurie sagged against her captors.

"Step away from my sister's patron."

The words barely registered. Aurie heard them from the bottom of a hole. When she blinked away the tears, she saw her sister, hands poised for spellcraft.

Aurie choked against the gag. *She's alive!*

"I'm thrumming with faez," said Pi, in her dirty bloodstained peasant dress that made her look like a child playing dress up. "So unless you want to find yourself launched into space, I suggest you step away from Semyon Gray, and let my sister go."

Celesse pulled her hands away from Semyon's head, but gave no indication that the other mages should follow. Aurie struggled against them, but they held her fast.

"You're no match for me," said Celesse, raising her chin with supreme indignance.

Pi raised an eyebrow and spoke with such icy calm she could have cut glass. "Think about how much faez had to be spent for the Temporal Engine to be stone quiet. I did that. And there's plenty left over." Her sister gave a bloody grin. "And if you even dent my sister's hair, I'll feed your bits to the Watcher in the pool."

Celesse looked to the runed brass cylinder on Semyon's chest and weighed the amount of power that had to have passed through Pi. And it wasn't just the Alchemist Patron. Everyone in the room, Aurie included, was visibly doing the calculations.

The only advantage that Aurie had was that she knew why her sister had survived such a display of power—the soul fragments. She should have seen that sooner herself. They'd been thinking about bringing other mages into Semyon's dreamscape to dissipate the energy faster, but Pi was the ultimate converter with thirteen souls at her disposal.

Celesse let the corners of her lips curl slightly. "While I respect your impressive display of magical aptitude, you cannot stand against our combined power. Plus, we have your sister, and while I'm rather fond of you both, I'll hurt you if it comes to that."

Aurie tensed for the impending battle. There was no way her sister was going to back down from such a threat. Much to Aurie's surprise, Pi said, "Fair enough." Then she walked over to Semyon's desk, grabbed a piece of paper, scribbled on it, and handed it over to Celesse, who'd been watching the sudden change with confusion and interest.

At first, Celesse looked like she was going to crumple up the paper, and then she glanced back up at Pi, who wore a grave expression that, combined with the state of her clothing, made her look like she was the last survivor of a horror movie.

"You know it's true," said Pi.

"How?" asked Celesse, a hint of emotion in her voice.

Pi did not answer. She only nodded towards Semyon,

which set Celesse's wheels spinning.

"We're stronger now," said Celesse defiantly.

"And so are they. That one nearly killed my sister before you got here," said Pi, pointing to the still body of Jade. "She got into Arcanium by herself, when none of the Cabal could. There's an army of them waiting to take control. You know the charter is the only thing that keeps them back."

"The other patrons will kill him, then it won't matter," said Celesse, seemingly desperate.

"We know how to operate the Engine now," said Pi. "And I can protect them."

"Doubtful," said Celesse, whose hands suddenly couldn't find a place to rest. She didn't appear to believe her own words, as she danced on her stationary feet.

"Fuck!" she finally exclaimed, squeezing her hands into fists. She snapped at her mages. "Let her go. It's over."

They did not question her, but Aurie could sense their stunned disappointment. Professor Mali and Longakers looked on in confusion.

When the manacles were off, Aurie rubbed her wrists. The rag they'd stuffed in her mouth tasted like mothballs, but there was no water around to rinse.

"I hope you know what you're doing," said Celesse to Pi before she left.

Once the Alchemist Patron was gone, Aurie threw herself into Pi's arms.

"You saved us," said Aurie.

"For once," laughed Pi. "I thought it was my turn."

Professor Mali rolled over to the bed, and before she could grab the scrap of paper on Semyon's chest, Pi snatched it up. The professor glared back with impunity before softening into a frown.

"I'm sorry, Professor. I have to protect certain secrets."

Pi snapped her fingers, and the paper burnt to a crisp.

"No need to apologize," said Professor Mali. "I was curious. I'm simply happy that everyone's alive, and Arcanium is safe."

Professor Longakers cleared his throat from behind his row of computers. "I do not think that girl who shot Aurie is alive."

It was brief, but Aurie caught her sister's jaw clench as she held back her grief.

"I'll take care of Jade," said Pi. "Though she didn't realize it, she was a big help in fixing this."

Aurie pulled Pi in for a long hug. Both of them kept their tears in check, but she sensed the floodwalls wouldn't withstand the pressure much longer. They had things to do first.

"What now?" asked Aurie, holding Pi at arm's length. "You look like you got dragged behind a wagon for a few miles."

"I'd like a hot shower, a warm meal, and a few hours' sleep, and then I'm ready to go back in," said Pi.

"A few more sessions like that and Semyon will be on the road to recovery," said Professor Longakers.

"Are you sure?" asked Aurie. "Should I come with?"

Pi nodded, a secret smile on her lips. "Only to get me inside, then I can do the rest. I'm much better on my own."

"That's what I'm afraid of," said Aurie.

"Don't worry, sis. I'm not going anywhere."

"Even after Arcanium is fixed?"

"No," said Pi. "I've given up on running away. Even if I'm not a part of the Halls, I'm still staying here. This place is too important."

"It's weird hearing that from you," said Aurie.

"It's weird hearing it from my own lips. But this year has taught me that even dysfunctional family is family, and keeping it together is better than the alternative."

33

After another week of trips into Semyon's mind to balance the Temporal Engine, Professor Longakers declared that Semyon's soul was reconnected with his body and would require normal healing from then on. The students of Arcanium could use magic again, though sparingly until their patron was back on his feet, which was estimated to occur before the new school year.

This freed Pi to return to Big Dave's Town. Jade's body had been sent down a few days before, and kept in suspended animation until the burial.

Pi had been in contact with the Misfits to coordinate the details. None of them planned to stay in the area after Jade's death, so they would entomb her on the little island. Aurie had found a couple of spells that would ensure no denizens of the Undercity disturbed Jade's final resting place.

The other women greeted her warmly when she arrived on the island, even Sisi, who didn't release their hug for a couple of awkward minutes. No one spoke really, but after the battle against the Cabal in the street, Pi felt no need for small talk until after the ceremony.

A solemn procession brought them to the back of the

island. Their living quarters had been dismantled, replaced with a stone cairn beneath which the body of Jade Umbra lay. The other ladies watched while Pi drew runes around the burial grounds with a gold-flecked paint that would last for centuries. When the last words of the enchantment fell from Pi's lips, the runes exploded white for a millisecond, before disappearing into near invisibility.

"I knew her longest, so I'll go first," said Sasha, straightening her black dress, which made her look like a fashionable Catholic priest. She took a spot before the cairn as if she were about to lecture her. "Jade Umbra—if that's what your name really was—you tried to kill our friend, betrayed us in the name of revenge, and nearly ended the lives of thousands of people. Pi tells me that you did this because you'd succumbed to faez madness, which you'd always told us was a myth, and now I'm forced with deciding between believing you, which would mean you're a liar and a killer or accepting that it's real. I'd be a fool if I choose to continue what you taught us, especially because that would mean we'd end up like you, and tarnish the memories of our friendship, which I cherished when you were alive. I guess I'm saying I forgive you, and miss you, and wish to God that we'd figured this out before it killed you. Peace to you, Jade. May you rest well in eternity."

After Sasha stepped back to the group, Bethany took her place at the head of the cairn. She held her jean jacket close to her body, squeezing it around her.

"Jade," said Bethany, choking slightly, then clearing her throat. "You took me in when I had nobody else. You didn't care that I'm a walking anatomy demonstration. And though I don't know what to think about what happened at the end, I'll miss you for all time. I...I honestly don't know what I'm going to do now, especially since we're all leaving."

Bethany was wild-eyed and frightened. Sasha pulled her

in for a hug when she shuffled back to the group.

Nancy stepped forward and saluted the cairn with her stone arm. "You made us family, when nobody else gave a shit. So I guess, thank you."

Yoko took her place, pulled a hunk of copper from her pocket, and set it on the closest rocks. She whispered to the lump and a flame flickered into life, dancing across the amber metal.

"This spell will last exactly one year. I will return every year and renew the flame as thanks for our friendship. I miss you, Jade," said Yoko.

Everyone's gaze shifted to Sisi, since it was expected that Pi would be last, but when they looked to the petite girl, she fled in tears.

"We each grieve in our own way," said Yoko, to which everyone nodded.

Pi approached last, kissed her fingertips and brushed them against the rough stone.

She didn't speak for a couple of minutes, but when she did, it felt like she was half stuck in a dream.

"I think I was in love with you. Not that forever-love thing that little girls dream about, but in the way someone says about another person, hey, I really like spending time with you and want to do it a whole lot more. Like every waking moment, you know." Pi bit her lower lip until she could speak again. "The thing that hurts the most was that my feelings made me blind to what was really going on with you. It makes me distrust that love, because I didn't know what the faez was doing to you. I mean, maybe you were already too far gone when I met you, but the rational part of me can't see that. It just sees that love as the shove that finally pushed you over the cliff." She blinked, looked around, felt the weight of the others' presence. "I guess, I have to say that even after everything that happened, I still love you, and am going to miss you."

She stumbled back to the group, delirious with emotion. They collapsed around her, and before she knew it, she was sobbing uncontrollably into someone's shoulder, apologizing about getting tears on their dress.

After they were drained, the Misfits moved to the front of the island, where a cooler of beer awaited. The first round disappeared during quiet reflection. Halfway through their second beer, they started making small talk. Sisi returned then, and Pi quieted them for an announcement.

"I know you're each planning on going your separate ways, but before you go, I want to give you something. You can use it or not, but know that the price for this gift has already been paid," she said.

They glanced amongst themselves at her cryptic words.

"I cannot, in good conscience, allow you each to continue your magic without some measure of protection."

Bethany blurted out, "Are you going to be our patron?"

There was a lot of excitement in their eyes, which tugged at her heart for multiple reasons—first, because they'd distrusted her so thoroughly when she'd first arrived, and second, because they would be willing to trust her with that kind of bond.

"No. No," said Pi, waving them down. "Maybe someday I'll do that, but not right now. I have some things I need to work on. But I do know someone that can help you find a patron. Not from the Hundred Halls, of course. His name is Radoslav. He'll speak with you individually and determine the best person who you could pledge to. I promise none of them are scoundrels, though many—probably all—are linked to the criminal underworld. I'm sorry, it's the best I can do. You don't have to use this, but it's there if you change your mind. I don't want to see anyone else getting hurt."

Everyone thanked her, and she could see they each had to

do some soul searching before they decided. Feeling suddenly like she wanted to be alone, Pi said her goodbyes, made them all promise they would contact her if they ever needed help, and took the rowboat back to the far shore.

She went back to Big Dave's Town, returning to the room above the Devil's Lipstick where she and Jade had last spent the night together. She went through her things, partially hoping to find some clue to Jade's condition, and also hoping not to find anything, because then that meant her death was preventable. When no signs amid her belongings were uncovered, Pi poured a glass of whiskey and sipped it while sitting on the edge of the bed. When she no longer wanted to be awake, Pi curled onto the bed in her clothes, pulled the pillow to her face, and inhaled the lingering perfume.

34

The waterfall thundered against the pool beneath Arcanium, spreading a mist across the floor near the stairs. As the light spray kissed Aurie's ankles, she motioned to her sister, who was following behind with her leather jacket slung over her shoulder.

"Did you really swim through the moat?" she asked.

Pi crouched by the water, ran her fingertips through it. "Thanks, buddy, for not squishing me down there."

To Aurie's surprise, a dark shape passed under the surface. A semblance of a wave if she judged her cephalopods right.

"Let's go," said Aurie. "We have an errand to attend to after this."

"Always the taskmistress," said Pi.

They found Semyon in his apartment, sitting on the couch with a blanket over his legs, the glow from a tablet highlighting his face as he studied an electronic text. His face was gaunt, and his eyes were hollow.

Professor Chopra was sitting with him, and got up the moment they arrived. He looked like he didn't know what to do with his hands at first, then to Aurie's surprise, he reached out and offered a handshake.

"Thank you for what you did," he said, then without another word, hurried from the room.

"The Silverthornes," said Semyon with a grin. "Welcome, and have a seat. I have much to thank you for."

"We can't stay long. We have an appointment," said Aurie, glancing at the runed brass cylinder resting in an obsidian cradle.

"Yes, I see," he said. "Certain things must be attended to. I won't ask how you convinced him to give that up, nor how you even became aware of him. I promise I won't keep you too long. But I'm sure you have questions for me as well."

"Was that all true?" asked Pi suddenly. "What we experienced in there. Was it?"

Semyon took on a pensive cast. "I assume you lived through my memories."

Pi stepped forward. "You don't know? You didn't direct those?"

He shifted his blankets, cleared his throat. "I remember being stuck in a void, connected by the barest thread, floating in a vast endless nothing. Through the bond I share with Arcanium, I sensed the danger that the school was in. My mind was not clear in this place, I was a collection of thoughts, trying to rub enough together to create a spark of life. So I directed nothing about what you experienced, though I have a guess, based on where my thoughts trended in those times."

"We experienced the days before the Halls were formed. When you were a colonel in the British army hunting witches," said Aurie. "We met the other patrons too."

In her presence, Semyon had always been in complete control, from the time he'd rescued her after the trials, to when he'd battled the soul thief in the statue. He appeared suddenly sheepish, as if he wanted to be anywhere in the world but that location.

"That is, of course, something I am not proud of. Those were different times, and I was a different person," said Semyon.

"We understand," said Pi. "Invictus brought you together to fight the Riders."

Semyon raised a surprised eyebrow. "A convenient fiction. But it worked, for the most part."

"So you know there's no such thing?" asked Pi.

"I figured it out decades later. I always wondered if the others knew, but I guess we know what Celesse thinks," said Semyon with a rare smirk. "The other thing to consider is that the other patrons were connected to me in that place. The charter is a bond stronger than blood, but less than death. Those could have been their thoughts as well. It's possible that one of them might have directed the memories, consciously or unconsciously."

Her sister looked like she was holding back secret information. Aurie wanted to press her, but it was clear she didn't want to speak in front of Semyon.

"Have you ever been friends?" Aurie asked.

"Of course," said Semyon. "There were many good years, decades, in fact. Many more good ones than bad ones." He looked away. "These days there are far too many bad ones."

"What went wrong?" asked Aurie.

He set the tablet on the couch next to him and folded his hands in his lap. "At times I feel like we're a family that lost its last parent, and the children are fighting over the inheritance."

Before the events of the last year, Aurie had always struggled imagining the original patrons together in a familial way, but now she couldn't help but feel sorrow for the bonds lost.

Semyon's tablet chimed, announcing a call. Before they politely excused themselves, Aurie scooped up the Engine of Temporal Manipulation, placing the artifact in a magic-dampening backpack before closing the door behind them.

Without attacks from the Cabal to worry about, they took the Red Line to the twelfth ward. The old industrial area hadn't changed since their visit earlier in the year, but it didn't have the same menacing feel. Past the chained gate, the fallen barrels of waste contained rocks with sprouts of grass growing on them, rather than glowing puddles.

When they reached the area that had once been an autumnal forest frozen in time, they were speechless. The trees were gray, leafless, and unmoving. Aurie wandered to the nearest, running her fingers across the rough surface.

"They're petrified," she said in awe. "The whole damn forest."

"The sudden return to the present time must have petrified them," said Pi.

The ground was dead, dusty. Nothing was growing. Nothing was alive.

"I wonder if this place will ever recover," said Aurie.

"It reminds me of the desolation."

Aurie turned to her sister. "Back in Semyon's, it looked like you were going to say something, but you held back. What was it?"

Her sister glanced around as if she suspected they were being spied upon. "I'll tell you when we're in a safer space. This place gives me the creeps."

Their footsteps reverberated through the stone forest, making Aurie check over her shoulder frequently.

"I figured out who Jade Umbra was," said Pi, clearly trying to take the creepiness out of their journey. "Knowing she had faez madness helped me figure it out. Everyone in the Misfits had a slightly different story about her, but no one had ever heard that she'd had a sister. I think she picked that up because of us. She seemed surprised when I asked what her sister's name was, like she hadn't thought of that yet. It ends up that Adler was her name, and the Umbra part was partially right. Her real name was Adler Shade."

"Adler Shade," said Aurie. "Does she have family?"

"Her father died when she was younger, and her mother thinks she ran away. I found newspaper articles. They lived in a little town on the west coast."

"Where'd she get the name Jade?"

Pi squeezed her arms to her chest. "That's the street they lived on. 892 Jade Street, Chico, California."

"What about the Garden Network? Or the other things she knew?"

"Stolen knowledge, I guess. Same way she got me."

Pi's jaw pulsed with emotion.

"I still can't believe the Riders were just faez madness. I guess that's proof that perception drives reality."

"I worry about that."

Aurie touched her sister's arm. "How are you doing?"

The shrug she gave was exaggerated and obviously false, but Aurie wasn't going to point that out. It was going to take time to heal.

When they reached the area that had the two cottages, there was nothing that indicated they'd ever existed.

"They were right here, right?" asked Aurie.

"It feels like it. Let's look around."

They spread out, and within a few minutes, Pi called out from a petrified grove. A stone cap was set into the earth. Upon it was engraved: Boann Byrne - Beloved.

Aurie shouldered the backpack containing the artifact.

"What now?" asked Pi.

"I haven't the slightest. All I know is that I had a strong feeling I needed to bring the Engine back here. I was expecting to find Oba and the cottages. But I guess you can't live in a dead forest."

They walked around the area, looking for clues to what to do with the Engine.

"Maybe we're supposed to keep it."

Aurie shook her head vehemently. As soon as she'd heard the words, she knew that would be bad.

"No. I'm absolutely sure we're supposed to leave it here."

Pi pulled a pair of welder goggles from her leather jacket. She looked like she was cosplaying a steampunk airship captain when she slipped them over her eyes.

"Whoa, this place is covered in enchantments. Like I'm not sure why we're not crispy critters right now. I see triggers everywhere."

Pi pulled off the goggles and handed them to Aurie. She had to adjust the band to get them over her head, but when she did, the world lit up. It looked like a picture of the earth at night, when the cities glowed across the landscape. Aurie followed the lines and runes, teasing out the purpose of their construction.

She handed them back to her sister. "I know where it goes."

"Please don't say in the tomb. I'd really rather not desecrate a grave."

"Don't worry," she said, and stepped to the edge of the capstone. The Engine was light in her hands. Before she placed it on the spot she'd seen with the goggles, Aurie weighed the things she could do with it if she kept it, but decided against, because Oba seemed like the type of individual who would not appreciate being ignored.

When she set the runed brass cylinder on the grave, it immediately sunk beneath the surface, disappearing as if the capstone had been quicksand. A bell chimed once.

"I think that's our sign to get the hell out of here," said Aurie, walking in the other direction. "That place is covered in traps. As soon as we leave, or some number of bells toll, they'll activate, and I really don't want to be here."

The sisters jogged back to the industrial park. The bells only chimed one more time, at least that they could hear.

"So what were you going to tell me back there?" asked Aurie as they stood amid the ruined buildings.

Pi cast a spell that would hide their conversation.

"When I was in those memories," said Pi, placing a peculiar emphasis on the word *those*, "I found someone else before I reached the well of power."

"Someone else? Like did you finally get to see who's behind Malden's shield? Or did you meet Oba or something?"

"No, but close. It was Invictus."

"Merlin's tits. Why didn't you tell me this before?" asked Aurie.

"We haven't been alone so I could tell you, and I feared that someone might overhear," she said.

"Was it the real Invictus?"

"Of course not," said Pi. "He's dead, remember. But they all remember him, and it's his bond that created the charter for the Hundred Halls. They had enough memories between them to make him real enough."

"What was he like?" asked Aurie.

"Not as tall as I thought he'd be. Cryptic and threatening. Stereotypical for a wizard, I guess, but let's be honest, all the fiction anyone ever wrote about that involved magic was going to pay homage to him. On the other hand, this might have been a terrible representation of him, but there was something he said that's been bothering me since."

"Was that what you told Celesse?" asked Aurie.

Pi shook her head. "No, I told her about the Riders. What

he said was: *When the error of the quarterarch you shall know, then through the thresholds you shall flow.*"

Her sister's voice even took on a wavery, prophetic tone when she spoke. Aurie checked her arms, and they were covered in gooseflesh.

"What does that mean?"

"I wish I knew. I've been racking my brain since I heard it. When I went back into the memory, I always went back to that cottage. I never encountered him again, but his books and belongings were there. I read them all, examined every item, trying to find some clue to their purpose or the reason for the riddle."

"What if it's...?"

Pi shook her head right away. "No way. More than likely, it's one of the other patrons messing with me. Remember what Semyon said. The memories could have been directed by one of the other patrons."

"Are you planning on ignoring it?" asked Aurie.

Pi put her hands on her hips. "That's why I told my know-it-all nosy sister. Because she does riddles and wordplay better than me. And you research like a fiend."

"Flattery will get you everywhere."

"And gourmet cupcakes," said Pi. "All this skulking around makes me hungry."

"Who's buying this time?"

Pi tilted her head. "Who was it again that saved everyone?"

"Fair enough," said Aurie with a face-splitting grin, holding out her arm. "I'll buy."

Her sister linked their arms and leaned against her. It was comforting that way, having her around. The last year, with them being apart, had been hard on Aurie. She knew it'd been hard on Pi, too.

"Hey, sis," said Aurie.

"Yeah."

"Let's not be apart again. That sucked."

"Absolutely," said Pi. "And because I'm the bestest little sister in the whole wide world, I will definitely not bring up the fact that you were the one that convinced me to leave."

"You're really trying to get those cupcake privileges revoked."

Pi mimed zipping her lips closed.

As they neared the Red Line, Aurie said, "Let's make this last year our best year."

"Agreed. Can't be hard, right?"

"Yeah, true. Things would have to really go to hell to be any worse than our previous years."

"Shut up, Aurie. You'll jinx us."

§ § §

Find out what happens
in the final book of The Hundred Halls

CITY
OF
SORCERY

January 2018

Also by Thomas K. Carpenter

ALEXANDRIAN SAGA
Fires of Alexandria
Heirs of Alexandria
Legacy of Alexandria
Warmachines of Alexandria
Empire of Alexandria
Voyage of Alexandria
Goddess of Alexandria

THE DIGITAL SEA TRILOGY
The Digital Sea
The Godhead Machine
Neochrome Aurora

GAMERS TRILOGY
GAMERS
FRAGS
CODERS

THE DASHKOVA MEMOIRS
Revolutionary Magic
A Cauldron of Secrets
Birds of Prophecy
The Franklin Deception
Nightfell Games
The Queen of Dreams
Dragons of Siberia
Shadows of an Empire

THE HUNDRED HALLS
Trials of Magic
Web of Lies
Alchemy of Souls
Gathering of Shadows
City of Sorcery

ABOUT THE AUTHOR

Thomas K. Carpenter resides near St. Louis with his wife Rachel and their two children. When he's not busy writing his next book, he's playing soccer in the yard with his kids or getting beat by his wife at cards. He keeps a regular blog at www.thomaskcarpenter.com and you can follow him on twitter @thomaskcarpente. If you want to learn when his next novel will be hitting the shelves and get free stories and occasional other goodies, please sign up for his mailing list by going to: http://tinyurl.com/thomaskcarpenter. Your email address will never be shared and you can unsubscribe at any time.

33114566R00192

Made in the USA
Lexington, KY
08 March 2019